ANNO DOMINI

2064

Jacob Clearfield

JACOB CLEARFIELD

Copyright ©2020 Jacob Steven Clearfield

All rights reserved. No part of this publication may be reproduced, stored in a retrieval system or transmitted in any form or by any means electronic, mechanical, photocopying, recording, or otherwise without the prior written permission of the author.

This is a work of fiction. Names, places, characters, and incidents are entirely the product of the author's imagination or are used fictitiously. Any resemblance to actual persons living or dead is entirely coincidental.

ISBN: 9798619931600

ANNO DOMINI 2064

For my family. Whatever the future may
hold, may Grace still find you there.

Acknowledgements:

A special acknowledgement must be given to my wife. Without her this book would never have reached a publishable state. Her thoughtful critiques and aid in editing were indispensable in writing this book.

I'd also like to thank Timothy Gordon for his advice and insight, and especially for providing an impartial opinion at times. Finally, I'd like to thank Cecilia Lawrence for collaborating with me so much on designing the book's cover. It was such a pleasure to combine my vision for the novel with her artistic vision to create something unique and beautiful.

1.

The slow crescendo awoke him, as it always did. Groggy, he spent a moment gathering himself and wishing he could stay in bed a minute longer. The tones of, "Together We Are Better" continued to grow until they were too loud to ignore. Mark reached for his C-All glasses and put them on. As the data overlay turned on and his schedule loaded in the right upper corner, the melody tapered away.

Leslie also put her C-All on. As her data overlay booted up, Mark heard the click as the monitoring devices in the room turned off. He couldn't help but steal a glance at her as she pulled herself from the bed. She had a sleek, toned physique combined with proportionately generous curves. Even straight out of bed, her looks would be the envy of most women.

"I see that look. You know there's no time for that if we wait until the anthem to get up," Leslie teased him. Her warm voice was just shy of scolding him. "True," Mark replied. If they wanted to be ready in time for their commute, there was barely enough time to shower, dress, and eat a quick breakfast before heading out the door. Further recreational activities with Leslie would have to wait.

It felt a shame though. For more reasons than just her body, Mark truly enjoyed being with Leslie. Mark had been lucky enough to move to Milwaukee during the same four-year shift as her. As so often happened, the "newbies" tended to socialize chiefly with each other at first. He and Leslie had gotten to know each other quickly.

Two years out now, it said something that they remained together like this. The four-year shift was meant to be a full

ANNO DOMINI 2064

uprooting. Often the "newbies" would quickly form haphazard romantic attachments to cope with the new environment as much as anything else. Break-ups around the three-month mark were commonplace. For many people, they became almost a way of life; routine even. People would go about three months, then take a month off, and then find a new (or perhaps the same) partner for another three-month period. Mark had had several such relationships himself on other rotations.

Pulling himself out of bed, he walked across the room into the adjoining bathroom. Though his hair had been tousled from a night's sleep, he had to admit he didn't appear half bad either. He wasn't finding much time to work out these days, but he stuck to the Party's dietary guidelines well. At 32, his youth and natural metabolism kept him trim. He took a quick shower, used a little product, and shaped his brown hair into something socially acceptable. With a little oral hygiene, he was ready to go.

Meanwhile, Leslie had showered the night before and used the time to allow her make-up app and dispenser to produce her preferred pre-programmed facial coloring. He'd noticed she had three designs she used the most, with a few extra variances that took longer for special occasions. Today she used her office favorite. The coloring accentuated her smooth cheeks and darkened her thinned eyebrows. The slight eye shadow brought out her light brown eyes together with her auburn hair. Meanwhile, as her make-up applied, she worked to style her hair in a modern angular style. At 28, she was a four-year cycle younger than him. However, people often mistook her to be in her early twenties.

Of course, generally Party members looked younger and more attractive than the greater mass of society. A stricter adherence to the dietary standards, purposeful work, mandatory thirty minutes of aerobic exercise daily, and regular six-month health check-ups all benefited them.

As his hygiene routine ended, Mark put his C-All glasses

on again. Still powered up, they confirmed that breakfast was now waiting. As he approached the apartment's dining room, he heard his robot assistant "Sarah" stepping in from the kitchen with their meals.

Leslie was also ready for breakfast. Sarah retreated into the kitchen after placing their breakfast trays. Leslie sat down across from him. His glasses informed him they had approximately ten minutes to eat before their car arrived. "Do you think Don will notice us coming in together again?" he asked.

"Probably, but I doubt anyone really cares," Leslie replied. Taking a few bites, she mulled the question over a little more. "It's not like we're planning to go off cycle, right? I don't think anyone is getting that impression. They all know we value our careers too much for that. Besides, that's so uncommon nowadays. No one really does that anymore." Leslie went back to finishing her meal.

"I suppose," he agreed. "The last time I saw someone go off cycle was eight years ago, in San Diego. At least the weather was always nice there. I doubt anyone goes off cycle to stay where there are winters like here."

"Pansy," she replied. Mark grinned. He hated the cold. His previous cycles in California and Virginia had left his body far too used to pleasant weather. No matter how he seemed to dress, be it in layers, using heated undergarments, or just using the warmest coat he could buy, the Wisconsin winters still seemed to chill straight through to his bones whenever he went outside. Which was why he had barely been outside between the months of December and April since coming onto this cycle.

They finished their meal and signaled for Sarah to clean up. They then headed for the door. After putting the requisite coats, hats, and gloves on, there were only 30 seconds left on his glasses. After a brief ride down the elevator, he saw the car pull up just outside the apartment door. He gave his thumbprint for identification, and the passenger doors swung open. They each clambered in, avoiding half melted puddles of snow from the light December fall the night before. The front screen came up with a confirmation window querying whether they would like to proceed to city hall. A quick press "yes," and the car started in motion.

From his apartment in the Third Ward, it was a quick drive to city hall. The building stood as a testament to the city's past. With the addition of the new central tower, it had also become a symbol of the city's glorious present and future under the Party's leadership. Springing from the middle of the old 19th century brickwork, the steel and glass of the new tower tapered upwards a full thirty-three stories. It was buttressed by elegant arches connecting to attached buildings on either side of the street (and in fact anchoring through the heart of those buildings into the bedrock below, serving as a focal anchoring point for those buildings as well). These arches represented the interconnectivity that supported the Golden Republic. Atop the great tower perched a pedestal upon which the words "Together We Are Better" were engraved. Standing above was a statue of an arm bearing a torch with the old Wisconsin motto on the side, "Forward."

When he'd first seen it, he'd found it as inspiring as any piece of Party architecture. Over time, the novelty had slowly worn off. He now sometimes wondered whether keeping the old city hall building had really been wise. After all, the Party meant to throw off the dust of the old order. Why keep any remnant of the old building? The two styles had nothing in common. Then again, perhaps that was the point. The new towered over the old, springing forth from it and dominating it. No one could see the two and believe the old was better, could they?

Mark and Leslie arrived just as Don did. Mark couldn't help but notice Don shooting him a wink as they entered the elevator when Don thought Leslie wasn't looking. Mark knew better than to think Leslie had missed it and so pretended not to have seen it. Leslie exited at floor 28, and he rode with Don the rest of the way up to the 32nd (and penultimate) floor.

Stepping out of the elevator, he made his way to his desk. A modern-looking aluminum affair with crisp angles and a chair with a thin but comfortable black leather padding, the desk was practically his home away from home. It sat within an open office space, affording easy viewing across the city. His work space was on the north side of the floor to overlook his special project.

At the founding of the Golden Republic, it was declared that the country was to begin a new history "unstained by the filth of past hatred and ignorance." This had not always been easy to put in practice. Milwaukee had long been marked by segregation, and the Party saw this as an old stain in need of erasing. Unfortunately, solutions proved elusive. While Party members routinely moved every four years and were assigned in ways that produced diverse and representative groupings in every major administrative center, the greater masses of the population could not be moved in this way. Logistically, it appeared all but impossible. Even in areas where it had been attempted, people who lived in the blighted areas had proven surprisingly resistant to being moved.

Efforts to integrate these areas by moving people into them also often produced unwelcome results. There were spikes in criminality and assaults, small enclaves quickly formed, and gang violence followed. Such neighborhoods were often the same places already practically immune to policing. The continuous monitoring devices ubiquitous in most populated centers would never last more than a few hours in these neighborhoods. In such places, Party members were generally-safe because of the constant recording of their C-All glasses. In fact, the data analysis engines monitoring their recordings often would call police forces in before a Party member even realized they were in danger. But for non-party members, such areas were extremely dangerous.

So had proven Milwaukee's north side. Mark had been

part of a new approach to the area. When he'd arrived, an argument was being put forward that these areas need not be forcibly desegregated. After all, these communities had been some of the strongest bases of support for the Party since the earliest days of the Golden Republic. The people there were amenable to the Party's doctrines. The only element needed was time. Through education in the schools, the mobility provided by the Party for those who joined it, and the continued draw from the area of young men and women into the Golden Republic's armed forces, the old stains of segregation would eventually disappear. Mark had felt this was a productive approach, if for no other reason than all previous efforts had failed. Soon after arriving in Milwaukee, he had become a strong advocate of the new approach. He ended up on the winning side of the argument when the idea was adopted by the local Inner Party representative. Within the office his star had been bright ever since, leading to his position now on the 32nd floor.

Backing this approach had been successful in part because it had justified increased military recruitment efforts using the funds of his department. This had paid off with significantly higher recruitment numbers for the city, making the higher echelons of the Inner Party immensely pleased. The peacekeeping efforts in Europe, Africa, and the Middle East required a constant flow of new soldiers from the Golden Republic and its steadfast ally, the People's Republic of China. The two great pillars of the East and West seemed to be forever forced to use their strength to bring order to the messy and constant internecine strife in the globe between them. While casualties usually remained low, with most fighting being kept to guerrilla tactics and small-scale skirmishes, the number of garrisons needed to prevent collapse in these regions was staggering.

Mark's time at work was now largely aimed at targeted recruitment. In early efforts, his office had advertised defending the ideals of diversity, inclusivity, and equality abroad. This had failed to inspire many recruits. Efforts aimed at promoting "defending the homeland" and "stopping terrorists there, before they come here" had been somewhat more successful, though not as much as in other areas of the country. Mark had realized that his target demographic was, despite the Party providing the same stipends and material rations as in all other areas of the Republic, still suffering from lower standards of living. He therefore created recruiting materials that promoted the financial benefits of military service. To join the armed forces was to become a de facto Party member. After completing ten years of service, Party level housing, food, and stipend were provided for life, and service members could settle in the area of the Republic of their choosing.

This approach has boosted recruitment a full 45% year-over-year since the program was started, and he'd been recognized for the success. There had already been friendly hints from coworkers that he was sure to have his next assignment be in the Golden Capitol. Success there would mean access to the very upper echelons of the Party.

Looking through recent recruiting statistics, the possibility couldn't help but present itself to him. He indulged himself by imagining it. Inner Party members didn't have to rotate and could "reserve" property. Children of upper echelon Party members could even be entrusted to stay with them to raise for the Party. He wasn't sure about that final benefit. However, staying in a permanent post in California (or at least some place warm) certainly appealed.

He focused again on his work. Today, Mark was busy signing off on new recruiting pamphlets and reviewing the campaign for the upcoming spring. The work went quickly and soon the morning was over. Between noon and two o'clock, thirty minutes was allowed for lunch. This meant taking the elevator down to the 15th floor and then choosing food from a rotating menu before finding a table. Mark usually preferred to take his lunch around 12:30PM. As the time approached, he wrapped up most of what he'd planned to accomplish in the morning. He just had a few things to finish in the afternoon before taking transportation out to visit some of the Party centers on the North side.

Walking toward the elevator, he saw Allison heading that way as well. Allison was close friends with Leslie. He assumed Leslie had already headed down to the cafeteria. This would be good, as he'd avoid the awkwardness of sitting with people he didn't know.

"Hi Allison," he said. "Oh, hi Mark," she replied, a little unevenly. Even though she'd seen him approaching the same elevator, her manner gave off a sort of surprise that he'd greeted her. Allison was always nervous around men. Despite knowing her over a year, she was still apprehensive towards him. She pressed the button to summon the elevator almost a little too forcefully, underlining his impression.

"How are things in the education department today?" he asked.

"Um, good, I guess," she began. After a moment's consideration, she suddenly launched into what sounded like a prepared speech. "The new textbooks for next year are almost done. We're still working on some of the teaching guides for the younger ages. Our psychologists have found that for more violent boys under age four, rough play is required to reduce the incidence of long-term aggression and social non-conformity. Unfortunately, most young age caretakers at present are female and encouraging them to undertake rough play is proving difficult."

She took a breath, "Meanwhile, there have been experiments with adding male Party members to the young age caretaker ranks. Unfortunately, they generally perform at a lower efficiency than the female caretakers. We have been developing a curriculum guide to help caretakers identify higher risk young males who can be transferred to centers where specialist male caretakers can engage in the needed forms of play." As she finished, a look of satisfaction had taken hold of her face.

"Huh, that's interesting, Allison," Mark replied. Though honestly, he had merely meant to engage in some light conversation while in the elevator. He thought for a moment how to respond. "Being a young caretaker was never a career I considered. I imagine if that's where the Party assigned me, I'd be rather lost." This was an understatement. The only times he saw children were when he was travelling through non-Party member residential districts. The children there seemed to run about like wild animals.

Indeed, he'd heard it said that for those without C-All glasses, you had to watch out for any small items you were carrying when around such children. They were liable to sneak off with any trinket they could snatch. He had to imagine the children in the Party education centers were more disciplined. Even so, he could hardly imagine actually being in charge of raising them.

Allison nodded. "Most Party men aren't very interested, which we think is why they are generally less efficient than female caretakers. Still, the Party has been making great strides in its education program. Before the Golden Republic, education was so disorganized, it was literally a Dark Age! Now that we have defined goals for our children and the controlled settings to test theories and experiment, we can learn the best way to raise them.

Can you imagine, before the Golden Republic all the children were like non-Party member kids! How was society supposed to learn anything about educating children when the children would spend most of their time at home with total non-professionals mucking everything up? I mean, when you think about it, our generation really missed out by still having parents. The next generation, they will be the ones to really bring mankind into the future."

Her hope seemed infectious. "I suppose that's true. I guess I'd never thought of myself as having been raised at a disadvantage. My parents were always fervent Party members from the beginning, which was probably as good as anyone could have hoped for at the time." Truth be told, he still enjoyed talking to his parents now and then. He could even occasionally visit them in Vermont where the Party had retired them. He wondered what it would be like to have no parent besides the Party.

The elevator finally arrived. Allison pressed the button for floor fifteen. After the two of them stepped into the elevator. "Yeah, you're right about that. For us, having parents in the Party was as good as it got. I suppose there's no sense in begrudging the next generation when we have it so much better than generations before us," she replied.

"Huh," he paused, "Another good point. How are you not head of the education department yet?" An expression almost like terror came onto her face at the suggestion. "I'm kidding, I'm kidding. I'm just saying you're clearly very good at your job, and insightful to boot!"

"Oh, um, thanks Mark," she replied. At this, the conversation went dead. Mark realized he should have known better. Allison was hardly the ambitious type. The idea of managing people probably terrified her. Complimenting her hadn't helped things. Thankfully, the elevator moved quickly. As it opened, they joined several other people walking into the food selection area.

The food choices were always excellent, with a mix of healthy options locally sourced as much as possible. They also sourced across the country and sometimes from countries friendly to the Golden Republic that produced foods unavailable within the nation's borders. With the increasing robotization of agriculture and the use of more indoor high-density farming, there wasn't much that couldn't be grown locally. There were still goods though that could only be grown with certain soils and climates. As Party members, access to these foods was a definite perk.

While picking out food, Mark spotted Leslie, already seated at the end of a table. Finishing his selections, he used the auto-scan feature of the C-All to confirm them and then walked over to her table. Allison had already sat across from her. Mark was irritated to see that Don had also grabbed a seat next to Leslie, but at least Mark could grab a seat kitty-corner to her still.

"How's it going?" He greeted them. Don had been in the middle of some sort of diatribe and looked faintly annoyed at the interruption. Leslie and Allison had looked more than a little disinterested as Mark approached. "Things are good," Leslie replied.

"It's good you're here, Mark. I'll bet given what you do you'll have some perspective on the news today. Leslie here doesn't feel it's a big deal." The expression Don gave while stating this made clear he had little respect for such an opinion.

"What news is that?" Mark asked.

"The French Caliphate has invaded the Republic of Brittany. Poland and the Eastern League are threatening war if the French don't pull their troops back, and the East German Republic and the German Islamic Republic are at each other's throats over it," Don reported. "It sounds like Russia is supporting the Breton's too, even if it means being on the same side as the Eastern League." He gave his report with considerable eagerness. Don always felt unrest or war in other parts of the world would inevitably lead to opportunities for the Golden Republic to spread its influence.

"Sounds like another mess in Europe. How many times have we seen these types of conflicts? One minute it's the Muslim states putting down some secularist or primitivist uprising in France or Italy. The next it's a neo-capitalist uprising in England, or the East German Republic saber rattling against the German Islamic Republic and trying to rally the Eastern League for some kind of primitivist crusade. That is if the GIR isn't trying to get France to join in a jihad against the East German Republic or the Eastern League," Mark replied.

"Maybe so, but if the Golden Republic steps in and guarantees Brittany, they'd pretty much *have* to accept some of our educators. Brittany is still more native French than Islamic, so they'd probably be much more open to our ideals," Don countered.

It was true that the Islamic world had proven the most resilient to the Golden Republic's ideals. While Asia and much of Africa largely fell under Chinese hegemony, and the Western hemisphere under the Golden Republic's, Europe and the Middle East formed a sort of zone of chaos between the two. It seemed a shame to Mark; the world was so close to being at peace, but these two areas were as violent and chaotic as ever. Keeping the peace in these areas and breaking up the worst of the various malefactors was a large part of why his recruitment efforts for the armed forces were so needed.

"It's possible, but it's not like making inroads in Brittany would really change much," Mark replied.

This response seemed to deflate Don for a moment. However, after a second, he replied, "It wouldn't, but even small victories for our cause would be worth celebrating, eh?"

"True enough," Leslie chimed in. "But I think those are matters for the Inner Party to decide on, anyway. Not something we need to worry about."

"Well, maybe not now, but we're all still young; maybe we will have to make those kinds of decisions for the Party someday. It doesn't hurt to practice," Don replied.

At this, the rest of them shrugged modest agreement. On the surface, Don's statement seemed like a good loyal statement, so disagreeing seemed wrong. However, it also sounded rather ambitious, and there was a natural danger in that to which Don always seemed somewhat oblivious. Not that people, "disappeared" much anymore like was necessary in the early days of the Party. Usually, people would simply be sidelined. Mark was fairly sure the Inner Party kept lists of Party members who were worth promoting or being given good positions. Others were simply kept on the periphery. Obviously, treason or sedition was still punished harshly. Lack of tact, like in Don's case, could be dealt with in more subtle ways.

Thankfully, Leslie changed the subject to discuss some new programming her division was creating for the winter season. She was sure a new science fiction program would be very popular. It imagined a future where the Chinese had created robots with too much intelligence, and they had rebelled. The Golden Republic had to come to China's aid to save humanity from the robot menace. It followed the exploits of a brave GR commando and his unit as they fought within the course of the larger war. The rest of the lunch passed swiftly. Soon Mark was heading back to the elevator for the second half of his day.

Today his afternoon would be spent visiting some Party education and recruitment centers on the North side. Mark returned to his office briefly to finish up a few loose ends. After, while riding the elevator down he used his C-All glasses to confirm his scheduled car. By the time he'd reached the ground floor, he saw the car pulling up to the curbside. Wrapping a scarf around his neck, he braced himself and made the brief walk through the biting cold to the car wherein a warm seat awaited him. Once the door closed, he happily confirmed the first location to the Party center on Wright Street.

Watching through the windows as the car sped by, he couldn't help but think about how strange it was that despite all the changes in the world in the last few decades, how unchanged much of Milwaukee was from even a hundred years ago. So many of the buildings he passed had been built in the 1930s. Many were even older, dating back to the 1800s. Cream city brick still stood proudly as the core component of many a sizable house or commercial building.

It was amazing to think the lives being led within those homes were not substantially different from those being led in the early 2000s. There were no robot assistants, C-All's, or virtual reality systems in these homes. Most tasks were still done

ANNO DOMINI 2064

by hand or with dumb appliances. Television was still the main form of entertainment. A bus was still the main form of transportation. Families were still common, usually matriarchal in nature and multigenerational in each home. For all the changes the Party had brought to America, in places like this you could hardly tell.

The building his car now approached was an exception. Smooth curves of polychromatic steel tapered upward to a graceful point, resembling something like an ancient mariner's sail tilted slightly askew. It was an excellent example of the beauty and resilience of Party architecture. Holograms of proud soldiers, wise teachers, and caring healthcare providers projected from the building, declaring the benevolence of the Party and the benefits it brought to all who accepted its tenets. Far smaller than the headquarters downtown, it was probably only 20,000 square feet or so total between its four stories. Yet, it stood out prominently among the simple square one and two-story buildings that surrounded it.

Stepping from the car, he tucked his chin to better cover his neck with his scarf as he hurried through the cold. Walking in through the automatic rotating door, he felt the immediate relief of the warmth inside. The interior featured sleek modern curves, accented with metallics and tasteful lighting. His C-All informed him that the building's chief was waiting for him on the fourth floor. A short ride in the building's single elevator brought him to the top floor where the local manager awaited him.

The meeting that followed was fairly tedious. They discussed the station's compiling of data from the precinct regarding reports from local informers focusing on the population's feeling toward the Party and overall morale. They also discussed recent recruitment numbers from the district for the Party and the Armed Forces. The most recent advertising campaign was going well, and the manager was careful both to promote herself as an effective agent for implementing his cam-

17

paign and to compliment him for creating the campaign.

As boring as Mark found these meetings, he had to admire just how much planning had gone into the woman's efforts to balance her shameless self-promotion with her even more shameless brown-nosing. At the end of the meeting he made sure to give several compliments in return to her. After all, there was a good chance this woman would go far in the Party one day.

Two further meetings followed that afternoon at very similar stations spaced around the North side, before he could finally ride back to his home in the Third Ward. As he returned, the headlights of the car plowed through the dark and frigid December air while a mild snowfall gathered on the streetlights and sidewalks. Finished with a day's work, Mark's mind turned to how he would fill the remaining hours before bed. His stomach sank. The restlessness and emptiness he struggled with when alone began to swell like a wave that would overwhelm him. He searched his mind to consider the ways he could distract himself in order to keep afloat.

2.

If he wasn't alone, Mark was usually ok. Leslie wouldn't be joining him tonight. There were good reasons why she couldn't. Mark reminded himself of those reasons every night she was away. He had no great illusions about living with her permanently. He'd heard that some Inner Party members would take permanent lovers. He was, however, nowhere near advanced enough in his career to do this.

Mark was attached to her, though, to the degree that he couldn't see being with other women right now. He'd never discussed it with her. But it seemed like they had made an unspoken commitment for now to only be with each other. Speaking about it would have made it public to the C-All. So, they didn't. Even if there was nothing explicitly against monogamous relationships in Party policy, it was still frowned upon. Even serial monogamy had too much in common with the old oppressive idea of marriage.

Mark considered why he missed her on these nights. It wasn't really about sex. Certainly, he enjoyed that part. Having Leslie around for the night was about more than just that physical act. Leslie was interesting. He loved talking with her. She was also comfortable for him to be around. Her presence filled the night up, so that his thoughts didn't stray as they did when he was alone.

Entering his apartment, he faced emptiness. After a moment, his robot Sarah came into view and greeted him. "Welcome home, Mark. I received your C-All request for lasagna tonight for dinner. It will be ready in fifteen minutes. Is there any other way I can assist you?"

"Thank you, Sarah, that's fine for now," Mark replied. Mark took a seat in his most comfortable chair and used the time waiting for dinner to review the headlines from the day. The Brittany story was among them, as were troop actions in the Levant and several local interest stories. There was nothing else of particular note.

Sarah finished readying the lasagna. It was good. Mark enjoyed a new episode of one of his favorite sit-coms during dinner. With dinner finished and Sarah cleaning up, Mark had completed everything productive he'd planned for the day. At this point he had about four hours left in his day. It was up to him how he would entertain himself.

The Party made sure a great array of entertainment was available. Television shows, movies, and music were the primary entertainments available to everyone. Party members had an even wider array of options. The C-All glasses could easily portray theater size screens upon any wall or even floating in mid-air. On such screens, he could watch Party shows from both the past and present. He could even watch some older pre-Golden Republic films.

Similarly, many games were available through the C-All glasses. The Party issued a standard controller and a mouse and keyboard he could use with the C-All. Video games were exceptionally popular amongst both Party members and the general masses. Playing video games was one area of life where the two groups would commonly interact with each other. The Party actively encouraged Party members to play multi-player games. Individuals who reflected the Party well to the greater masses would even be rewarded for doing so. Some of the greatest players would play in competitive leagues. These games were broad streamed regularly each night.

A wide array of sporting competitions also took place within the Golden Republic. As a Party member, it was standard to have access to essentially every organized sport filmed. Mark usually enjoyed watching basketball, but there were no games tonight that interested him.

The Party encouraged playing sports as well. In fact, engaging in physical fitness was mandatory. Mark had regular gym nights, and on weekends, he would take part in a local basketball league. It was nothing serious, his team rarely bothered to meet on weeknights to practice.

Beyond physically playing sports, the C-All allowed for the virtual simulation of sports. Activities such as boxing, tennis, golf, and bowling were all easy to replicate in a virtual form within a Party member's standard apartment space. Virtual spaces were also used to enjoy concerts or theater productions. He could tour many of the great museums of the Golden Republic and even elements of some foreign ones virtually using his C-All.

Mark considered all these options. The trouble was, he couldn't decide between them tonight.

There were other possibilities too. Some of the most popular entertainments were erotic in nature. The Party had cracked down sharply on unregulated prostitution and human trafficking. It had likewise curtailed much of the violence that marked pornography prior to the rise of the Golden Republic. However, the Party acknowledged pornography as having been one of the chief elements that had helped it liberate the masses from the concept of marriage. The Party saw it as a needed outlet for human sexuality and expression. To that end, the C-All could be used for a tremendous range of pornographic purposes. Robot assistants like Sarah were even designed to be integrated with it, so that witnessed sex acts could be simulated in real time for the user.

In his younger years, Mark had frequently used these entertainments. The Party had taught that use of them was natural and even laudable. Even then, he'd felt like there was something lacking. At the time, he assumed it was just the fact it wasn't the "real thing." But as he'd gotten older and engaged in sex with real women, he often found the same sense of hollowness afterwards as with the C-All. It wasn't quite as bad now with Leslie. There was a physical relief with the act that he felt almost had to be obtained, so he'd never considered quitting it altogether. But over time sex had become almost as irritating as satisfying for him. He never used the C-All for it anymore. Even with Leslie, he pressed for it less often than before.

He wondered if feeling this way made him strange. It wasn't something he discussed. He wasn't sure if it was something the Party monitored, and if so, whether there was an ideal amount of sexual activity it would prefer he maintained. He got the sense it wasn't too concerned about it. As long as no one was trying to restrict the sexual activities of others and no one was attempting to force non-consensual sexual activity, the Party didn't seem to care.

Nowadays no one was trying to restrict other people's consensual sexual activities. Non-consensual sex was the issue the Party still spent effort on. Maintaining sexual freedom risked people abusing that freedom on unwilling partners. This was one of the major arguments for the widespread availability of pornography and the sexual programming of robots. Sex was always available. No one had any cause to desire sex with someone else against their will. Thus, rape was inexcusable.

When rapes happened, police forces were always quick to respond. The punishments were swift and brutal. Chemical removal of the libido combined with implantation of pain chips was the most common punishment. The Party made sex criminals experience a constant level of pain commensurate with the seriousness of their crime for the rest of their lives. Additionally, anyone who wore a C-All could identify a past sex criminal at a glance. As a result, such persons were utterly ostracized from the Party. These means almost eliminated rape amongst Party members. Unfortunately, in some non-monitored areas like the north side in Milwaukee, no one really knew how often it happened. Stories of rapes and assaults in such places were rife.

ANNO DOMINI 2064

Mark turned his thoughts back to the problem at hand. How was he going to entertain himself? Too often these days, when Leslie wasn't around in the evenings, he found himself paralyzed with indecision. Occasionally, a new video game or a new show would come out that he would find interesting, and he could dive into it for a while. But, inevitably, his interest would wane, or he would finish the game or watch all the available episodes. It seemed like after every time that this happened, it was a little harder to become as engrossed in something else. He was going longer and longer between finding entertainment that could fully occupy him.

Worse, when he couldn't find something to do, he'd often just sit and think, which worried him. He was concerned that the C-All was recording the time he would just sit with no activity or entertainment selected. He suspected too much downtime would be flagged and lead to Inner Party review. To combat this potential issue, he sometimes chose a virtual concert or music playlist and pretended to listen. Meanwhile, he was just sitting and thinking, as paralyzed as ever about what to do with himself.

During this state of paralysis, he often thought about the future. He could imagine it easily enough. He'd remain diligent and canny in his approach to work and would ascend the Party hierarchy. Eventually, he'd be rewarded with higher positions that in turn would provide him larger apartments or even houses, nicer climes to live in, greater prestige at work, and finer clothes and food. He envisioned this future with detailed clarity. But he also saw himself sitting at night, in a bigger house in a nicer climate, still paralyzed with choices to entertain himself, struggling more and more every day.

Eventually, he would get old. Eventually, he would die. His name would remain in the Party's databases, but hardly anyone would really notice or care when he was gone. Not that it really mattered. Even if he were remembered, even if he rose to lead the Party itself and did acts so memorable that humanity would always remember him, eventually the sun would burn out and everything would end. Even then, even if humanity had learned to travel the stars and had escaped the fate of extinction to that point, eventually all the stars would burn out and humanity would cease to exist. None of it really mattered.

Since none of it really mattered, why couldn't he stop thinking about it and enjoy himself? This was the heart of the problem, because he couldn't think of a damned thing worth doing that he'd really enjoy. At least not tonight. Perhaps never. This last thought scared him the most. What if he reached a point where nothing distracted him or pleased him anymore? He hadn't thought about this concept when he was younger. The older he got, the idea that the things he did didn't matter bothered him more. The notion seemed to suck all the enjoyment from the things he had lived for: the pursuit of his career, spending time with women, enjoying sports and food. It all felt increasingly dull to him. It was as if his world was slowly losing its color. The ridiculously early nights of winter in Wisconsin and the constant grey skies during the day felt like an outward expression of this inward reality.

He considered the possibility that he was depressed. He'd learned that people sometimes have chemical imbalances in their brains that cause irrational sadness or despair. He'd learned, too, that decreased sun exposure in the winter could worsen this. Yet, he didn't feel like what he was experiencing was irrational. Existence was meaningless, so wasn't it rational to be upset about it? A flare of anger took him for a moment. His frustration was justified. The universe had created mankind and then cursed him with the knowledge of his own insignificance. How was that just? How could this be borne? Why did the Party not address this concept? Surely greater minds than his own had struggled with this problem. Had they truly not come up with any answers? It seemed like all the great entertainments and the goals of the Party led to avoidance of this issue. Was avoiding the question the only real answer that could be given?

ANNO DOMINI 2064

Mark had known Party members who suddenly disappeared from a position, only to find out that the member had thrown him or herself from a building, or sometimes in front of a car at the last moment. A few managed to hang themselves or cut themselves so badly they would die before the help their C-All summoned could arrive to save them. Typically, it was said that they had been depressed and had hidden it well. Yet, these people had not seemed overly sad or unmotivated at work. Mark sometimes wondered if they'd struggled with this same issue. Maybe he was weird, and they had been, too. Maybe most people could avoid thinking about these things, but the ones that did were doomed.

Mark wasn't prepared to go that far yet. He did still find pleasures in life. Even if it was getting harder and harder, he figured if there was still some pleasure in life he could enjoy, then it was still worth sticking around. He still had hope too; hope that there was yet some answer still eluding him. It was probably a forlorn hope, but a part of him didn't think so. He was modest enough to acknowledge there might be an answer out there he simply wasn't smart enough to find. If so, there was always the chance he could still stumble upon it. Some people said age and experience bring wisdom, so maybe that's what he needed to find the answer. It wasn't the sort of thing people discussed. For all he knew, perhaps many others had found an answer to the problem, and it was only a matter of time before he did as well.

With that thought, Mark decided the only thing he could do for now was distract himself. There was a new game on the C-All that taught virtual fencing lessons. Some movement would be good. He pulled up the game. A virtual instructor appeared before him and a weightless rapier seemed to appear in his hand. He spent the next few hours learning the basic rules and techniques of fencing. He ended with a reasonably successful tutorial match against the instructor. It was enough to work up a sweat, and the complexity of the rules and learning the fencing positions kept him occupied. By the end, he was tired and wanted nothing more than a good shower and a light snack before bed.

Sarah cooked popcorn for him while he took the shower. Then she moved herself to the closet to recharge for the night. After the snack, Mark felt ready for bed. As he ordered the lights out, he removed the C-All, and heard the usual click as the recording microphones kicked on. Mark always smirked a bit at that noise. The microphones didn't have to make a sound; it was just a reminder. People had no trouble remembering that their actions were being monitored while wearing the C-All. Sometimes with the devices off, people forgot. The sound was really a courtesy; a reminder from the Party that one was never truly left unmonitored. It was in some ways a comforting thought. With that, Mark drifted into a dreamless sleep.

....

The next day was much the same, both at work and at home. In fact, the rest of the week passed with little change from day to day. Leslie was able to come over on Friday night. They both had off from work that weekend. Leslie had planned on Saturday for them to see a new exhibit at the local art museum. She would stay over Friday night and then they would go Saturday morning before it got more crowded in the afternoon. With a new exhibit opened, Saturday afternoons could get very busy. Mark had been by the museum several times but hadn't yet gone inside. The novelty alone would make it worth the trip.

Friday night went well. Having Leslie over always made the night go quickly and saved Mark from the boredom and anxiety that increasingly marked his nights alone. The next morning, Mark woke up looking forward to their trip to the museum.

They both went through the usual morning preparations and meal and then took the auto-car they'd reserved. In the summer, the museum was close enough to walk to. However, walking through the snow and ice such a distance was the last thing Mark wanted to do with his day off. Instead the car would take them to the heated underground garage. The snow and ice could get along well enough without him, Mark thought.

"I'm so glad I'm finally able to take you today," Leslie remarked as the car got underway. "It's a perfect day for it too. The sun is out, and the lake will be beautiful from the main level."

"I'm sure it will be. I'll admit I've been feeling down with all the gray weather. It will be good to get out and see the sun today." Mark replied. The museum was located right next to the lake. The view of the waterfront was something Mark always found inspiring. He was really looking forward to seeing it today.

"The exhibit is supposed to be good, too," Leslie continued. "They even have some pre-revolution pieces! I guess a lot of them are originals rather than reproductions. Some of the art is over a hundred years old!" Leslie was quite animated about this. She'd always loved history and would often get excited by old artifacts. She even had a small collection. Most of the pieces she had were old technology. She'd also found a few old maps, and once had managed to purchase several old children's toys. This toy collection included some blocks, a few model vehicles, and a strange small hat with circular black ears on the top with a sticker of a cartoon mouse on the front. The Party was generally uninterested in the past, aside from ensuring no subversive elements from the old order crept into the present. So long as old items were essentially harmless, as these were, the Party rarely cared if someone kept them.

Mark nodded. "I looked at the summary page for the exhibit. 'The Art of Revolt: A Look at the Art That Inspired the Revolution.' I recognized a few of the pieces from my school days. Should be cool to see in person." Mark wasn't sure that any of the art was "good" per se. But it was historic, and that, he supposed, was interesting in and of itself.

A few moments passed as the car travelled the few blocks before nearing the museum.

"I'm not sure anything in the exhibit will beat the museum itself," Leslie remarked. She timed her remark to coincide with the appearance of the "sail" of the museum. Mark could hardly disagree.

"I've heard people say the design was so forward-thinking it was undoubtedly a representation of Calatrava's dream of the coming Revolution," Mark commented. One of the bureaucrats in the arts and recreation department had mentioned it to him when they were planning a brochure for the city. This meaningless bit of lunchtime chat had somehow bubbled back into his consciousness.

The clean lines of the building's white sail rose over the brilliant varied blue hues that made up the horizon of Lake Michigan behind it. Accented with crisp snow and a clear blue sky, it seemed hard to believe such beauty could be real.

The thought occurred to Mark that it wasn't really like a sail at all, but instead, the museum had wings. Wings that were soaring between two horizons of endless blue. His heart ached a little as he looked at it. "A mistake," Mark murmured.

"What's that?" Leslie was thrown off guard by the remark. "Sorry, I was thinking about the advertising campaign the person who told me about the museum ended up launching. Nothing important really," Mark replied. That had been too close. An unguarded thought had led to dangerous speech!

Mark realized the sight of the museum had struck him so profoundly that it had moved him. As a result, he'd unwittingly let his guard down. The mistake he'd thought of was nothing to do with the faceless bureaucrat. The mistake was on the Party's part for leaving such a building standing. The building had wings. It was free. Looking at it gave one a yearning for something similar. The building was anathema to the control needed by the Party to keep order. Had they really not seen that?

ANNO DOMINI 2064

An abrupt change in light pulled Mark from his reverie as the car entered the underground parking. Mark and Leslie exited the car and walked up the spiral staircase into the main entrance hall. Mark was now more on guard but still could barely believe the feelings inspired by the soaring ceiling, the light streaming through the glass walls, and the stunning blues of water and sky that came through the east end of the building.

"It's incredible," he managed.

"It really is," Leslie replied. Mark felt a small squeeze from her hand. The two stood for a moment taking it in. In the distance, a tour group was checking in. A young man at the back of the group noticed the way he and Leslie were staring around them. Mark realized they'd been spotted and couldn't help looking back. The man was of average height with a handsome, confident face. Mark wasn't sure whether his skin was naturally light brown, or he was very tan, which would mean he was new to the area. He seemed to have a friendly disposition. The man shot Mark a grin before turning and joining his group as they headed into the exhibit.

Being noticed had snapped Mark out of the moment. He took Leslie's hand and gently tugged while taking a step towards the entrance counter. The two approached and their C-All's linked with that of the visitor assistant at the desk to confirm their identity and register the visit. "Welcome to the museum. Your C-All can provide all necessary information regarding the layout and exhibits. However, please do not hesitate to request museum staff if you should require any assistance," the woman said.

"Thank you," Mark and Leslie responded in unison. The woman gave a small grin in response. Mark thought he saw a bit of red creep into Leslie's face.

At they passed the entry point the grand hall sprawled in front of them with soaring windows framed in white steel looking out at Lake Michigan and the matching sky above it. To the left was the walled special exhibit. The entry was at the east end of the wall. The wall was painted in light browns serving as a background for outlined images in stark reds and yellows of famous artists, architects, and sculptors of the early Party. These images surrounded "THE ART OF REVOLT" in large lettering across the wall and beneath it in more stylistic cursive "A Look at the Art That Inspired the Revolution."

A line of people waited outside for entry into the exhibit. Another museum worker sat by the door. Occasionally she would receive a message in her C-All, at which point she would open the door and allow a set number of people into the exhibit.

"Looks like we're not the only people who thought it would be a good day to visit," Mark commented.

"Well, the new exhibit did just open, and it's a Saturday so more people will have off to come see it. If you took in some culture now and then you wouldn't be so surprised," Leslie teased.

"Hey, I read. I take virtual tours. I even go to virtual live shows sometimes. I'm plenty cultured," Mark jokingly countered.

"Right, I'll believe it when I see your C-All logs," Leslie returned.

"I'll show you mine if you show me yours," Mark grinned. Leslie blushed. Apparently, he'd called her bluff. It was funny, Mark mused, we all have secrets, secrets known only to us and the Party. Maybe that was fitting. The Party was everyone, everyone had secrets, and the Party knew those secrets, because the Party was everyone. It felt like there was a germ of a recruiting campaign in there. He'd have to think about it more later.

3.

The museum worker beckoned them forward as she opened the door. They were greeted with a large panel of introductory text:

> *The era immediately preceding the Great Revolution was one of tremendous upheaval and societal chaos. Primitive power structures and ideologies were dying, but it was not yet clear when or if they would fully die. The old system needed to be destroyed, and humanity needed a new dream for its future to replace it. Before the great revolutionaries and statesmen articulated that dream, it was first expressed in the Arts. The exhibits here on display are a sample of works from artists in the decades preceding the revolution that served to destroy the old system and usher in the Golden Republic.*

From here, the wall channeled them to the right through a corridor into a large rectangular room containing several paintings, photographs, and sculptures. The museum had arranged the artworks to flow toward the left where another corridor formed leading to a further room beyond. On the right, just ahead of the artwork, there was another text panel:

> *Early Revolt:*
>
> *The works in this room are from a period in the early 21st century wherein the ideals of the future Golden Republic were first being formed. Often, these ideals were defined through opposition to the existing system. These works served to present to the viewer the possibility of a better world and to thereby destabilize the existing primitive societal systems holding back such a world from emerging.*

JACOB CLEARFIELD

The first image was a print of what appeared to be a woman of Middle Eastern descent, wearing what Mark recognized from foreign news reports as a hijab. The image was strange in that it was made up entirely of red, white, and blue coloring, with the hijab on the right being blue with white stars, and on the left being red and white in stripes. A small plaque next the image gave a description of the work.

The plaque explained that the piece was a striking example of the sophistication used by artists of this time period to undermine the existing societal structures. At the time, many of the people of the United States of America were deeply worried about the possibility of terrorist attacks from Muslims, and at a deeper level, also feared the threat that Islam posed to the still widely held primitive religious beliefs of their own society. At the same time, the society was worried about being racist for ascribing these fears onto individual Muslims who likely had no personal connections with terrorism.

The work was created to give the viewer a sense of wrongness without it being obvious why it should feel wrong. In turn, this would cause the viewers to reflect that they might be racist for feeling this way. The goal was achieved was through the flag that symbolized the country being used as the material for the hijab. Previous generations had felt that use of the flag in any sort of clothing would be disrespectful, but this taboo had weakened. By this time, it would not be obvious as a source of discomfort. The combination of the flag with the hijab, which, more than a piece of clothing, was often seen as a symbol of female oppression and Muslim dominance, would be sure to spark discomfort immediately in those seeking to maintain the present order. If they did not understand why the symbolism upset them, they would feel that the image confirmed they were racist.

Mark wasn't sure he fully understood the concept. The image didn't seem wrong to him so much as just sort of odd. It

ANNO DOMINI 2064

was strange to think just a few generations ago an image like this could mean so many things to people, while now it bore no relevance to anyone.

The next piece was more visceral and easily understood. The left side of the piece was a panoply of old black and white photographs of black men who had been hung or shot. On the right were high resolution, color images of black men who had been shot, often with law enforcement officers found within the images. In the middle of the display, hanging from the wall, was an actual rope tied into a noose.

Next to this piece there was another small plaque explaining how the piece had been displayed in many museums after its creation and shows the way the concept of racism was used to attack the social structure of the United State. In its early history the people of the United States had enslaved black men and women, and even after freeing them continued to treat them contemptibly for many generations after. By the early 21st century, most people viewed all of this as a stain upon the country's history. Artists at the period would show the horrors of black treatment from earlier in the country's history and place it side by side with events from a more current context to argue that the existing society was no better than it had been in the past. This action played to the guilt of the society and was used as an argument for why the existing social structure needed to be destroyed.

Mark understood the power of this argument immediately. Even nowadays, the Party was careful in its approach to the black population. The injury done to them by the prior society had in many places left them still segregated from the larger society and less open to full compliance with the Party's programs. Such was the case in Milwaukee itself. Many Party members felt that successfully addressing this problem would likely be the work of generations.

Mark and Leslie continued to move through the room,

taking in more artworks. The theme of race was a prevalent contribution, and other artwork featured themes of sexuality/gender, care for the poor, and destruction of the environment. Each case showed the society to be oppressive, uncaring, or wantonly destructive. Although he'd been taught history in school, it was still striking to Mark just how miserable life must have been for most people before the Golden Republic came into being.

Toward the end of the room before narrowing again into a corridor, there was another picture. Standing in front of it, Mark recognized the man who had grinned at him in the entry hall earlier. He seemed to be lost in thought as he stared at the picture. As Mark approached, the man seemed to startle. The man looked over and, recognizing Mark, smiled and gave a small nod before moving on from the picture.

Mark looked at the image the man had been staring at. It was a photo of a sculpture within a container of yellow liquid. Initially, Mark was not sure what he was looking at. He did not remember this image from his history books. The sculpture appeared to consist of a man, naked except for a small loincloth who was nailed to a set of crossbeams and wearing thorns around his head. The sculpture was submerged in a glass vial containing yellow liquid.

A look at the plaque revealed that the liquid was in fact urine. The sculpture was apparently of symbolic significance to one of the dominant primitive belief systems still practiced by many people within the United States in the early 21st century. This belief system continued to be a significant factor in the make-up of the corrupt society, and as such it needed to be eliminated if society was to be revolutionized. The artist used this work to mock the beliefs held by those who valued the sculpture as a symbol. By being able to have it publicly displayed, the artist also mocked the waning influence of those believers in society and thus demoralized them further.

"This is a mistake." Mark had to stop himself from uttering the words aloud. Usually, the Party was good about catching this sort of thing. Perhaps this piece held historic significance and was worth including from that standpoint. However, from Mark's experience within the Party, he knew there were several things wrong with displaying an image of the sculpture.

First, it showed a symbol from one of the pre-existing belief systems that the Party had worked so hard to abolish. Some foreign belief systems were still major forces on the global stage and as such their existence still had to be acknowledged. However, the Party was strenuous in its efforts to erase the memory of the belief systems that had once held society back within the territory of the Golden Republic.

Another problem with the piece was that instead of attacking the failings of the previous society or pointing out why the beliefs of that time were wrong, this piece only served to crudely mock the society. Certainly, mockery was a strong force. Sometimes it was still used to caricature foreign powers that were hostile to the Golden Republic. But good mockery used an element of creativity or wit to show mastery over the subject being mocked. A jar of urine certainly wasn't witty or creative.

At this point Mark realized he'd probably been staring at the piece for a bit longer than might be wise. Leslie had been behind him before and had now started to move on towards the corridor to the next room. Mark wondered whether spending too much time looking at a Party approved image might not somehow still trigger the AI in the C-All. It probably wouldn't, but being too far out of the normal was generally a bad idea. Of course, the man he'd seen earlier had clearly spent a while looking at this image too, so maybe his reaction was normal?

"Are you coming?" Leslie asked, a note of irritation was in her voice as she raised her right eyebrow. Clearly, she wasn't sure why Mark would want to spend any more time than necessary looking at a jar of urine.

"Definitely. Interesting exhibit so far," Mark replied while turning and walking up beside her as they entered the next room.

At the end of the corridor another large room opened and bore another introductory text:

The Ascent Toward Glory

The works in this room show the acceleration of both art and society toward the new societal order that would replace the ever more rapidly collapsing social order of the 20th and early 21st century in the United States of America.

The room had a considerable number of pieces. Mark and Leslie steadily made their way through them. By this point, the crowd had thinned slightly, so that it was possible to view the pieces in a less linear fashion. Most of the artworks were like those in the previous room. However, they were all from the ten years just preceding the revolution itself.

Dominating the room was a three-part piece that took up the entirety of a wall. A plaque larger than those used for individual pieces explained that this was a set meant to commemorate some of the momentous events the artist felt had been changing society for the better. It was a set of oil paintings completed only a year prior to the revolution. The paintings were each nearly five feet high and another five feet across. The first showed a large group of couples, each comprising of either two men or two women. The couples were in the center of the frame and back lit by a radiant sun. The sun's light dominated the center of the painting. Surrounding the couples were people of every race coming towards them, many laughing and celebrating, some extending arms in congratulation. Meanwhile, in the corners of the painting were men in strange robes and hats, some carrying curved staves, or wearing symbols like the one

ANNO DOMINI 2064

Mark had seen in the photo earlier. The light from the center was dim in these corners where the men seemed to be dourful and downcast, or in a few cases visibly enraged. Next to the grand painting was a small plaque:

Exempt No More

Prior to the Golden Republic, people would often live together as couples, being bound in an oppressive system that limited them to sexual relations with a single other person throughout their life. Oddly, the system reinforced this practice by limiting those who could participate in it to only those who would join a couple consisting of two persons of opposite sex. Eventually, this restriction was legally eliminated. Many of the primitive belief systems of the time insisted that the practice could still only be entered into by two persons of opposite sex. This painting marks the passage into law that any such belief system that refused to participate in the binding ceremony of two members of the same sex into the practice would no longer be exempt from taxation upon the donations made to that belief system (this being their primary income, the law considerably reduced their wealth and influence.)

The next painting showed a young woman wiping a tear from her cheek as an older woman placed her hand on the first woman's shoulders, comforting her while bearing an enthusiastic expression and pointing towards a line of men. The men were gagged and handcuffed while several police officers led the men towards a waiting prison. Mark read the panel next to:

Hatred Silenced

This painting celebrates the passage of universal hate speech laws. These laws prevented the use of speech as a weapon for the purpose of oppression. The ability to say whatever one wished had been a primary tool the oppressive masters of the past social order had used to maintain their control and enforce the continuation of the system. By taking enough power to end oppressive/hate speech, the soon-to-be founders of the Party and the Golden Republic all but ensured the destruction of the old order.

The final painting in the set was a little harder to interpret. It showed four smaller images. In the first a man and woman were sitting down to a large dinner with several children. They were grinning and looking toward what was clearly an early model android similar to Mark's "Sarah" robot bringing in a large turkey. The next image showed a group of men at leisure playing pool and enjoying alcohol. Another image showed several women lounging on a beach with an android serving them drinks. Last, there was an image showing both men and women playing instruments, painting, and writing. Surrounding these four images were scenes of automatic assembly lines, and outward from these were individual robotic cooks, waiters, maids, and assistants. Mark surmised the painting glorified the advances in using robots for the workforce but wasn't sure how the painting fit with the Revolution. He looked at the plaque and read:

Universal Prosperity

This image celebrates the passage of a universal income law. Up to this time, the ongoing robotization had been seem as a threat to commoners and a way in which the old social order could be upheld indefinitely. As more and more wealth became concentrated in fewer and fewer hands, human labor became unnecessary for most tasks. The passage of the universal income law ensured that all persons could enjoy the fruit of robotic labor. The artist turns the idea of robots as a means of oppression on its head, and shows their labor as a means of liberation from work and allowing the pursuits of camaraderie, leisure, and art.

Leslie joined Mark. "Wow, what do you think? How do you suppose people felt finding out they'd never have to worry about getting a job again?" She asked. "It must have been such a relief. Imagine all those people on the edge of desperation for so long suddenly having all their necessities taken care of."

Mark nodded. "I'm sure it was. It's funny, nowadays, no one really needs to work. But so many of us still want to. It's practically the thing that defines joining the Party officially: getting a Party job. Maybe that's part of the genius of the Party. People who don't want to work don't have to, but those that do can always find a job."

"That's true. I suppose that's really the best, isn't it? Work for those who want it, leisure and plenty for the rest. I'd never really thought about it, but I suppose some people need to feel like they are doing something or need to stay busy somehow. It probably wasn't enough just to give everyone an income."

With that, Leslie turned away from the painting. Mark followed her into the final large exhibit. This room was the largest of the three exhibit spaces. There were literally hundreds of works inside. Here were busts and portraits of the great politicians and leaders of the early Party and the Revolutionary period. Here were statues of soldiers firing towards unseen reactionaries, and paintings of jubilant masses celebrating after the Great Election. Mark noticed the works seemed to be grouped by time period within the Revolution and centered around three major events that gave structure to the timeline of the Revolution.

The first part of the room contained works dealing with the Great Election and the New Constitution. Some were campaign artworks promoting the politicians advocating the New Constitution. Others were paintings, photos, and sculptures showing the tremendous celebrations following the election night. There was a huge painting showing the signing into law the revocation of the old Constitution and the beginning of the Golden Republic. A quote threaded across the painting in gold "unstained by the filth of past hatred and ignorance." Finally, a projector was set up showing real photos from the election campaign, the Great Vote, and the Signing.

The second part of the room showed the battle that ensued as reactionaries attempted to overthrow the new Golden Republic. Here were sculptures, paintings, photos, and even holograms of various soldiers, police, and famous generals. Mark recognized a particularly famous sculpture of a sniper from Chicago who was said to have personally killed over 200 reactionaries. The area also held images of great battles, such as the Battle of Atlanta and the Battle of Chicago. Near these were memorial artworks to victims of terrorist attacks and posters calling for people to report any suspicious behavior or speech. Images glorifying the execution of traitors and the triumph over reactionary forces were also quite plentiful.

The last section of the room was smaller and much more familiar. The space featured artworks that praised the triumph of the C-All and its public emplacement form. It was credited as the device that ultimately ended the terrorist attacks of the reactionaries and ensured the continuance of the Golden Republic for all time. Mark noted several abstract paintings and even VR 3-D renderings of complex moving shapes meant to simulate visually the complexity of the AI that was developed to make the C-All possible. There was also a large stylized painting of the C-All device itself.

Leslie was staring at this painting longer than she had looked at any of other works so far. Mark came to stand next to her. He took a closer look at it. The painting was a skillful render, but he wasn't sure what about it had caught her interest.

"I suppose I owe my childhood to these things." Leslie gestured toward her own C-All. She had a strange look in her eyes, as she pursed her lips. Mark had the sense she was trying very hard

ANNO DOMINI 2064

to hold back emotion.

"What do you mean?" Mark asked. He wasn't sure how he should proceed. He had the distinct impression of danger but wasn't sure why. As far as he could remember, Leslie had never said or done anything in his presence that would arouse suspicion of her loyalty to the party. But the way she'd spoken, Mark felt like there was dangerous ground here.

"If not for the C-Alls, I'd have probably never been brought to the Academy. Who knows if I'd have even made it into the Party?" she answered.

Her answer wasn't what Mark expected, but he did feel safer again. "How did the C-All get you into the Academy?" Mark asked.

"About two weeks after the C-All's were introduced, police arrived at my parents' home at night. Let's just say my parents were less than happy when the police arrived. The police took me to the Academy, and I never saw my parents again. Plenty of kids at the Academy still saw their parents. I've always assumed my parents said or did something that put their loyalty in doubt, but I never knew what it was. I suppose it's better that I don't know. I'm better off having been raised in the Academy than by reactionaries..." She turned from the painting and looked at Mark. "Otherwise, who knows where I'd be now?"

Mark wasn't sure how to respond. Leslie had seen enough and began to walk toward the room's exit. Mark followed her. Outside of the exhibit was a small gift shop with picture books, miniature copies of the artworks, and biographies of some of the artists that had been featured. Mark thought it would be proper to buy something, and his place could use a little art on the walls. He decided to purchase a print of *"Universal Prosperity."* Leslie briefly considered seeing more of the museum, but they decided to save it for another visit.

On the ride home, Mark was quiet. The experience had been more profound than he'd expected. The sense he'd had walking into the building contrasted markedly with the emotions that built as he and Leslie toured the exhibit. At first, he'd felt a tremendous sense of openness, and, some other indescribable feeling, like being a bird upon the wing. As they had made their way through the main exhibit, he'd felt a growing sense of entrapment. Even after leaving the exhibit and entering the main entrance hall he couldn't help feeling as though he was being put back into a cage. Worse, there was the sense of resenting the cage more than before because of the few moments spent outside it.

While Mark was lost in his thoughts, Leslie was unusually chatty. She seemed determined to keep a conversation going. Mainly she brought up things going on at work, recent interactions with co-workers, or even their style choices. Mark tried gamely to keep up but couldn't help but be a little distracted. Halfway through the ride, he could tell Leslie was getting a little annoyed with him. He tried to shrug off his thoughts about the museum and engage more fully.

Mark's efforts must have paid off. When they got back to his apartment and closed the door, Leslie suddenly turned and pulled herself up to him, giving him a rather hard kiss. She followed this with further repeat kisses, rather insistently. Leslie hadn't been flirting with him beforehand, so her actions took him by surprise. As she unzipped his coat and started to unbutton his shirt, he couldn't see a reason to object, and so again set out to keep up with where Leslie was leading.

Afterward, they had a late lunch together. Leslie had an athletic engagement that evening and so departed soon after. Mark would be playing in his basketball league much of the following day. He headed to the gym that night for a little practice. In this way, the rest of the weekend passed normally enough. However, now before bed both Saturday and Sunday night, Mark found himself thinking about the museum. Two images kept repeating before him, the wings of the museum spread against the blue sky, and the stylized image of the C-All. The

ANNO DOMINI 2064

images seemed to flit back and forth, elevating him into the sky one moment, then pulling him mercilessly back to earth the next. He wrestled with this for over an hour each night, until finally his fatigue overcame him. Mercifully, his sleep both nights was the dreamless sleep of temporary oblivion.

4.

Resuming work on Monday felt like a return to normalcy. Mark spent the day planning the spring parades necessary for morale after the gray Milwaukee winter. Being at work made the weekend excursion feel as if it were from another life. The monotony of routine suppressed the last vestiges of freedom he'd felt seeing the wings of the museum. He missed Leslie at lunch and instead ended up sitting with his coworker Steve. The two men discussed nothing of importance. In the spring, Steve had taken the notion of purchasing a small boat to take onto Lake Michigan. Steve figured when he was next reassigned it wouldn't be too hard to sell it to someone here, if he wasn't able to take it with him should he have another coastal assignment. Mark followed along and tried to sound interested. When he wasn't actively working, he noticed all of his social interactions were similar. Everyone engaged in careful small talk. The same was true outside of work in social gatherings.

For a moment at the museum, Mark had felt like he'd experienced something profound, but there was no one with whom he could discuss it. Mark did his best not to think about it. By Wednesday, he had almost put the museum completely out of mind. That morning, one of the image processors for the next virtual poster campaign began to malfunction. Mark contacted IT. Mark immediately recognized the man who came up to the floor to repair it. He was the man Mark had seen at the museum. The man recognized Mark as well and grinned as he walked over and introduced himself.

"Nice to meet you, I'm Christopher, from IT. I hear you're having a problem with one of your processors." Christopher had a ready smile with brilliant white teeth that contrasted with his light brown skin and dark hair. Standing about six feet tall, he was trim and fit, with a neatly shaven face and brown eyes.

"Nice to meet you, I'm Mark. I think I may have seen you the other day." Mark was sure it was him, but felt he needed the confirmation. It felt important, as seeing Christopher brought the memory of his feeling from the museum rushing back to him.

"At the Art Museum. Yes, I remember you. They have quite the exhibit there now, don't they?" Christopher then looked toward the image processor. "Well, why don't we take a look here?" With that, he was opening the casing to look at the chips and wires beneath. He moved with practiced hands and a look on his face of intense focus. Mark sat down at a nearby desk to work while awaiting the processor coming back online.

"I noticed you were there with one of our female colleagues. Was it her idea or yours?" Christopher suddenly asked. Mark looked over. Christopher was working at removing some chips with specialized tools and appeared fully focused on his task. Apparently though, he was interested in making conversation while he worked.

"Hers I guess. I'd never been to the museum before that. I honestly hadn't thought of it before she decided she wanted me to go with her," Mark replied.

Christopher continued to work as he replied, "Good for you then, trying something new. You never know what you'll enjoy until you try it." He paused. "Though I suppose there are some things you can be sure of one way or another beforehand." He turned to smile at Mark and then turned back to his work. "It's a shame about this processor. I'll bet this is really slowing you up."

"A bit," Mark replied. "I was using it to process up the next set of recruiting VR posters. I was going to present them later today to a few of the Inner Party heads who are visiting. If you can't fix it quickly, this might turn into something of a bad day for me."

"A bad day…" Christopher mused. "Days are funny like that. One moment they can be fine, and the next something happens, and they go bad. Still, most of the time it's not the random things that make up the day, is it? It's what already happened in the days before that decide how most of our days go."

The remark seemed innocuous enough. Yet Mark got the sense that Christopher was saying something deliberate, although he wasn't sure. He started to pay close attention.

Christopher paused before returning to his subject. "For instance, suppose today is a good day for me, but the day before was miserable. You can almost bet that if the day following a miserable day is decent, it's because the day before that miserable day, and likely a good many other days before that miserable day, I'd done things decently enough so that the effects from those other days overwhelmed the bad day and I could go back to having a good day again. If I was having a miserable day, but the day before had been good, you could again almost guess there had been a series of days with bad decisions before the good day whose effects meant I was back to being miserable today."

"I suppose that's why we always try to make good decisions," Mark replied. Christopher's statement seemed obvious enough on its face and enough like common wisdom that it wouldn't alert the AI of the C-Alls. It was a bit odd, though, for a day-to-day workplace conversation.

"Very true," Christopher replied. "Now, lucky for you, in this case your day isn't likely to be ruined by a random happenstance. There is a small defect I can fix easily. I suppose if you've been making good decisions long enough before today, your meeting will be fine, and you'll still have a good day." Again, a bright smile flashed across Christopher's face.

"Thanks! Hopefully it will," Mark replied. Christopher

ANNO DOMINI 2064

continued to work on the processor. Mark wasn't sure why, but he felt compelled to ask, "What time do you normally get lunch?"

Christopher's grin broadened. "I usually have a break around 1 PM. Maybe I can meet you in the cafeteria sometime. I just got here on a new rotation. The group you saw me with at the museum was a bunch of other new year ones. There's a new initiative for the rotation program where they show us local sites before we start. I think the idea is to orient us to the city and give us a chance to get to know some other new Party members before we begin our duties." Christopher stood up. "The processor works again. Hopefully now you'll be all set."

Mark stood up to say goodbye. "Great! Thanks again. It was good to meet you. Hopefully, I'll see you in the cafeteria or around the office." Mark shook his hand, and Christopher walked towards the elevators. Mark got back to work for his upcoming meeting.

Luckily, his preparations had been more than adequate, and the meeting went well. That night, he met Leslie at her apartment. While they were eating, he asked whether the new rotation had affected her department at all. There had been a couple of new people in his department, but no one who would work directly with him. Although individuals were usually on four-year rotations, the rotations didn't always align across departments. Sometimes the Party allowed individuals a few extra months to help finish up work at the old rotation or moved them sooner if their work finished early.

Leslie replied, "There were a couple new people starting today in my department. One is a slightly older woman who will mostly be working on the organization end of local community events. The other is a young man fresh out of college. They are putting him in as an understudy for some news shows."

Mark raised an eyebrow and teased, "He must be good-looking if they are grooming him for news announcements.

47

Should I be jealous?"

Smirking, Leslie replied, "Oh yes. I'm afraid I've gotten quite bored with you. Obviously, what I need is a new young man in my life to bring back some excitement." She took a bite of grilled chicken from her salad and speaking with her eyes, dared him to reply.

"Excitement? I seem to recall suggesting we try that rollercoaster VR game last week and you said your life had enough excitement in it already without adding rollercoasters into the mix."

Leslie's eyes picked up, and she swallowed hurriedly to respond. "I said I'm looking for excitement from a young *man*. Not junior high excitement from being with a *boy* riding a rollercoaster."

"Touche," Mark replied. "Anyway, I met one of the new IT guys today that just rotated in. I recognized him from the Art Museum the other day."

Leslie's expression changed briefly before she regained composure, "That's funny, there were an awful lot of people at the museum that day. I don't really remember noticing anyone in particular."

"We were right behind him for a little while when we first went into the exhibit. He recognized me, too. His name is Christopher. He seems nice."

"Well, that's good. I suppose we'll still be around here long enough that it's worth getting to know new people. Another year and a half, and you know neither one of us will care one bit about any new arrivals," Leslie replied.

"Ugh, I don't want to think about that," Mark said glumly. "That'll mean things will end with you around then. I've never really been with a woman this long before. I'm not looking forward to it ending."

Leslie put down her fork. "I've never been with a man this

long either. I know there's not really a law against it, but it is kind of frowned upon." She paused for a moment and then continued, "I've talked to a few other women who've had longer relationships. One said that after a few times the endings were hurting so much she decided to avoid long-term relationships completely. Another one gave up on dating altogether after a long romance. I don't know. A few women also told me they still felt it was worth it, even after how much it hurts when it ends." She stopped speaking. Mark wasn't sure what to say.

After another moment Leslie went on, "I want to say thank you for the day at the Museum. I didn't mean to talk about my parents like that. I could tell after we walked out I'd upset you and you were quiet at first in the car. I really didn't mean it like any kind of resentment against the Party or anything, and I definitely wasn't trying to get either of us in trouble. It just kind of hit me, you know? Looking at that image. I mean, even if it was for good reasons, it's still hard to lose your parents when you're a kid. So yeah, thanks for still being with me after that. I know you really tried to be sweet to me on the way home once the shock wore off. I really appreciated that."

Mark again didn't know what to say. He felt bad. While her story had surprised him, the reason for his disquiet after the exhibit had nothing to do with her revelation. Nor had he really been worried about getting in trouble or that Leslie might be at all disloyal. He wasn't sure though that it would make Leslie feel any better to tell her this.

Mark decided it was best not to contradict her. "It was no problem. I can't imagine how tough that must have been at first. I was lucky that my parents were always big supporters of the Revolution and the Party. I mean, geesh, I still see them every couple of years in their retirement community in Vermont. I don't even know what it's like to not have parents."

Leslie nodded. "It's not just that, though. My parents were *traitors*. You don't know how embarrassing it is. It's not just that

I don't have parents. I don't want to talk about them. I don't want anyone to *know* about them. *That's* the hard part."

Mark realized this went way beyond what he could ever really empathize with. He couldn't imagine what that would be like. "I'm really sorry, Leslie. I didn't realize. I'm so sorry..." Mark put down his fork and took Leslie's hand from across the table. They held each other's hands for a long moment. Then, somewhat awkwardly, they resumed eating.

Eventually, Leslie brought up how the recent games Mark had played in his gym league had gone. Mark's team had been doing well and had a chance of being competitive in the tournament in the spring. Mark discussed how he felt like the team was beginning to gel and work together more instinctively than last year. He had high hopes for the tournament.

When they'd finished, Leslie used her C-All to order her "Sarah" to clean up. He and Leslie teamed up together in some multiplayer VR games, and Mark ultimately stayed the night.

The following day, Don was walking in as they entered City Hall. Seeing the two of them together, he smirked. "Had a good night, did we?" His tone held the smug satisfaction of having one over on Mark.

"That's hardly your business, is it?" Leslie replied. She turned to Mark. "I'll see you later. Don't let this buffoon tease you too much." With that, she quickened her pace and reached an elevator that closed immediately behind her while Mark and Don walked through the lobby.

"Sorry about that, she's been a little out of sorts lately..." Mark offered to Don. There wasn't much point in antagonizing him, even if he was a jerk at times.

"Oh, it's no problem. I'm just surprised you're still with her after this long. Guys like you and me, rising stars in the Party and all, it's not like we don't have our pick of the women around here. I'd have thought you'd be ready to be with someone new

ANNO DOMINI 2064

by now." There was a note of curiosity in Don's voice. Mark suspected he was being sincere.

Mark replied, "I've had a few other women try to flirt with me. I've caught a few glances, too, that I'm sure I could have followed up on if I'd wanted. So yeah, I suppose you're right that I could have found someone else by now if I'd wanted." Mark wasn't sure why he was opening up to Don of all people. But Don had seemed genuinely interested, and Mark felt like he wanted to put his thoughts into words.

"There's a lot to Leslie. I guess I still just find her fascinating. It's fun to spend time with her. It's interesting to get to know her better. You don't get to do that with a woman if you don't stay with her for very long." It was more complicated than that, but this was close to the truth. If the C-All AI, or worse, a human monitor, had been listening the night before and then listened again to this conversation, the pieces would fit together.

"Huh, I guess I can see that. Not really what I'm looking for, but I suppose I can respect that. Well, good luck with it then." At this, Don extended his hand to Mark. Surprised, Mark took it and the two shook hands just before the elevator opened. Don road the elevator up to the 32nd floor, Mark and Don exchanged nods as Don exited ahead of him and turned toward his desk at the opposite side of the floor.

The conversation was still on his mind when he ran into Christopher at lunch. Christopher greeted him with an easy grin and a wave. He had picked out his meal and asked if Mark would like him to save a spot for him.

"Sure, I'll be there in just a minute." Thinking Leslie was likely to eat around this time and would probably give him a hard time if he loaded up on junk food again, Mark tried to make several healthy choices that wouldn't be too tasteless. He found Christopher seated back toward the left corner of the seating area. He took a seat across from him.

51

"How are things going in IT?" he asked Christopher as he sat down. He picked up a rice cracker and mixed it with a curry paste while letting Christopher open the conversation.

"Well enough. Mostly today I've been handling some bugs that have been cropping up with the new C-All updates. There's a bug in the software that deals with shared AR vision. Some of the meetings people have been hosting have had delays because not everyone can see the graphs or figures at the same time."

Mark ate his curry covered cracker and then replied. "Yeah, one of our meetings early today things seemed a little glitchy. It was nothing that halted the meeting, though. It seems like every major patch update has something that goes a little wrong." He took a drink of his hot apple cider and then continued, "How have the people in your department been?"

"Everyone has been really welcoming. IT is funny, sometimes we're all just hanging out together with nothing to do, and at other times, we're all off taking care of different problems around the building and barely see each other. Today with the patch roll out, we've all been super busy. Yesterday though, we were goofing around playing virtual table tennis most of the day."

"Well, that sounds awesome. Beats making pie charts and talking about military recruitment figures all day," Mark replied.

"Yeah, but there's not a lot of advancement opportunity. What you're doing really matters to the higher ups. It could get you a nice rotation next time around or even a promotion," Christopher countered.

Mark paused for a moment. "Yeah, lately I've almost been questioning if that's still what I want. I mean, I think I still do, but... I don't know." Realizing he couldn't just leave it at that, he quickly joked, "Maybe I'm just starting to get lazier as I get older."

ANNO DOMINI 2064

For a second, Mark thought he caught Christopher looking at him thoughtfully. However, he quickly followed Mark's joke with a quick laugh. "I hear that's what happens to everyone, eventually. The body slows down, and you just stop feeling like working as much. Then before you know it, you're in a retirement home watching your stories all day long."

Mark laughed. "Maybe I'll need an early retirement then. I don't know. Probably just the cold weather and the gray skies getting to me. I was out in Virginia before this rotation. I don't remember ever feeling so drained out there." Realizing he was neglecting his food, Mark ate a baby carrot and then started to work on the sub sandwich he'd made for himself.

"You should try one of those light therapy devices. I hear they work for some people on rotations in places like this. I knew a guy at my last rotation in Seattle who swore by them," Christopher remarked.

Mark heard footsteps approaching from behind. Glancing over, he saw Leslie approaching. She took the chair next to him. "Hello." She reached a hand to greet Christopher. "I'm Leslie."

Christopher took it. "Hi, I'm Christopher. You and Mark must be friends. I believe I saw you with him at the art museum together."

"Oh yes, you must be the new IT staffer Mark mentioned to me. It's nice to meet you. How are you liking Milwaukee so far?" Leslie warmed to making small talk with Christopher. Mark made use of the interruption to eat more of his food. He had a tendency when talking with people to forget to eat.

Leslie got Christopher to talk a little about the IT department and how he was getting on with the other staffers. In turn, Leslie discussed some of the work being done in the media department. It relieved Mark to see the two getting on rather amiably. So far, he rather liked Christopher (he made a mental note to ask if "Chris" would work), and he felt he could really use a male friend around. He had a couple of male friends from

53

his last rotation in Virginia with whom he still met up for VR multiplayer games. But he knew it would be good to have someone more local to hang out with as well.

"Hey, why don't we meet up some time for drinks after work?" Christopher was looking at Mark as he spoke, pulling Mark back into the conversation. "I hear Milwaukee is famous for its beer. I guess the cheese and bratwurst are good, too. Maybe we do a little post-work beer and snacks?"

"Yeah, that sounds good. There's a place on National Avenue close to the old baseball stadium and the Veterans Hospital. It's a little drive from here, but the food is fantastic, and they have an old-fashioned bar that I like," Mark replied.

"I think I'll pass," Leslie interjected. "I'm not a big beer drinker. We should meet up some other time to do something else, though."

"Definitely. That place sounds cool. I'm free tonight. Want to meet up and head over after work, Mark?"

Mark thought for a moment. He didn't have much planned tonight. He wouldn't mind getting a drink after work. "Yeah, signal my C-All when you're wrapping up. I'm usually done around five. I don't have any off-site visits today, so I can just meet you down in the lobby. Should be fun."

"Great. I'll see you then. For now, I should get back to it." Mark noticed Christopher had finished his plate during his conversation with Leslie. Christopher shook his and Leslie's hands again and proceeded off toward the cafeteria exit.

"He seems nice," Leslie commented. "You could probably use a guy friend here, too. It would take some load off me," she teased.

"Gee, didn't realize I was such a burden." Mark used a low-pitched, somber voice, one that resembled a cartoon donkey he vaguely remembered seeing as a child who was always glum. He

ANNO DOMINI 2064

continued with the voice, "Guess I'll have to try extra hard to be his friend. Wouldn't want you to feel like you have to spend more time with me when it's been this hard already." Mark smiled.

"Ha, ha." Leslie's face then turned serious. "But really, he seems nice. I'll bet you two will have fun. I'll come hang out with you guys some other night. You should try to get to know him." A soft earnestness had replaced her earlier teasing.

"Thanks. He does, and you're right. I was thinking the same thing, honestly. It should be good." They shared a little more about their mornings while finishing lunch and then split off to resume the workday.

Mark spent most of the afternoon in strategy meetings. Word had it that the Golden Republic might intercede in the Breton affair. There was concern that a failure to calm the situation was likely to lead to a wider war across Europe. The Golden Republic planned to play an intermediary role, but troops might be necessary to help enforce a peace. This action would increase recruitment needs and so new inducements were being offered by the Party. The question would be how to market these inducements to raise recruitment by the desired level. Mark felt that while the Party should highlight the new pay raise, the new guarantee of higher priority in healthcare queues for families of soldiers should be the primary selling point. Most Party members took it for granted they could easily see a doctor when needed. Mark had now had enough contact with non-members to know that being able to see a doctor when needed was a great worry for most people. Wait times could easily be several months for non-emergencies.

By the end of the afternoon, he had mostly convinced his coworkers of the approach. After a solid day's work, he was enjoying the thought of heading over to Kegel's Inn to meet Christopher. He rather imagined there was something old-fashioned to getting a beer after work. The restaurant itself was a true relic from the past. Dark European hardwoods made up the lower walls and the bar, while the upper walls consisted of plaster with painted scenes of rustic German peasant life from the 1800s. The food was as authentic German as could be found in Milwaukee, which was saying something, and the menu had not significantly changed in over 100 years. The restaurant itself was older yet. Mark signaled Christopher as he was finishing via the C-All and then waited for him in the lobby.

Christopher soon joined him from the elevator. "Ready to go?" Mark asked as he approached. "I think so," Christopher answered. "I feel like I could use a good drink after this afternoon. One of Leslie's colleagues in media decided it would be a good idea to open an attachment from an outside email. Turned out it was some ransomware from a hacker in Russia. Idiot probably didn't realize he'd gotten a Party position e-mail address. Our folks at the embassy assure me the FSB there will be knocking on the moron's door by tomorrow. Something tells me the Party won't be paying his little ransom for the password to unlock that particular computer. Still, we had a heck of a time locking it down to make sure it didn't contaminate any other accounts or devices."

"Wow. Well, that sounds like a busy afternoon. Let's get a drink then." The auto-car he'd summoned was waiting outside. The drive took about fifteen minutes. On the way, they discussed the ransomware attack in more detail. Mark shared what he'd been working on regarding the new recruitment inducements. At the mention of the Breton crisis, Christopher seemed to turn pensive.

"It's a tough situation over there. I feel for the soldiers who end up going. I can see the reasoning since the different factions in Europe will see the Golden Republic as being neutral on the matter. We're not exactly known for favoring either side since they are both primarily motivated against each other by religion. Or at least that's what they say. The Bretons are mostly native French, while the French Caliphate is mainly populated by people of Middle Eastern descent nowadays. It's hard to say how much of that is playing a role in the conflict."

Mark thought about this. "I'm sure it plays a role. In any case, the Poles and the Eastern League are threatening intervention and are mobilizing. Russia is also promising support for the Bretons, so now the German Islamic Republic is threatening to go to war to support the French Caliphate. That has the Eastern Germans in an uproar... Then the Turks are announcing they would support the GIR. The Chinese don't want to see Europe spiral out of control, but they see this as more our area. So unless we want to see another major war in Europe I think the Party is right to take the lead in breaking this up before it gets out of hand."

Christopher nodded. "I definitely understand the thinking. Put a significant force in the field to stop the Caliphate's invasion and then use diplomacy backed by force. It seems like the best way to go. I was just thinking about what it will be like for the soldiers when they get there. It's hard to say whether the Caliphate's troops will back down."

The car turned off National into the old parking lot. With the advent of auto-cars most parking lots in the city had been replaced or repurposed. However, this far west from downtown many lots survived. Mark led Christopher to the front door. As they stepped through, Mark felt himself transported back in time. Christopher smiled in delight. The two found places at the far end of the. On the opposite end, they saw a doorway into the restaurant proper. Beyond, they could hear sounds from a few restaurant patrons. Meanwhile, three non-Party men, all middle-aged, sat with each other in the central area of the bar. The bartender was tending these men but nodded toward Christopher and Mark as they sat down.

"This place looks great. How did you find it?" Christopher asked. His eyes darted about the room, taking in the small details in the woodworking and the old photographs and paintings that dotted the walls.

Mark had to think a second. "I think when I first got here one of the outgoing fourth years I worked with in the office mentioned it. I didn't have a lot to do yet so I figured it would be worth trying it out. I've been coming back now and then ever since. Sometimes I take Leslie here for supper, too."

The bartender finished with the men in the center of the bar and came to take their drink orders. Mark chose a dark ale he'd tried here previously and liked. Christopher chose a locally brewed lager he'd noted on a chalkboard behind the bar listing specials for the night. The bartender quickly returned with their drinks, and they continued talking.

"So, I take it you and Leslie have been together for a while then?" Christopher asked.

"We have," Mark replied. "I know that's not very normal. We hadn't really planned it or anything; we just sort of... never broke up, I guess. We're not planning on going off rotation though, so I suppose it will eventually end sooner or later."

Christopher took a drink before responding. "I've seen a few people go off rotation. I've heard from them later that it's hard to adjust to at first, and the Party frowns on it. But after a few years, they just kind of melted in with the larger population of non-Party members. Whether that's what they'd been hoping for or not, I guess I can't really say."

Mark finished a gulp. "It's hard to imagine what that's like. I mean, I guess I've taken a lot of my purpose in life from my work. Most non-Party members don't work. I mean, I know a lot of them do side jobs for extra money, and a few even own businesses like this place here. A handful do full-time jobs that aren't managed by the Party. But you know what I mean. Most people just live off the universal income." Both he and Christopher paused for a bit at this and continued to nurse their drinks.

Mark continued, "I've worked enough now in the different neighborhoods and the local Party centers to have some idea what it's probably like. I hate to admit it, but I'm not very impressed. Most of the people are listless, or... just filled with drama. When you talk with the people, it's all about who did what to who and who ought to be helping care for whose baby, and often why this person hates that person. Or else, you meet these people who say little, and when you press them, you find they don't really have much to say. They seem to watch the other people who have all the drama while they just kind of float along. Honestly, something tells me if I didn't work for the Party, I'd probably be one of those people. I don't care much for drama."

Christopher fixed him for a moment with a piercing look. "That's true, I think. What you said doesn't fit everyone out there, but it fits a lot of people. There are also the bad ones out there, the predators who stay within the lines just enough so the Party doesn't go after them, or at least doesn't punish them harshly. But they prey on the weak and the naïve and cause considerable drama without sticking around to fix it afterward. They don't really talk about the drama, and sometimes they'll look like the floaters. But then when they find the right victim, they become all charm and kindness. They keep that act up until the point they get what they want from a person. Then they either move on, or else stay a little longer to take enjoyment in torturing the people who relied on them or cared for them."

"You sound like you've had some experience with these people." Mark commented. Thinking back, he could remember cases where people had talked about someone who would fit the description. He didn't think he'd met such a person though, at least not knowingly.

"Not personally, at least in a direct sense. But I've had close friends who were badly hurt by such people. I've also met plenty more who tell similar stories. The predators are out there. But anyway, I take it then your work is meaningful enough it wouldn't be worth giving up, even if it meant getting to stay with a particularly good woman?"

For someone he'd just met, Mark thought, Christopher had a way of getting right into the heart of matters. Oddly though, he found he didn't really mind.

"Well, I've thought about that. I really like Leslie. I'm not sure just being with her would be enough; especially if that was basically all I had to live for at that point. I doubt we could fill the days just the two of us. Plus, if we had kids, since we would still be Party members, the Party would take them to the academies right away. So it's not even like we could put our time into kids like the general masses sometimes do. I don't know… There's some attraction to it, but it doesn't seem like it's enough on its own." At this point Mark gazed somewhat morbidly into his beer. He then looked over to Christopher and found him studying Mark with a look of intense interest.

"It probably wouldn't be enough. Not on its own, especially without being able to raise children. The only thing you'd have to live for is each other. That might sound romantic, but I think with nothing else to support it you'd both sense it wasn't enough and a bitterness would set in. You'd probably both be miserable and maybe even angry with each other before the end."

Christopher delivered these words with a slow thoughtfulness and precision. Mark had the sense that Christopher had probably only just reached this conclusion. But having arrived at it, he seemed certain it was true. The words, spoken with such weight, appeared to end any future Mark might have still considered where he and Leslie went off cycle together. "I suppose the question then is, what are the alternatives?" Mark asked.

Christopher suddenly continued, breaking into Mark's reflection on his early pronouncement. "You seem to do well at work, from what I hear you are a real up and comer. Perhaps you could work your way into the Inner Party?"

Mark took another drink before answering. In his mind, he could see himself back in California, living in a large individual house by the ocean. Comfort, power, and women: it was hardly a secret that for a man high within the Party, all these things were attainable to a degree far beyond what was available to the common man. Mark also considered that it was possible someone would analyze the C-All recording of this conversation later, so he needed to be careful with his answer. At the same time, he felt a need to express his real feelings on the matter with Christopher. He sensed Christopher might be someone who could help.

Mark swallowed and then began, "It's possible. I'll admit I'm good at what I do, and I suspect the Party could have uses for me at a higher level. I do feel, though, as I get older, some of the passion and drive, maybe even ambition, which I used to feel.... I can feel it wearing away. I used to feel like if I were an important man within the Party, well, then that would really be the pinnacle of life. At that point, I'd be satisfied with things and could just enjoy it until I got too old and had to retire, and then hopefully I could retire comfortably and enjoy that for a while."

Christopher broke in here. "That sounds pretty nice. I think that's what a lot of people hope for out of life." It sounded both like support, but also a prompt, and Mark took it as such.

"It probably would be nice. I'm not even sure why I'm not feeling as driven to achieve it as I used to be. I think it's still basically my plan for now. I guess I can't really think of anything better to aim for." At this, Christopher gave him a sympathetic smile before taking another drink of his lager.

The two sat in thought. Christopher then asked whether Mark wanted to get some food and stay a bit longer. This seemed like a good idea, so Mark got up and talked to the hostess. She ushered them through to the restaurant side of the first floor.

Old wooden tables sat on older wooden floors, surrounded by slowly fading painted walls showing various German huntsmen seeking prey, peasants in the fields, and pastoral scenes with various animal life native to Germany.

Christopher told Mark about some of the goings on within IT and his experiences on his previous rotation. Mark shared a little more about some other restaurants and forms of entertainment he'd tried around Milwaukee, including several theater venues and local music groups. Mark couldn't help but feel Christopher had steered the conversation back to safer topics, after what had been initially a rather deep conversation.

"Do you play VR games?" Christopher suddenly asked. He shot Mark a conspiratorial grin. "I'm pretty good at them. I'm always looking for people to play either with or against."

"I do. Not as much as I used to, but I think I hold up reasonably well with most kinds of games. Is there a server you tend to play in?" Mark replied.

Christopher tapped into the air a few times. Mark could see behind his C-All as he picked through a few windows. A link appeared on Mark's own C-All screen floating just before him. He reached up and clicked to save it. "There," Christopher replied, "I won't be on tonight, but can you meet me after work tomorrow night around 8 PM at that server?"

Mark thought about his schedule. He was pretty sure he would be free then. "Sure," he replied. He set himself a reminder in his C-All. "Sounds like a plan. What games do you play?"

"I've been playing paintball a lot lately, but I enjoy a lot of the strategy games, too. Once we get into the server, we can decide on whatever we want. There are lots of options available on it I play with other friends. Hopefully, I can introduce you to a few of them sometime." The two finished their meal and were sure to tip the waitress and bartender as they headed out. As they were walking out, Mark remembered to ask Christopher about his name.

"By the way, do you prefer Christopher or Chris?" Mark asked. Christopher chuckled in response and then replied, "I don't really mind either. Plenty of people call me both." Separate autocars awaited them in the small lot beside the building, and they exchanged farewells before each heading home.

On the drive back, Mark noted how quickly the sky had gone pitch dark. He could see only a few stars between the clouds that covered the sky. Between the winter clouds and the light pollution, he realized he hadn't seen many stars of late. Looking at them, he reflected on how universal stars were for humans. You could live anywhere in the world, amongst nearly infinite varieties of peoples, plants, animals, and terrain, but the stars were the same for everyone. As the autocar dropped him off, he took a moment to look at the stars a little longer before heading in.

Feeling the crisp winter air on his face, the stars felt almost as if they fit with the winter, as though they possessed a cold beauty that could only be experienced when surrounded by snow with steam coming from one's breath. Mark rethought his earlier assumption that the stars were the same for everyone. Looking on the stars from a place of heat could never quite feel the same, and he realized the stars would hold a different meaning, a different beauty when viewed elsewhere.

He thought back to a time when he was a kid and his dad had taken him camping in the summer. He and his dad had spent a night with a campfire looking up at the stars. The night had surrounded them with warm summer air, the scent of pine, and the sound of leaves rustling. At the time he'd seen the stars with a sense of wonder. They had felt vast and gave a feeling of nature, wild and untamed. They were different tonight. The stars back then didn't hold the cold and austerity that they held for him tonight.

As he proceeded into his apartment, he wondered how

other people might think about the stars. It wasn't something he'd ever really thought about before. Maybe he'd ask Leslie about it. With that thought, a small stab of pain shot through his thoughts. Eventually, things would have to end with Leslie. He'd not really faced it until now. But after his conversation with Christopher, it had become real to him. He realized he really had been keeping going off cycle as a possibility in his mind. Even as they'd both rejected the idea talking to one another, he'd held it out as an option for himself to avoid facing the reality he would eventually have to lose her. Now the only question was when would be best to end it, and he understood he had no answer to this question.

Getting into his apartment, he decided there was no sense rushing any decisions. To distract himself, he tried practicing VR paintball for a while in case Christopher and some of his friends decided that's what they wanted to play. He logged in to a public game and was promptly trounced. He played about five games, getting a little better each time, although he was no asset to his team on the fifth game, even if he wasn't as large a liability as he was in the first. He was sure he'd have to play for quite a while to be any good, but maybe he wouldn't be a complete embarrassment to himself tomorrow.

With that, he finished and got ready for bed. He tried to keep his thoughts on the games he'd played and how he might improve. It was better than thinking about Leslie.

5.

The next day, Mark went to work feeling unsettled about Leslie. He felt anxiety and confusion that tugged at his chest almost palpably. He nearly panicked when his C-All received a call from Leslie during his commute in the autocar. It was uncanny. They saw each other often. She called occasionally, but it was rare. Generally, they would send text messages when not with each other.

Mark accepted the call. Leslie's face materialized in miniature appearing a few feet in front of him through the C-All. Her stylishly angled auburn hair framed her light brown eyes. It struck Mark again just how beautiful he found her.

"Hi Mark, I thought I'd just call since it would be easier. I wanted to check if you'd be free tonight. Allison wanted to have a get together after work at her place. I guess it's her birthday and somehow, she forgot to tell anyone until literally the day of. Personally, I think Allison was nervous to have a party. But then Michelle was talking to her last night, and when she found out she pretty much forced Allison into it. I'm sure Allison must have blundered by even saying something to Michelle about it, because she never told ME it was her birthday or I would have made sure we were doing something. Anyway, would you be able to come?"

Mark thought for a moment whether he should try to reschedule with Christopher. "Well, I promised Christopher that I'd meet him tonight in VR to meet some of his friends and do some gaming. But I'm sure it could wait…"

Leslie smiled. "Oh, no don't back out on that. Not right

65

away when you're just getting to know him, that would look bad. You don't have to be at Allison's tonight. It'll probably end up being mostly women, anyway. I mean, I wouldn't want any of them stealing you, with you being probably the only attractive man in the room and all..." She gave him a flirtatious grin.

"Gee, when you put it that way, maybe I *should* go," he teased back. "I think you're right, though. It wouldn't be good to back out first thing. Plus, I spent a bunch of time last night prepping my skills..." He grinned. "Wouldn't want all that practice to go to waste."

"Uh-huh," Leslie mocked seriousness. "Well, try not to make *too* much of a fool of yourself hon. Tell me about it later."

"Will do." With that, they exchanged goodbyes, and the call ended. While they were talking, the feeling in his chest had abated, but it now came back full force. How could Mark leave her? But then, if being together would really make her miserable, how could he try to stay with her? Leslie loved her career; he could see her becoming bored just as much as he would if she left it. If he had been the one to push her to go off rotation, he could also see her eventually resenting him for it. It was an impossible situation.

The day proceeded at what felt like a snail's pace. Meetings filled Mark's morning. Mark could barely stay focused enough to tell what they were about. He occasionally gave appropriate answers to prove he was listening. He couldn't help being distracted, though. So on occasions where usually he would have spoken up, he was content to let others direct the flow of the meetings. At lunch he was relieved when neither Leslie nor Christopher were present. He sat a little way off by himself and ate quickly. He then went out to an autocar he'd summoned for his planned afternoon rounds at the local education and recruitment centers.

The weather reflected Mark's mood. A gray pall had fallen over the city. Clouds had swept in off the lake to add fog to the damp grayness of dirty, partially melted snow. Even the cream city brick seemed gray in the fog. As he approached the first station, the sharp metallic lines of the building's architecture rose through the fog like a knife cutting through smoke. The building seemed to lunge suddenly toward him in the last fifty feet as sharp details came into focus. A feeling almost of dread seized him as the car came to a stop. He had to work to calm his breathing before he composed himself enough to get out of the car.

Once out the door, the dread passed. The normalcy of his routine took over again. He made his way inside, completed the inspection, reviewed the latest recruitment files, and congratulated the station workers on the uptick of two additional recruits from last week's five to this week's seven. It might have been chance, but the new incentives and good work from the Party members at the station may have played a role too. Either way, it was worth congratulating them. As Mark exited the building, he felt sure no one would have noticed anything different in his mannerisms. It was only as he got into the autocar and sped toward the next station that some of his previous anxiety took hold again.

He realized that for the first time he had a desire significantly at odds with the Party. He wanted to be with Leslie, with no definite endpoint. Such relationships were against the Party's plan for its members. It seemed unfair to him, and the fact he felt that way filled him with fear. This feeling was dangerously close to resenting the Party. People who resented the Party had a way of disappearing.

Still, it didn't seem fair. Why not allow Party members to stay together? Why not allow Party members to start families like everyone outside the Party? The parents could still send children to the academies during the day. Why shouldn't the children be able to stay with their parents the rest of the time? It had worked well enough when he was growing up.

The autocar approached the next station. Mark realized

he might as well wonder why the sun rose in the east. The Party would not change its policies on his account. Maybe things were different within the Inner Party. There were rumors. Of course, by the time he made it anywhere within the Inner Party where he could bend rules, it would have been years since he'd have last seen Leslie.

Again, he set his thoughts aside during the next station's inspection. Like the first station, recruitment was up. He congratulated the local Party staff and encouraged them toward further efforts. The next four stations passed in the same manner. He continued to mull the problem between stations, but there were no solutions. At some point, he would need to let go of any resentment for the Party regarding the situation. He just wasn't sure how long it would take to get him to the point he could.

By the end of the day, he nearly forgot about the meet-up with Christopher. Eating the supper that Sarah had prepared, a message suddenly came up from Christopher: "ready to join?"

"Almost ready, just finishing supper," he responded. "I'll be ready in five." Finishing his plate, he ordered Sarah to clean up and went over to his couch in the living room. Retrieving the VR attachment, he fit it around the C-All. The C-All responded by shifting to create a virtual space of black emptiness around him, with the contours of his room outlined by glowing blue lines to form a cube around him. A prompt came for a server to join. "Can you send me the link for the server?" Mark messaged.

A link promptly came back, and Mark directed it into the prompt. A small connecting symbol appeared, and then the world became a hazy green that steadily resolved into a lush garden surrounding him. Mark could see bright flowers and fruit trees in every direction. At the far limits, Mark saw a stone wall encompassing the grounds. He stood in a grassy clearing within the garden. Christopher was standing directly in front of him.

"You made it!" Christopher smiled. His avatar was a near

perfect match of his real-world body, only here he was maybe a little taller.

After looking around a second longer, Mark replied, "Is this where you play paintball? It doesn't look much like the public servers I've been on. They usually go for more of an urban setting or look like real-life indoor paintball centers."

"No. We rarely play here. This area is more of a welcome and meeting area. We set the server up to have multiple rooms, and we move between them. This is meant to be a starting zone. There are a few guys on playing tonight, and we'll be using more of a forest zone. Before we go, though, I need to tell you a bit about the server and its rules. If you agree to them, then you can join in tonight."

"Well, I promise I'm not a creep or anything. Beyond that, I think the C-All does a good job keeping people in line, since anything you do ends up getting recorded." Mark grinned. "So, I'm sure I can agree to whatever the rules here are."

Christopher's face took on a serious look. "Mark, have you ever heard of dark zones?" The look of confusion on Mark's face showed he hadn't, so Christopher continued. "Not everyone is okay with being monitored all the time. Especially within the Inner Party, sometimes there's a strong need for privacy for important decisions to be made. Also, sometimes people with power and influence are also just people and want to engage in certain activities without being observed."

Mark's face dropped. This was not at all what he'd been expecting tonight. What had he gotten himself into?

"It's quite safe, I assure you. The server projects false data back to the C-All AI. Anyone who tried to view through your C-All would see avatars playing various sports or games. The audio also gets tricked to match. This kind of tech has been around since the first C-Alls were rolled out. There are enough such servers being used by Inner Party members that people in IT basically just avoid them whenever they come across them in server scans. The upshot is, when you are in here, you can say or do anything, and the Party won't know about it."

"Okay, but just what kinds of things are you doing that you need a space like this? It's not like you need it just to play paintball." Mark considered disconnecting. At the same time, the thought of such a place was intriguing. He was too curious to leave straight away.

Christopher grinned. "Well, we're not planning to overthrow the government, if that's what you're worried about. Sometimes we just need a place to think out loud and talk to other people, without having those thoughts monitored at every step. You know?"

Mark thought about the inner dialogue he'd been having with himself all day. He knew. Still, he didn't enjoy being surprised like this. It was obvious why Christopher couldn't have told him about it ahead of time, but still. Another thought came to mind.

"How do I know this isn't just some way to set me up? Maybe you're testing my loyalty? Maybe the Party was worried because of my relationship with Leslie. They could have sent you to see if I was slipping because of her."

Christopher smirked. "I'm not sure saying that suspicion out loud would have been the right course if that were true. You'd have been better off just taking off the VR and then reporting me to the authorities."

"I still could, I suppose." Mark realized they both knew he wouldn't. "Well, crap." The software Christopher was using had better work. If it really was a trap, then it was too late, anyway.

"Lucky for you, I'm not here to trap you. Maybe someone else out there is, but it's not me. Let me know if anyone seems to be trying to set you up though. I am taking a risk by bringing you here. I'd hate to lead the Party back to any of us, you included."

ANNO DOMINI 2064

After a brief pause, he continued. "Anyway, shall I go over the rules?" He looked expectantly at Mark.

"I guess I may as well hear them at this point." Even though everything Christopher had said would probably have been what someone trying to trap him would have said, it came across as genuine. Mark couldn't help but believe him. More than that, the idea of talking to other people without being monitored intrigued him. The thought of it seemed almost exhilarating.

Christopher took a breath and then began, "First, you may only come to the server by invitation. The link I sent you will not work a second time. If you wish to come, you must message me, and I can send you a current link to connect. Do not invite other people to the server. You won't be able to unless someday we give you the ability to do so. That day is a long way off at this point."

"Okay. Noted. What else?" Mark could see the sense in the first rule. Spread something like this too easily, and it would only be a matter of time before you got caught.

Chris took a breath. "Within this server, there are different rooms. Sometimes we call them different channels, sometimes we refer to them by name as different places. You only gain access to them when someone with access invites you. It is possible you will meet people here who have not been to rooms you have been to. Accessing someone's profile lets you see which rooms a person has been to, but you'll only see the rooms you have also been in. You are not to discuss with people any rooms they have not yet been in."

Mark didn't see the reasoning for these rules as clearly and worried a little over the secrecy implied. But he was in it this far already. Besides, he hadn't really seen anything yet anyway. He could always judge for himself once he'd seen more. "Fair enough. I can do that."

Christopher smiled. "Good! The last rule is simple: treat

everyone here with respect and strive to avoid any personal conflicts with others. We all have enough problems in the real world without creating problems here, too."

"That sounds like a good rule in general," Mark replied.

Christopher nodded. "So it is. Now, we have a few minutes before the rest of my friends are on. Several are in the paintball channel already. I wasn't lying when I said we'd play paintball tonight. We could go join them for some pre-match rounds. Otherwise, if you want to spend a little longer here and ask any questions you have, we could do that first."

Mark was not done with questions yet. "So, you guys are maintaining a secret server that could get you all arrested or worse, and you use it to play games together and just talk?"

"Mostly. The games are a way to build friendships and a sense of community. A lot of the men like to play competitive games as a way of hanging out together. Some of the women play too, although not as many."

Mark looked at him quizzically. "So, this is more than just you and a few of your friends?" The situation was getting stranger and stranger. He wondered again just what Christopher was introducing him to.

"There are a few hundred in our community. No one knows exactly how many similar communities exist. The network was built that way on purpose. Only a very select few individuals maintain connections between communities, and none of them know more than a handful themselves. It's probable a few communities have lost their connections with the broader network. Perhaps sometimes lost communities will have members who find members of other communities in the real world that then bring them back into the network." Christopher seemed rather thoughtful in countenance as he explained this. Mark wondered whether he was truly conjecturing or in fact speaking from experience.

ANNO DOMINI 2064

Another thought occurred to Mark. "You're saying there's a broad secretive network of communities, each with hundreds of members, that maintain connections to each other, but they aren't at all engaged in revolutionary activity?"

"I suppose if you consider free speech and free thought to be revolutionary activity, then our network is revolutionary. But we aren't terrorists, and we're not plotting a government overthrow or anything like that, if that's what you're asking."

"That still doesn't really explain what the purpose is then," Mark pressed. He realized just being here was illegal. But for his own principles, he wasn't onboard with hanging out with a group of people just to find out later they were a bunch of violent extremists.

Christopher thought for a moment before replying. "There was once a man named Aristotle. The schools of the Golden Republic don't really talk about him. He was once required reading for anyone who considered him or herself to be educated. He talked about how in every action and choice we make there is an end involved. He observed that we attain immediate ends for the purpose of greater or longer-term ends, which can in turn be for still further ends. He postulated that there is some ultimate end to which we humans aspire, some simple complete thing for which everything else we choose, and act, is directed towards."

"Aristotle thought about what that end might be and decided (here Christopher's voice took on a professorial tone) 'The simply complete thing is that which is always chosen for itself and never on account of something else. Happiness above all seems to be of this character, for we always choose it on account of itself and never on account of something else. Yet honor, pleasure, intellect, and every virtue we choose on their own account...but we choose them also for the sake of happiness, because we suppose that, through them, we will be happy."

"So... there's a large network of communities that have

73

gotten together using secret server channels... in order to be happy?" Mark let his face show his incredulity.

Christopher laughed. "Well, you asked what our purpose was. Happiness is the ultimate end we are all aiming for, isn't it?" Mark wasn't exactly amused. He felt like he was getting the runaround.

Christopher continued, "Look, there's too much to it to explain all at once. But we're not out to hurt anyone if that's what you're worried about. The guys are all on too, so we should move to the paintball channel. But I tell you what: have you ever really thought about happiness? As a concept that is."

Mark shrugged. "Not really, I guess. I mean I want to be happy and I think about what might make me happy, but not a lot beyond that..."

Christopher nodded. "I would have said the same thing when I first started out here. Think about it a little after tonight, and the next time we get on here we can really talk about it."

"Okay, I guess. This, uh... None of this was what I was expecting tonight Chris. Can I call you Chris?" Mark replied.

Christopher nodded. "I suppose you can. The other guys are ready. Why don't we go play some paintball?" Christopher tapped his wrist and a small menu opened before him, though Mark couldn't see the details of it. He selected a few menu items and then the world around them shimmered briefly into a sparse world of blackness delineated by bright cubical lines before transforming again into a verdant forest surrounding them.

"We use the teleport system here, same as any standard paintball server, to get around long distances. Your right hand carries the paintball gun, but you can switch it. You can also find power-ups that give you a paintball gun in both hands. You get 30 shots before having to wait three seconds for a reload. We set the server for a team deathmatch. We're both on blue," Christopher quickly outlined.

Mark looked down and could see they'd dressed his avatar in blueish camouflage. His right hand had a digital paintball gun attached. He tested mimicking pulling a trigger and a paintball fired. He noted that the server mimicked real world physics, giving the paintball a realistic speed and arc due to gravity. He pointed with his left hand to a spot and made a fist. The teleport beacon opened as it would on most servers. He directed it a little more to his liking and then opened his fist. Instantly he teleported to the spot. He nodded at Chris. "Right, I think I've got the basics. Seems similar to standard servers."

Christopher nodded back. "Good. This match is already in progress, so we should stick together and look for the opponents on red. When the round ends, we'll get teleported back together with the rest of the team. Keep your head on a swivel." Christopher then teleported a little further ahead. Mark followed suit.

For the next two hours, they played a series of intense matches. Christopher briefly introduced Mark to two other players, though he barely caught their names and soon forgot them. Aside from getting to play with Chris, it didn't seem all that different from playing on a public server. By the end, he had almost forgotten the strangeness of the initial introduction to the servers. When they'd finished Christopher wished him a good night and reminded him to think a little about happiness before next time so they could talk about it more. Mark agreed and said goodbye.

As the server rescinded and the real again appeared before Mark in his apartment, the enormity of what happened struck him. A cold fear gripped him. He had to stop himself from rushing to the windows to check if police were outside. There was no point in panicking. If Chris had been lying or if the secrecy he'd discussed really didn't work, then Mark was already as good as arrested no matter what he did. On the other hand, if it had worked, then he had to act like nothing had happened at all. Mark resolved that he could give no appearance that he'd done anything more than just play a normal set of paintball games. He showered, spent a little time reading the news, and then headed for bed. Thankfully, exhaustion allowed him to fall asleep quickly.

6.

The next day Mark awoke, as he always did, to the rising crescendo of "Together We Are Better." He reached for his C-All and adjusted it into place. He heard the slight click as the monitoring microphones switched off and his C-All took over. As always, he had the brief thought that the click was unnecessary from a mechanical standpoint. It was purely artificial, to remind the person activating the C-All that he had still been monitored when the C-All was off. The artificiality bugged Mark every time he heard it.

This time a new thought occurred to him: they had good reason to be monitoring him. For the first time he could recall, he'd done something that the Party would consider rebellious, maybe treasonous. Not that they had discussed any actual treason. Still, obviously there was a lot more there than just paintball happening.

As he got up and showered, he thought about what he could do now. He could probably report Christopher. They might question why he hadn't gone immediately. But he could say he waited to avoid arousing suspicion from Christopher and so they could arrest him at work without a chance to escape. It was a believable lie. There'd still be some suspicion cast on him. It might damage his career. On the other hand, it might also be seen as a strength. He'd been tempted, and he'd rejected the temptation. He was true to the Party and had even brought in a traitor.

This course of action meant sacrificing Christopher. Whoever Christopher was, he seemed like a good guy. Mark wasn't sure what Christopher had involved himself with, but something about Christopher made him the sort of person you wanted to be around. Flagging him to the Party to arrest didn't sit well with Mark.

Working shampoo through his hair, he also reflected on the fact he was genuinely curious about what Christopher had to say. Happiness? It was such an odd topic to discuss. People didn't have conversations of that nature. You simply couldn't. He was sure the answer you were supposed to say to such a question was something like "happiness is serving others through the Party, for the greater good of the Golden Republic." The conversation would end there. He was sure any other answer would get flagged for further inquiry.

Finishing the shower, Mark dried off and dressed. He thought about that answer. Was there some truth to it? It was what he'd been taught, but he wasn't sure if he'd ever really believed it. Obviously, the answer was self-serving for the Golden Republic. At the same time, it was an answer that was being used by a society of over 300 million people. Did that mean there was at least something to it?

Sometimes at work when he accomplished a significant goal, he felt a real satisfaction. His accomplishments raised him above his peers, even if only momentarily, and led to congratulations and respect from others. Sometimes a significant achievement yielded material rewards as well. Mark had assumed his happiness came from these elements of his life. But as he thought about it, maybe he really took some pleasure from feeling he was helping the Party.

Yet, he wasn't entirely sure he believed in the Party. He thought about the nights of boredom and restlessness he'd been having. About the way the entertainment, comforts, and even sex didn't seem to satisfy as much over time. Didn't the Party existed to provide these things? If they left him feeling unsatisfied, then did he really feel helping the Party was serving others?

A darker thought occurred to him. It had nagged at him

ANNO DOMINI 2064

on those nights when he'd felt most restless and alone: what good was it to help other people, really? How was helping other people really any better than helping yourself if you're all going to be dead soon, anyway? Nothing would last. A few short centuries and all signs of not only your own existence, but that of everyone you ever knew would disappear.

Some part of him felt that this couldn't be entirely true. He'd drawn back from the thought before, and he did again this time. The thought itself seemed menacing, like a hungering beast. He could see in it a potential for destruction that was palpably wrong.

Mark realized then that he would talk to Christopher again. He had wondered before whether other people thought about these things. It seemed he had his answer. Perhaps more answers would follow. This thought alone brightened his mood considerably.

Mark ate breakfast and finished getting ready. During his commute to work, Leslie messaged and asked how the night with Chris had gone. "I didn't make too big a fool of myself... I think," he replied. Leslie responded, "Glad to hear it, hopefully I'll see you at lunch."

It felt a little weird, keeping a secret from her. Mark had never truly had a secret he'd needed to keep like this. Obviously, he couldn't tell her. He wasn't even sure how he could tell her without also effectively telling the Party, given the constant surveillance. It was a moot point. Still, it was strange to think he now not only had a secret he had to hide from the Party, but from Leslie. He wondered what it must be like for Christopher. How long had he been keeping secrets now? Who had he needed to keep them from?

Mark considered it was stranger still to think now he had a secret he'd have to keep to his grave. Even if he decided not to talk to Chris again and to pretend the whole thing had never happened, he'd still have this secret to keep.

79

Reaching the city hall, a feeling of hesitancy struck him. Here was the heart of the Party in this city. Now he, with this secret, was entering it. Realizing any significant hesitation would be suspicious, he tried to look as normal as possible. As he walked through the door, the familiarity of the action felt comforting. Making his way through the hall to the elevator, the surrounding people were going about their business the same as any day. The ride to the 32nd floor was the same as every other day. By the time Mark sat at his desk, the rhythms of everyday life had returned to him. His anxiety eased.

The next few days continued in that rhythm. Nothing seemed to change at work. There were no odd looks, no unfamiliar faces around. If the Party knew what he'd done, they were making no sudden moves in response. It was often easy to forget anything had changed at all. When Chris invited him to another round of paintball after work three days later, he did it so nonchalantly that for a moment Mark forgot what it meant. Mark had plans to go to the gym that night. He answered he could meet a little later after he got home. The plan worked for Chris.

It worked out well, as exercising at the gym gave Mark time to think about what he would say to Chris. He'd taken the homework, as it were, seriously. It surprised him how difficult it was to answer the question of what happiness is. Despite thinking it over for an hour while working out, on the ride home he felt like a schoolboy about to hand in a rather lame essay to his teacher.

When he got home, he messaged Chris to let him know he was free. He figured there was still a good chance that they'd play paintball, so he might as well wait to shower afterward. A link appeared in his C-All. Upon activating it, the world once again went dark into a loading screen before resolving into the virtual forest he'd met Chris in before.

Christopher was waiting just ahead on the trail. He smiled as Mark approached. "Glad you could make it."

ANNO DOMINI 2064

Mark smiled back. "Me too." Chris gestured toward the ground and sat down. Mark followed.

"I figure tonight we'll mostly talk. We might as well get comfortable, I figure." Chris smiled and then seemed to wait. The moment drew out, and Mark realized Chris was expecting him to start.

"So, uh, I thought about what you said last time," Mark began. "I realized I don't really know what would make me happy. Sometimes I think I'm happy when I'm doing something I enjoy or maybe eating food I like or learning new ideas. The problem is, the enjoyment never lasts. I can't even count on the same things always making me feel good. Something that I used to enjoy I can do again and feel bored or distracted during. Sometimes other emotions overpower the thing that would make me happy. I might have an amazing meal and still feel sad. So, nothing that I listed can be happiness."

Chris nodded. "That's very good, and quite insightful. Some people spend their whole lives chasing distractions. There are many people who think if they could just have enough good things or access to enough fun activities, their lives would be perfect and happy. Since they never seem to have enough, they keep chasing more and more, not sure why it doesn't seem to work, but assuming it's because they just haven't been successful enough or lucky enough to have everything they need to be happy."

Mark found himself encouraged by the compliment. Maybe he didn't need to feel so inadequate about his thoughts. "Well, so then I thought more about when I feel happy. Sometimes I've felt good when I accomplished something. When I got top grades in a class in college or when I've been promoted at work. Having people respect me and look up to me can be a good feeling."

Chris nodded and waited. Mark cleared his throat. "But at the same time, I'll realize there are people still doing better

81

than me. I may have got top grades in one of my classes, but I didn't have the best grades in all my classes, much less among all the students. I'm doing well at work, but I'm not even a member of the Inner Party. Then who knows how many levels are within the Inner Party?"

"Suppose you rose above everyone," Christopher interjected. "Suppose you rise through the ranks to become the most powerful member of the Party. Let's say you become the most powerful man alive on Earth. What then?"

Mark hadn't considered that. He thought for a moment. "I suppose if I did, I'd have to worry about someone overtaking me. I'd have to worry about maintaining what I had and whether someone was coming to steal it away from me. I'm not sure I'd really be all that happy."

"A good point. Beyond that, though, you'd be more powerful than everyone else. So what? You'd probably feel good at each step as you rose. But where do you go once you are at the top? Would you really feel good just because you're the most powerful? Would you be able to walk around happy all the time because of that power?" Chris responded. He watched Mark intensely, as though the question were more than just rhetorical.

Again, Mark took a moment to think before responding. "I guess not. What good would all that power be just for the sake of having it? I can see where some people might find amusement in using such power to hurt people or use people. But I wouldn't really enjoy that. I'm not sure what I would do with that power. Just having it probably wouldn't make me happy."

Chris nodded. "People often try to find happiness by comparing themselves to other people. We do often seem to enjoy it when we can rise above others and gain power and respect. Power also brings the material goods and enjoyable activities we talked about earlier, too. So it's even easier for people to think the combination would make them happy. But if neither

ANNO DOMINI 2064

of the things bring happiness on their own, there really is no reason to think the combination would do any better in the long run."

This made sense. Mark reflected on how radical a proposition it really was. He had led much of his life with the pursuit of power and wealth in mind. Mark could see where it might not lead to happiness, but he wasn't sure with what to replace it.

Mark countered. "The problem is, I'm still not seeing what leads to someone being happy. I mean, maybe wealth and power are just distractions that don't let us have any lasting happiness. But how do we know that's not the best we can do?" Chris looked like he had a reply, but Mark decided to get out his full thought from earlier before Chris could answer.

"I thought about another option. I thought about what the Party would probably want someone to answer. I think it would be something like 'happiness is serving others through the Party, for the greater good of the Golden Republic.' I realized that sometimes when I accomplish something at work or do something that helps someone else, that makes me feel good, regardless of any material or status reward I might get for it."

"Do you think then that the Party would be right about happiness?" Chris asked. Mark had thought perhaps Chris wouldn't care for this idea. After all, what they were doing here was illegal. It seemed natural Chris would somehow be against the Party. However, Chris's question sounded genuinely curious and thoughtful.

"Well, there were a couple of issues I had with that thought. One was that, really at best, the main aim of the Party seems to be to provide everyone with enough material goods. But I already know that just having material goods isn't enough to be happy. Not having enough material goods leads to suffering, which seems like the opposite of happiness, so I guess serving the Party helps people, which seems to feel good. I guess, though.... I'm not sure if it's enough if the only end is to get everyone enough material goods." Mark took a breath.

"Then there's another thought I've been struggling with. This is something I've been thinking about for a while, not just after our last talk. I guess at the most basic level, it's death. Happiness is great and all, but what is really the point if we're all going to be dead soon? Even if helping people makes you happy, does it really matter? They will all be dead soon too, just like you. Everything we do will eventually fade away. So, what is the point to any of it?" It felt good to get that out. It was the worm that had been eating at him for some time. He didn't really expect Chris to have an answer to it. But even voicing it aloud made Mark feel a little better.

"Vanity of vanities!" Christopher grinned. It was not the response Mark was expecting.

"What?" Mark replied.

"Vanity of vanities! All things are vanity! One generation passes, and another comes, but the world forever stays." Christopher paused, thinking, and then said, "Another line says, 'Nothing is new under the sun. Even the thing of which we say, "See, this is new!" has already existed in the ages that preceded us.'" Christopher smiled again.

"What the heck are you talking about?" Mark asked. He was a little annoyed. He'd just voiced his deepest fear of existence being meaningless. Yet, here was Chris spouting weird lines from something he must have read once.

"It's from the book of Ecclesiastes. The whole book is basically a reflection on how life appears to be meaningless and men can't find happiness within it," Chris answered.

"Okay, that doesn't sound very helpful. So, why are you smiling?" Mark asked.

"Because the author of that book saw life as a riddle that mankind couldn't answer, but he still enjoined people to a certain approach to life. Why would the author do that if he didn't still have a sort of hope? That author had more cause for hope than you do right now. But I can tell you have some hope, too, don't you?"

Mark sighed. "Honestly, my hope has been in the fact that I'm not the smartest or wisest person in the world. There are questions I have that I can't find answers to, but I haven't really had access to materials that would tell me what other people have thought about those questions. So, my hope has been there are answers out there, I'm just not smart enough to find them myself. Now, you're quoting to me from some book that seems to say there are no answers. If you weren't smiling at me as you tell me about it, I'd probably be a lot less hopeful now."

Christopher responded, "Thankfully, there are answers to your questions. People throughout history came up with several answers to your question, and there has been plenty of arguing about it in the past. Most of the people who were giving answers, though, stood in the Party's way. So now you don't really get to hear what any of them had to say."

"Is that what this place is then? A place where people talk about those answers?" Mark asked. It seemed a little too good to be true. A place where people like him came just to talk about these sorts of questions?

"This place serves several purposes, but that is definitely one of the primary ones. Here, let's change the surroundings a bit." Chris activated a pop-up, Mark could see him pick something from a drawdown menu. The surroundings blurred into darkness before resolving back into a new place. Mark sat on what looked to be a vast expanse of grayish rock, utterly barren and devoid of life aside from Chris who was sitting where he had been before relative to Mark. Above them, the stars were incredibly clear. Mark could see the Earth large and bright in the sky.

"There's really no place on Earth where you can see stars like you can on the moon. Cool, isn't it?" Chris asked. Mark spent

85

a few more moments taking the view in. The vast expanse of stars shining amongst the inky blackness was breathtaking.

"Why did we switch to here?" Mark asked.

"I think we've covered a lot of ground today. You did a superb job with both your answers and your questions. It will take a bit to answer your questions. There's no saying you'll agree with the answers I have. But, for now, I don't want to overload you with too much at once. So I thought it would be nice to hang out and look at the stars for a bit before calling it a night. Plus, I wanted to show you where we'll talk next time." With that, Chris laid back and looked upward.

Mark followed his lead. He looked at the globe of the Earth. He wondered how Chris's people had made this channel. Like most VR channels, the graphics were true to life. Mark wondered how they had gotten a view like this from the moon. Sure, the Party maintained a space program and occasionally sent probes to the moon. But getting the data feed from those probes meant having someone highly placed within the space program. Whether or not he meant to, Chris was showing that his group had people well placed across the Party.

The thought occurred to him, "vanity of vanities." Was it worth caring where they had gotten the feed? Mark decided just to enjoy it. He looked away from the Earth out towards the stars again. He thought about the night he'd looked at them through the winter air. The sense of stark beauty again came to him. You could easily feel tiny and meaningless amongst the vastness those stars represented. There was a sense of awe and beauty from them, though, that overtook those feelings of smallness. Mark wasn't sure why that was important. But if Chris was planning to use this place for their next conversation, Mark felt sure it had something to do with it.

The two stayed there another ten minutes, each with their own thoughts. Then finally Chris indicated it was time for him to go. They each said farewell. Chris made a few menu picks and the moon and the stars faded from view. Mark found himself back in his apartment again.

7.

The next Saturday, Mark finally had the chance to spend a day with Leslie again. They mulled the question of staying in versus braving the cold December air to get out for a while. It was the 29th of December, with only two days left before New Year's Eve of 2064. The Party was being generous: both the Monday of New Year's Eve and the Tuesday of New Year's Day would be work celedays (celebratory days). A four-day weekend stretched before them.

"Let's just stay in today. Tomorrow will be less busy, so it'll be a good time to do something without the crowds. You know we'll go out for New Year's anyway. We may as well use today to rest a bit. Maybe we can use actual New Year's for resting, too, after going out the night before," Mark reasoned.

Leslie finished hanging up her coat and scarf and turned to him. "It's not that bad out today though. It's supposed to snow tomorrow. We'd be better off going out today. Besides, who said I was spending the whole four days with you?"

"Aren't you?" Mark asked. He'd assumed as much. Leslie's work had been very busy of late, and she'd still been keeping up with her normal social activities. On top of that, her friend Allison had been dating a man for longer than anyone had realized. The man had now rather messily broken up with her. Leslie had been using most of her free time to hang out with Allison to help her move on. Given all of that, Mark had been looking forward to spending a nice bit of time together with her again.

"Well... We rarely talk about this, but... Spending that much time together, wouldn't it look rather... committed?"

Leslie replied.

Mark nodded. "It would. But I've been thinking about that. It's not like there's a rule against it in the Party. It's obvious we've been together for a while now. It's not like our coworkers don't know. Would it be so bad if we stopped trying to hide it so much?"

Leslie sighed. "There's a difference, though, between doing this covertly and doing it openly. If you do it covertly, you keep up appearances. People may know, but they also know you are hiding it. There's something to that. It means something different if you do nothing to hide it."

"I'm not saying we go off rotation or something. We don't have to hold hands or kiss at work. I don't think we have to do anything extra to show we're together. But, do we have to try so hard all the time to make it look like we're keeping it a secret? If we want to be with each other for the weekend, why shouldn't we? Isn't that basically the Party's approach to romance? People can be with whom they want to be with when they want to be with them? If we want to be together, why shouldn't we be?" Mark pressed.

"If you stay with someone too long, it looks old-fashioned! Before the Golden Republic, people used to trap themselves in relationships. We know that's how people became oppressed. Maybe you don't remember your history books, but I do. Maybe I remember better, because the Party is also clear that women in particular were oppressed through relationships. My eighth-grade teacher told all of us girls, 'Never stay with a man over three months, or he'll try to use you or trap you somehow.' Before the Golden Republic, she'd been 'married' for a while and she told us how awful it was. The standard income gave her the means to break free. But before that, she felt trapped because she relied on a man for an income. When the Golden Republic came, she used her standard income to become a teacher. One thing she taught was not to make the mistakes she had!" Leslie had become increasingly impassioned as she told the story. Mark realized he'd really touched a nerve.

A silence descended. Mark wasn't sure what to say. Leslie seemed to realize she had said more than she'd meant to say. Finally, Mark responded, "I'm not trying to trap you or use you. I just enjoy spending time with you. You don't need to spend all weekend with me. I'd just been hoping we could because we haven't been seeing each other as often of late."

He paused for a moment. Leslie seemed to be thinking of a response, but Mark went a step further. "I realize if we're too open about being together, it looks bad. I know you're not exactly comfortable being in what has become a longer-term relationship because of how it looks. It might even hurt our careers, at least temporarily. I guess I realized this week I'm ok with that. But if you aren't, I understand. For your sake, I'm willing to do things however you want."

"I don't really think you're trying to trap me or use me," Leslie replied. "But you should know, I never intended for this to go on so long. It just kind of happened. I enjoy being with you, too, too much so to just end it just because it's gone on for longer than I'd planned." Leslie paused.

"But we know this can't go on forever, so there's no sense letting it hurt our careers. Let's spend today and New Year's Eve together. The rest of the time we should do our own things. Okay?"

"Okay, that's fine. I guess in that case, we still need to decide what to do today. Do we want to go out or stay in?" Mark asked.

"I say we walk down to the old Public Market, grab lunch there, and then walk to the lake. It's not all that cold out. We can check out the science and technology center there. It's just south from the art museum, practically a straight shot east from the market." Leslie replied.

ANNO DOMINI 2064

Mark nodded in agreement. Leslie summoned an auto-car as Mark got his boots out. The two bundled up, and a couple minutes later headed downstairs to the waiting vehicle. A short ride brought them to the market. They probably could have walked, but they would do enough walking later if they went by foot to the lake.

The Public Market was in an old two-story building that was mostly an open space filled with restaurants and stores selling local foods and craft. The smaller second-floor space housed a couple bars and restaurants along perimeter, leaving the middle open straight to the roof. Local non-Party members ran most of the stores. Meanwhile, it was Party members who could afford the luxuries on offer who primarily frequented them.

Mark recognized at least half a dozen people from work, most of whom shot him and Leslie conspiratorial grins or small head nods. None approached openly. Leslie shared small waves with several women he didn't recognize but were likely also from work. While ostensibly they'd come for a meal, they spent the first half hour looking around at the various shops and restaurants. Finally, they settled on the fish from a Cajun themed restaurant. Mark went with a shrimp po' boy while Leslie tried a gumbo. The meals were warm and a bit spicy, which seemed perfect before venturing back into the cold.

Eating his sandwich, Mark thought about how much he was enjoying the moment. He was spending time with a woman he loved doing something they both enjoyed. After the recent talks with Christopher, he felt like it was more enjoyable than it would have been before. In part, he thought this was because he had decided he didn't care so much about getting ahead in his career. Realizing his career wouldn't be enough to make him happy, he was more willing to be happy in the moment. He wasn't spending his time worrying about who saw him with Leslie and whether it might get used against him somehow.

Still, he wasn't sure why the moment felt so *right* to him.

91

It wasn't just the enjoyment of the food, or any kind of status of being there. Neither was he doing anything that particularly helped someone or something. Except, Leslie was also having a good time. He could tell by the smiles she had often been giving him as they'd browsed and ordered the food. While they were eating, she'd been telling him about some ways she'd been trying to cheer up Allison. She clearly enjoyed relaying the silly plans she'd thought of to cheer up her friend. So, maybe he was doing something good for Leslie by being here, and maybe that was part of why he was happy. He decided it wasn't worth analyzing too much for now, but he'd think on it later.

After finishing their meal, they started out for the lakefront. As they walked, Leslie asked him, "How have things been going with Christopher? You were all excited about that first laser tag match with him and his friends, but you've barely talked about him since."

"Well, you've been busy lately. It's not like we've talked a lot since then," Mark replied.

"I guess. How is it going, though? He seems nice. I was thinking maybe he'd be a good match for Allison? Maybe it would help her bounce back a bit..."

"Oh no, I don't think that would work well." Mark replied, maybe just a little too quickly. He tried to think of a good excuse for his disagreement.

"Why not? He's friendly. He's in the Party. Not to make you uncomfortable, but he is fairly good looking..." Leslie replied.

"Maybe I'm worried you're just setting him up with Allison, so you can make your move with him when she's done," Mark teased.

"Ha ha. Seriously though, I think it's a good idea," Leslie continued. "But it would be easier if you asked first. I don't want to hurt Allison if he says no."

ANNO DOMINI 2064

"I'm just not sure he'd be all that interested. He doesn't really talk about women much. I wouldn't want her to be embarrassed...." Mark said.

Leslie raised an eyebrow. "Are you trying to tell me he's gay? Why not just say so? Or are you not sure?"

Mark realized he was, inadvertently, in the clear. "I guess I don't really know for sure. I just get the feeling he wouldn't be that interested. So it's probably best not to try right now."

Leslie nodded. "That makes sense. But if you find out he isn't gay, let me know. Allison could use the rebound."

"Ummm sure. But's that's not really the kind of thing I'm likely to bring up. So, I guess, don't hold your breath," Mark replied.

Leslie laughed. "You are so immature sometimes. Really, how hard is it to bring that up with someone? Whatever. Just let me know if it comes up, I guess."

"So, if you aren't talking about women, what are you guys usually talking about? I assume you're not just blasting each other with lasers the WHOLE time," Leslie continued.

"Well, there's plenty of laser blasting, but I suppose that's not all we do. Mostly we talk about work, a little about where we've been before, places we liked, things like that. Nothing important really." It felt bad to lie to Leslie, but Mark didn't see a way around it.

Leslie shrugged. "I'm not sure why I'd expect much else. That's good though. I'd noticed you hadn't been talking to friends from past rotations much of late, and you haven't made a lot of friends here in Milwaukee. It's good to have someone local to hang out with."

"Yeah, yeah, thanks, mom." Mark put a heavy dose of sarcasm into his voice. Leslie looked irritated in response.

93

JACOB CLEARFIELD

"I'm just looking out for you." Leslie's features softened. She continued with concern in her voice. "You had been seeming more and more irritable and, just, tired lately. You seem better today. I don't know, whatever you two are doing seems to be helping. Keep it up, I guess." She shrugged. "I don't understand guys. If blasting at each other with fake lasers makes you happier, then I guess just keep doing that."

Mark laughed. "Okay, then I guess I will." The two were approaching the lake now. A crosswalk light went their way, and they reached the pedestrian area that fronted the lakefront. Mark motioned for them to continue straight toward the lake rather than turning to the science and technology center. Coming to the shore, they paused to look out across the water. The day was calm, and the lake rippled in a million places across Mark's field of vision. The sun reflected off the ripples in a bright array of dancing lights. It was strikingly beautiful. The desire to continue to watch it battled with the desire to get indoors from the cold. After about a minute, the cold won out, and the two proceeded to the science and industry center.

Out front, a model 4 robotic assistant greeted visitors. The Party had designed the model 4 for outdoor and all-weather use. Leaving it standing outdoors in the cold was a way to show off this functionality. However, it was a very rugged model and did not imitate the human form the way most in-home assistant models like "Sarah" did. The "Sarah" model was much newer than the model 4, and in fact could also perform outdoor activities in most weather. Only extreme weather nowadays warranted a model 4. However, the durability of the model 4 also allowed it to perform much heavier industrial applications. So, it remained in significant production, especially for rural areas.

Behind the model 4, the grey steel of the science and industry center building stood, stretching back to a rounded section that overlooked the lake. Mark could still make out the old name for the building, "Discovery World," in faded scratches

94

ANNO DOMINI 2064

where the Party had removed the old lettering. Meanwhile, a new large rectangular building emerged vertically from the center of the older building, towering over the original building a full five stories before tapering a further two stories with a pyramid at the top. Near the top the was displayed the new name, "Science and Industry of the Golden Republic" in great brass letters.

It had been a while since Mark or Leslie had visited such a museum, but they both found them interesting. This museum focused on the Party's efforts to harness tidal energy from the Lake, the re-emergence of what had been called the "Rust Belt" under the old regime as a center for robotics and armaments manufacturing, and the tremendous agricultural equipment manufacturing that took place in the area to supply the surrounding breadbasket that was the Midwest. It was markedly different from the focus Mark had seen in a similar museum on the West Coast, which had been much more focused on the programming and software work done out there, and the long tradition of media that continued to produce most of the Party's major entertainment products. Both museums had a common theme that was unmistakable: the triumph of the Party through science and industry over material need. The Party fed, clothed, housed, and entertained everyone through its virtues of planning and direction.

After a couple of hours looking at exhibits, the tile floors began to wear on their feet. Mark and Leslie rested in the viewing gallery on the top floor. The top level had glass walls on each side that allowed visitors to look out over the city to the west, the shoreline north and south, and the lake to the east. They found chairs on the north end of the room and sat. Leslie replied to a few messages she'd put off while they had been looking at the exhibits. As she did this, Mark looked out over the shoreline. Several skyscrapers much taller than the science and industry center obstructed some of the view. Mark thought about all the effort that went into maintaining those skyscrapers, never mind the logistics behind providing for all the people inside them. He wondered if it would be possible without all the robots being used.

The majority of the agriculture, mining, manufacturing, transportation, and retail work that existed was done through automation and robots. The main challenge was just overseeing and managing the systems that ran them. This challenge was the heart of the Party's efforts outside of the Inner Party. The only other duties were producing entertainment and staffing police. Humans still had to perform those tasks. The military also still needed a lot of humans, hence his job in recruiting. However, an increasingly large share of combat was done by robots rather than humans.

In history classes, the Party taught that a lack of necessities among populations often caused societal instability, which led to the fall of governments and empires. No civilization had ever had the advantages the Golden Republic now had to meet the physical needs of its people. Mark wondered whether that meant a true end to the violence and rebellions that had once roiled societies. If so, who knew how long the Golden Republic might endure?

It was odd, Mark reflected, how that thought had once been more comforting. Now, with something he was hiding from the State, that State lasting practically forever was no longer so reassuring. It was funny how one's own stake and position in a system could so dramatically change his or her views about it. Before he saw the Golden Republic as something that was an overall good, something he cheered for. Now that he hid something from it, there was a certain dread attached to the thought of it.

Leslie finished her message and moved to put an arm around Mark's shoulder. "You look like you're having some serious thoughts there," she said with a light teasing voice. "I leave

ANNO DOMINI 2064

you to your own devices for just a few minutes and here you are brooding again. I guess I really need to get you out more." She gave him a little squeeze.

Mark shrugged. "I was just thinking. It really is impressive, isn't it? You look out over this city and think about all the activity keeping it running. It makes you feel small."

Leslie looked with him for a bit. Her face became serious. The two sat for a minute and then Leslie replied, "You're right, it makes a person feel small. But that's okay, we're all part of the Party and the Party gives us something big enough to be a part of that it's meaningful. As long as we have that, we're fine."

Mark thought about this. He wasn't sure he agreed, but disagreeing was sure to be flagged by the C-All. "I guess being small is okay if you're part of something big, eh?" He gave Leslie a small grin.

"Just as long as you're not TOO small," she responded with a wicked grin. "Then there might be some issues..." They both laughed. The tension Mark had been feeling lifted. The two made their way back down and headed home. Leslie had enjoyed scoring a laugh and continued to make jokes as they went. Mark tried to keep up and counter where he could. By the time they got home, they'd both been laughing so hard their sides were sore.

Leslie stayed the night, with the condition she would leave the next morning. They could then spend the night of New Year's Eve together and go back to her place for New Year's Day. Mark would just have to find things to do on his own the next couple of days before they met up again. It was better than she'd agreed to at the beginning of the day, so Mark saw it as a win.

Still, it felt all too soon the next morning when Leslie had gotten ready and went downstairs for an auto-car. After they had kissed goodbye, and the door closed behind her, Mark sat down on the couch. He realized he hadn't worked out with Chris when they would meet again.

He opened his contacts menu in his C-All and selected Chris. He sent a quick message that he was free the next couple of days and wondered if Chris would have time to meet in VR again. A few minutes later Chris responded with a link and the message that he would be free in about an hour and could meet then.

He'd lounged in bed while Leslie had showered and dressed. Leslie had been in a hurry and had just eaten a granola bar before leaving, so Mark hadn't bothered yet to eat. Mark took the opportunity now to freshen up and get changed. His "Sarah" prepped some bacon and eggs while he got ready and then had a real breakfast.

Still finding himself with a little time, he checked the news and read an article about further hostilities breaking out in the Breton area with several terrorist attacks being staged simultaneously the night before. Again, recriminations and counter recriminations were being thrown across Europe. Both China and the Golden Republic were trying to cool heads before anyone did anything too rash in response. Mark suspected the resources poured into his recruitment division were about to go up again.

Finishing the article, Mark noted it was about five minutes from the time Chris had suggested. He decided he might as well wait for Chris in the VR room. He got himself situated on his couch and then accessed the link. The sparsely decorated walls of his apartment gave way to a dark loading screen. Then he was once more sitting in a field surrounded by stars.

8.

Christopher was running late. Mark looked at his avatar's watch. Chris was at least 15 minutes late now. Mark wondered whether he should sign off. He had nothing planned. The simulation of the stars was enjoyable to sit under. He decided there was no harm in waiting. He wondered what Chris would want to talk about. Part of him worried whether this was a waste of time or worse. If there really was an answer to being happy, why not just say so from the start? Was Chris trying to add some dramatic flair to it? Chris didn't strike him as a guy who would do that. Still, it was annoying. He was risking everything seeking answers to questions he wasn't sure could be answered.

He thought again about logging out, maybe sending a message to Chris and seeing if he wanted to reschedule. However, as he was debating with himself, Christopher's avatar appeared. He looked a little flustered.

"Sorry about that," Chris said. "I hadn't expected to be held up. I'd have let you know, but I really couldn't send a message until just now when I got free. Thanks for waiting."

Mark was glad he'd waited. He could tell Chris was sincere and sensed something serious had happened. "It's okay, are you all right?"

Christopher sat down across from Mark. "I was given some bad news. I had to tell a couple of other people about it who needed to know. It's never easy. I'm okay though, just a little shaken for the moment." He paused for a moment and then gave a small smile. "I'm glad you messaged me today. I could use some time thinking about something else."

Mark felt a pang of guilt for his earlier annoyance. He realized he'd just been anxious to talk again and had let that anxiety play into his impatience. "Well, last time we were talking about happiness," he started. "Maybe that's not a bad topic for cheering up with."

"It's not. Although I think today we will have to take a more circuitous route before we can get back to that main topic again. That's why I wanted to talk here with the stars over us. They make for a good starting point."

Christopher motioned toward the stars with an expansive wave. "The thing about looking at the stars is, most people who look at them can't help but feel a sense of awe. There is a vastness and a distance that is almost incomprehensible to the human mind. It reminds us of just how small we are within this universe."

Mark replied, "That's true, but I'm not sure that's entirely a good thing. Feeling small and insignificant doesn't seem very helpful if the goal is to be happy." He looked at the stars a moment more as he saw Christopher nod. It was an odd feeling looking at them; they were beautiful, but they projected a vastness that seemed overwhelming.

"Tell me, if there wasn't a consciousness that existed to look upon those stars, would they really exist?" Chris asked. Mark looked at him quizzically. "Would they?" Chris asked again.

"Well, I imagine they would be there just the same whether or not we are here, so yeah, they would." Mark replied.

"What does it mean for an inanimate object to exist though, really, if there was absolutely nothing that could register it existing? Is that true existence? There was an old saying before the Golden Republic that asked, 'If a tree falls in a forest with no one to hear it, does it make a sound?' The question could as easily have been, 'If a tree falls in a forest and no one ever knew of it, did it ever exist?' Perhaps someone might find the remains of the tree. Or, it might decay and give life to other plants or animals that then affect someone. So, its existence would still have had some effect. Imagine, though, if there were truly no people at all. What then?"

"Well, I think it would still have been present, though you could make the argument it wouldn't have mattered."

"Just so. The concept of meaning is tied to the awareness of existence itself. Perhaps things can exist, but if they aren't aware that they exist then they can't pursue any meaning." Chris replied.

"We haven't even established that meaning exists though. What good is knowing you exist if you will stop existing soon and eventually there will be no one to know you ever existed? In the long run, how are we any different from that tree falling in a world without people?" Mark asked.

Christopher nodded. "That's the heart of the problem. It's the thing people have been thinking about since practically the beginning of history. In general, people have come up with three possible solutions."

Mark raised an eyebrow. "Three? I haven't come up with even one yet." How could there be three different answers? Worse, the fact there was more than one meant there would still be the question of which was right.

"Three answers, though one could debate whether one of them is truly an answer. But it has been argued for long enough that I feel we should include it. Let's start with that one: that the concept of meaning isn't dependent on how long it lasts. The argument is that even though the things we do won't matter in the long term, it can matter to us right now, therefore we can create our own meaning."

Mark shook his head. "I don't see that as an answer at all. *So what* if it matters to us, if we don't really matter in the scheme of things? If we're just bits of dust amongst all these stars," Mark gestured upward, "then how can it possibly matter what we do?"

Christopher smiled. "I agree. It seems like that answer works for a few people though. At least, there have been those in history who have argued so. However, few people have accepted it. So even if it works for some, it doesn't seem to solve the issue for humanity as a whole."

"So, what are the other answers?" Mark pressed.

"The next idea is that there is no meaning to life. Everything we know or care about and everything we do will eventually cease to exist or even be remembered. This means that there really is no point to any of it. Simple as that." Mark's heart dropped. This was the answer he dreaded. It was the answer he'd always feared might be true.

"If that's true, why even keep living then? Life is hard. Why put up with it if there's no point anyway?" Mark asked.

"Generally speaking, if you believe this answer, then that's true," Christopher replied. "If this answer is correct, it won't make a difference in the long run whether you die now or later, so rationally, committing suicide makes perfect sense. Some people who argued for this answer said the only reason we don't all commit suicide is because we evolved to keep ourselves alive. The reason our species did so is that only those who stayed alive could pass on their genes and kept the chain going that allowed us to exist in the first place. The fact that most of us don't kill ourselves would have more to do with our instincts for self-preservation than any rational reason."

"You said, 'if this answer is true.' So I take it you don't believe it is?" Mark asked. There was still one answer left. He hoped it was a good one.

"I don't," Christopher replied. "There is one other possibility. This answer is probably the oldest answer humanity found. It has always been the most popular answer. It's the idea that there is more to existence than what we see in this physical universe."

Mark laughed. He laughed partly in anger, partly in despair. This was it? This existence isn't enough, so we make up something beyond it? "That's it? That's what I've risked my whole life for now? Superstition and make-believe? Science ended that idea long ago."

Christopher's smile turned sad. "That's what the Party teaches now. They have their reasons, although I wonder what will happen when those reasons are lost in the mists of time." He pointed to the stars again. "Have you ever wondered how all those stars got there in the first place? What do they teach you in science classes?"

"They teach us about the Big Bang. Everything was condensed into a tiny little area, and then suddenly exploded outward to give us all the stars and planets, and, well, everything," Mark replied.

"Where did the Big Bang come from? All that matter crammed into a tiny space. How did that happen?" Christopher asked.

Mark shook his head. "I don't know. Maybe it was always there? Maybe there's some kind of cycle where things explode out and then eventually circle back and collapse in again before exploding once more?" Mark proposed.

"A cyclical universe? People have proposed it many times. Interestingly, science doesn't support the idea. Did they ever teach you about the second law of thermodynamics?" Christopher asked.

Mark tried to think. He'd *heard* of the laws of thermodynamics. He'd probably memorized them at one point, maybe. He hadn't taken that many science classes as it wasn't really what he'd planned to pursue. He definitely didn't see where something like that would come into this kind of discussion.

"They probably did, but I don't remember what it says."

"It states that in every process entropy can never be reduced, only increased or held steady in cases where a steady state has been reached. For any spontaneous process, the entropy can only increase," Christopher said.

Mark felt like Christopher was talking in another language. "You lost me. What the heck is entropy, and why does this matter?"

"Think about heat. Heat moves from warm places to cold places. It never goes back the other way. The new state, where the heat is more spread out instead of condensed, is a state of greater entropy. What's true for heat is true for every reaction. Every process leads toward a state of more dissipation, creating a system that is ultimately more stable. Sometimes you can use energy to create a more complex system. But the source of that energy is a reaction that is creating significantly more entropy than whatever bit of complexity you've created. So, the net equation still comes out with more entropy." Christopher was animated as he spoke. Mark thought he was getting the gist of it but wasn't sure.

"Think about our planet. All the life on this planet relies on energy from the sun. Without the sun, everything would quickly go cold and die. Maybe there'd be some energy stored within the deeper parts of the earth. Perhaps some form of life would exist off of this energy for a while. But eventually it would run out. So, we need the energy of the sun for all the complexity of life and movement that we see. But the sun is a massive ball of burning gases that are constantly moving toward a state of greater entropy. Someday the sun will reach essentially a stable state. At that point it will have burned out. So, all the complexity we see here is still a result of increasing entropy overall."

"Okay, I get the concept. But what does that have to do with what we've been talking about?" Mark asked.

ANNO DOMINI 2064

Christopher paused for a moment. "What I said for our sun applies to the whole universe. You could almost think of it like a sled sliding downhill. It started at the top of the hill with lots of potential energy. Now we are somewhere partway down the hill. Someday the sled will hit the bottom. There is no way for it to climb back up the hill on its own. The point being, it's not a circle. There's nothing we've seen to indicate the universe is stuck in a loop. Everything points to there being a beginning, and eventually there will be an end."

"But if it can't loop on its own, how did it start in the first place?" Mark asked, rhetorically as much as anything, as he could see the point now.

"Exactly! It doesn't make sense on its own, which points to the existence of something more than what we can see in our universe. Either we don't understand how our universe works well enough, or there is something beyond our universe in play. Even if you argue we don't understand our universe well enough, the fact that everything we see in existence abides by this law makes it hard to argue credibly that there might be an exception to it and the other laws of thermodynamics. For the universe to be cyclical, you'd need entropy to decrease or energy and/or matter to be created from nothing. That literally has never been seen outside of the claims people have made of miracles."

"Miracles?" Mark asked. He'd never heard the word before. Given the context, the idea seemed far-fetched.

Chris nodded. "Sorry, I forgot you wouldn't have heard of the concept. Basically, throughout history people have claimed to have seen or experienced events unexplainable by science, which were considered to be evidence of the supernatural at work."

"How weird. I mean, I get the idea you're proposing maybe something existing we don't know about or can't detect that would explain the universe. But supernatural stuff happen-

105

JACOB CLEARFIELD

ing directly to people? I've never heard of anyone experiencing things like that. How credible were the people who made these claims?" Mark questioned.

"Some people who make such claims aren't credible at all. There have even been many people who were just creating hoaxes to take advantage of people. But there have also been cases that were quite well documented and witnessed by a considerable number of very credible people. I'll give you an example. One of the most documented events took place in Portugal in 1917. Three children had been reporting receiving communications from a supernatural figure. They had been told a miracle would occur at a specific place in Portugal on a specific date in October but were not told what the miracle would be. As a result, a huge crowd formed. Crowd counting techniques were poor, so estimates ranged from 40,000 to 100,000 people. Amongst them were people who didn't believe in the supernatural at all, people who believed in different beliefs concerning the supernatural, and people who were convinced in the same supernatural phenomena as the three children."

Chris continued, "the day started out dark and rainy. Then, it was reported the sun broke through from the clouds and almost instantly the temperature became considerably warmer. The crowd was suddenly amazed to see the sun behaving strangely with it seeming to grow and shrink, display strange colors, and spin and move about in the sky. People reported the sun was duller than normal, so they could look at it without it hurting their eyes. The phenomena lasted about ten minutes. The observers were awestruck. Newspaper reporters who were present reported seeing the same movements of the sun as the rest of the crowd. Hundreds of the observers were formally interviewed afterwards who had seen the phenomena. It was exceptional among reported miracles because there were so many who witnessed it."

"Huh. I mean, that sounds incredible if it happened. Kind of hard to believe, though," Mark answered.

ANNO DOMINI 2064

"I agree, and it's not like everyone believed it proved the supernatural exists. There were at least some in the crowd who said they saw nothing special. As for the majority who did, some speculated that rare meteorological phenomena created an optical illusion. Others speculated that the crowd was looking for a miracle and so started staring at the sun, and simply looking at the sun too long caused people to see strange images as the sun damaged their eyes."

"Wait, tens of thousands of people all stared at the sun at the same time, but they weren't told the sun would be part of the miracle? I mean, wouldn't that hurt? Why would they all be looking at the same time?" Mark asked.

"Well, that's what some people speculated. Others speculated that the crowd had been so expectant of a miracle they basically all imagined the same thing. Some postulated a mass hallucination. The most common theory, given the number of people present who all reported similar experiences, was that a meteorological event caused an optical illusion affecting the sun."

Mark thought about that for a bit. "That would make sense. It's weird, though, that that would happen right where the crowd was exactly when it was predicted to happen. That's uncanny."

"It is," Christopher replied. "So, some people argued that there probably was a meteorological explanation. But that it happened exactly when and where a miracle was predicted to occur would practically be a miracle itself. In any case, it's hardly the only miracle that's been documented in history with a fair amount of evidence being obtained. However, there never seems to have been a miracle so universally experienced or so incontrovertibly to have occurred and been without other explanation that humanity as a whole could feel sure of the existence of the supernatural. Instead, there are lots of accounts of miracles that cause individuals, small groups, and sometimes

107

tribes or nations to conclude that the supernatural exists. I would say that we could think of miracles as partial evidence of the supernatural, but not proof by any means."

"So, you're saying maybe miracles happen, but you can't say for sure?" Mark asked.

Christopher nodded. "I tend to go back to the big question we started with. Whether our lives can have meaning, at least to me, seems to come down to whether this universe is all there is. I think the fact that the universe's existence can't be explained by the rules we've observed that appear to govern it is evidence there is something more out there. Beyond that, even if the universe were an infinite loop, philosophy shows that you still must account for its existing at all. Nothing in the material universe accounts for that."

"The stories of miracles are more evidence that something else exists. Maybe on their own they aren't enough. But added to what I know from science and philosophy, the case becomes strong. I still can't say I know for sure that the supernatural exists, but the evidence all points that way." He paused. "There are more reasons I think the supernatural exists. To discuss them I think will take more time than we have today. I think the main thing to think about for now is whether you think the supernatural is at least possible. If so, what would that mean for you?"

"All right. I guess I'll think about it," Mark replied. It seemed like these conversations were getting more esoteric with each discussion. He was enjoying them, though. If nothing else, it was stimulating to learn about new history and ideas he'd never heard of before. "When would you want to talk again? Tomorrow night I'm going out with Leslie for New Year's Eve, and then I'll spend the day with her for New Year's. I don't really have anything planned the Wednesday night, though."

Christopher thought for a moment. "I won't be free that night, but Thursday night I'll be available. Would that work?"

ANNO DOMINI 2064

Mark nodded. The two exchanged good-byes, and then each logged off. The grass beneath the stars faded away. The C-All screen cleared to reveal Mark's apartment.

The rest of the day passed uneventfully. Mark mostly killing time watching videos and playing a few VR games. The games held his attention, but he found his thoughts drifting as he watched the various shows and short videos he normally enjoyed.

It had been a strange conversation with Christopher, and not at all what he'd expected. Christopher hadn't really answered the original question about how to be happy, but Mark could see why. The feeling of emptiness, of meaninglessness, that had plagued him seemed to be an obvious impediment to happiness. It was relieving to have someone addressing the problem.

Still, it was an odd answer to say that there might be things that exist beyond or outside of the universe that could solve the problem of how to be happy. As a boy, The Golden Republic had taught him how people had believed in superstitions and nonsense about gods and magic and all sorts of bizarre things that weren't real. The Party had explained these as primitive beliefs that had existed before science could show humanity how the universe worked. Some of these superstitions still existed outside of the Republic, but the Party expected that in time they would all eventually fade away as they had here.

Mark had never expected to meet someone who believed in such things. He certainly hadn't expected such a person to seem intelligent and thoughtful. History classes had described how in the time just before the Golden Republic there had still been such people who had clung to the old superstitions. The Party described them as having been ignorant and backwards. They had been some of the primary resisters of the Founding. Most of them ultimately died in the rebel armies or were arrested as terrorists and traitors when the C-All's and mass AI surveillance made it all but impossible for them to hide. The portrayal had been of people who were brutish, violent, and stupid. They were supposed to have been an obvious impediment to the future, but fortunately were too few in number to stop the Party.

Christopher did not live up to these descriptions. He was only one person and might not represent such people as a whole. Perhaps all the violent and stupid ones had been arrested, leaving the more peaceful and intelligent ones to continue on in secret. Still, Chris's reasoning didn't seem all that unsound. At this point he'd left exactly what he believed about the supernatural to be vague. The reasoning that led him to the supernatural existing though Mark had a hard time refuting. It was possible that dumb people had believed in an idea that wasn't so stupid. Or, Mark admitted, maybe the Golden Republic had been rather self-serving in the version of history it taught. Mark knew enough about how the Party worked to know the Party wasn't exactly big on revealing bad news or highlighting mistakes. It seemed likely they had written the history books to put the Party in the best light possible.

Mark continued to dwell on this. By the evening, he was fairly sure there was more to the story regarding the people who'd resisted the Founding and what they'd believed. Still, if what they had believed had been any good, why had they lost? If belief in the supernatural would lead to happiness, as Chris now seemed to imply, then hadn't everyone wanted that? Clearly whatever beliefs or systems people had had in the past had failed, as the Golden Republic had now thoroughly replaced them. Even if there was some network of people like Chris in the shadows carrying on some old set of beliefs, didn't the fact that there were so few of them seem to discount their beliefs? If everyone wanted to be happy and a set of beliefs had led people to happiness, wouldn't everyone have come to believe them?

Another thought occurred to him. If the supernatural

truly existed, it would exist regardless of whether people believed in the supernatural. So, whether or not Christopher's beliefs were helpful in finding happiness, and regardless if anyone else believed them, there was still the question of whether they were true.

Mark could see how you couldn't really disprove the existence of the supernatural. Science couldn't test something beyond the physical universe, since science by definition could only test things belonging to the natural world. But obviously not disproving it wasn't good enough. It seemed like believing in such a thing required positive evidence for it, rather than just a lack of evidence against it. That the universe didn't make sense on its own could be seen as partial evidence for the supernatural. But it was still possible human beings still didn't fundamentally understand the universe all that well.

Mark reflected on miracles again. He could see where if they were real it would be hard not to accept such things as evidence of the supernatural. If there were entities outside of this universe that explicitly interacted with it in a way that couldn't be explained by science, that would be solid evidence. Strange then, that Chris made it sound as if this had happened many times but never in a way that made mankind feel sure of the supernatural. Why, if there were such entities, would they be playing coy with humans? Why let only some people know for sure they existed, but not everyone?

It was strange to think of the possibility that there might be invisible beings watching him right now. The thought made him smirk. He already had at least one entity, the AI of his C-All, watching him all the time. Wouldn't it be funny if there were even more invisible entities watching him? Perhaps science and superstition alike led to men knowing they were always being watched. There seemed an irony there that was almost too good to not be true.

With that thought, Mark pushed off thinking about his

conversation with Christopher for the rest of the night. It was getting late anyway, so he got ready for bed and turned out the lights. After he removed his C-All and the slight boom of the recording mics sounded, he quickly drifted off into sleep.

9.

The Golden Republic planned for New Year's Eve to be celebrated with the annual ball drop in New York, preceded by a
great parade of the many civic institutions the Party organized
for both Party members and the general populace. A massive
laser and aerial drone show over the New York skyline would
follow. Veronica, Mark's boss, had invited most of the more
senior Party members from the office to her apartment to celebrate the festivities. She had invited both Mark and Leslie. On
arrival, the door to the apartment had been open with scores
of people visible within. The two went midway into the apartment before Mark spotted Veronica standing by a window. She
was looking out over Lake Michigan while talking with a few
other colleagues. She was an attractive woman, with sharp
green eyes and fiercely dyed red hair. Tonight she was wearing a
provocative but not overly revealing modern dress.

Veronica was the highest-ranking Party member in Milwaukee. She was part of the Inner Party, and it was rumored her
beauty in part derived from special skin treatments and surgi
cal augmentations available only to Inner Party members. The
specific treatments and augmentations she'd had were a source
of considerable gossip. Thankfully, the C-All AI didn't really care
about intra-Party gossip. At least, there weren't any reports of
people being reprimanded or punished for it. However, it was
possible Veronica knew *exactly* what people in her office said
about her.

Leslie interrupted his thoughts. "Enjoying the view?
Maybe I should be jealous." Veronica was pleasant to look at, but
that was hardly why he'd accidentally been staring.

JACOB CLEARFIELD

Mark shook his head. "Sorry, just a little nervous around power sometimes. Believe me, you've got nothing to worry about." He pulled Leslie in for a quick kiss. Leslie smiled.

"Glad to hear it. Also, I'm sure you have nothing to be nervous about. Your numbers this year have been great. I'm sure Veronica hears nothing but good things about you." Leslie nodded toward the display on the inner wall of the apartment. "Hey look, the Equity for Women Association is marching. My friend Lisa from our local chapter got to travel to New York this year to march with them. Let's go see if we can spot her!"

Leslie pulled him hastily through the revelers spread about the spacious apartment to get close to the display. The display was actually a virtual one that was being recognized by all C-All's that were in the vicinity as being affixed to the wall. It was not mandatory for Party members to take part in the New Year's celebrations. As such, a portion of the C-All display was not mandatorily given over to showing it as would be the case for Revolution Day or important speeches given by the Party president. However, most people attended social functions like this one to mark the traditional celeday. It was generally expected that the host would make the official Party celebration visible at any such function.

The wall measured about 15 feet by 10 feet. The display took up half the wall space. As they approached, Mark could see people holding signs for the EWA approaching the grand parade stand. It looked like members of the Party Youth for Justice had finished passing by. According to the scroll at the bottom of the display after the EWA was the People for Racial Justice (a non-Party group designed by the Party primarily for racial minorities). Behind them would come the People for Global Justice (a group for both Party and non-party members primarily aimed at helping spread the Party's message worldwide.)

Leslie pointed excitedly. "Look everyone, it's Lisa! She's on the display!" Everyone turned. Several other women from

ANNO DOMINI 2064

the office also recognized Lisa and cheered. The revelers broke into a round of applause. It wasn't often a local Party member made it onto a national broadstream. "That's so cool," Leslie said to Mark. "Maybe next year I can get the chapter to send me! I'd love to go to New York!"

"Maybe. It would be worth a try," Mark offered in reply. He continued to watch the display. Thousands and thousands of people marched, passing the review stand with floats, flags, and banners. It was an awesome spectacle. For all his recent misgivings, Mark could still feel a thrum of the old excitement thinking about the great power and unity of the Golden Republic.

Suddenly the feed cut to a female reporter. More dramatically, everyone's C-All's also popped up a display of the reporter. Mark heard an audible gasp. An unexpected mandatory announcement was extremely rare. It had hardly happened since the rebellions were extinguished.

"We are sorry to interrupt the End of Year Parade broadstream. We will return to the broadstream shortly after this report. Today the Eastern League declared that if the French Caliphate does not remove its troops from the Republic of Brittany within twenty-four hours, they will declare war on the French Caliphate. The Russian Republic has announced that it will join the Eastern League in its declaration. The German Islamic Republic has in turn declared it will join the war on the side of the French Caliphate to repel the 'crusaders.' East Germany has declared that if the GIR does so, they will join The Eastern League and Russia." The reporter looked very dour, but also nervous. This was likely the biggest news report of her life. Mark wondered how it must feel to have the eyes of an entire nation watching you all at once.

A quiet murmur developed amongst the guests as the report went on. Mark overheard Don say a bit too loudly, "Europe is going to f*ing pull itself apart!"

The reporter continued. "To avoid a potentially cata-

115

strophic war, our great Golden Republic has declared it will intervene to guarantee the sovereignty of Brittany. Troops from forward bases in the British Isles have already landed and are advancing Southward. We have warned the French Caliphate it must retreat from the country or any soldiers met within Brittany that are not actively pulling out will be engaged as hostile.

The Eastern League has now stated it will hold back from declaring war so long as the Caliphate retreats or the Golden Republic is actively driving them out. The League however, demands that Brittany not be annexed by the Golden Republic which our president has given assurances will not take place. Brittany will, however, accept Golden Republic outreach centers as an alternative to the primitivist beliefs held by the people of that nation. The People's Republic of China has supported this intervention, though they have likewise demanded that the Golden Republic refrain from annexation."

Don muttered a bit too loudly, "It figures the Chinese don't want to see us get a toehold on the mainland. Such great allies…"

Meanwhile, the reporter continued. "It remains now to be seen what action the French Caliphate will take in response. A war with the Golden Republic would be near suicidal. While the Caliphate possesses a limited number of nuclear weapons, they are old and would likely be intercepted by the Golden Republic's missile defenses. The Golden Republic would counter any such use in reprisal with our much larger nuclear arsenal. Meanwhile, the Caliphate, while possessing a large ground army, is poorly equipped with conventional weapons, and its air force is nearly non-existent. In any protracted war, we predict the Caliphate to lose overwhelmingly. Republic forces stationed in the British Isles alone would likely be sufficient to take Paris. Meanwhile, reinforcements are already being flown from the American continent."

Mark whispered to Leslie, "I can't believe the French

would be that stupid. They'll back down. They have to."

Leslie nodded. "I hope so. A war would just be crazy. I can't believe any of this is happening. What the heck are they fighting for, anyway?"

Mark thought back to his talks with Christopher. The Caliphate was fighting, at least in part, for its beliefs in the supernatural. He wondered if Christopher was a Muslim. He resolved to ask Christopher about the matter. If believing in the supernatural was supposed to lead to happiness, then why would people be fighting over it? Where was happiness in war?

"I don't understand it," Mark replied honestly. The reporter had finished. The feed switched off from the C-All's, and the parade returned to the broadstream. The marchers had also gotten the report and had stopped marching for the duration. The parade restarted, albeit with a sense of nervous uneasiness at first, as though people weren't sure when to start or what to do. Meanwhile, the guests at the party began to talk more animatedly, mainly about the potential war. It seemed 2064 might be more eventful than anyone would have predicted even an hour ago.

Mark considered that if a true war broke out, his day-to-day life was about to transform. A war would call for long hours and a lot of regional travel. Recruitment quotas would increase. The strategies for recruitment would need to change to face the reality of a shooting war. Despite this, he felt oddly detached. He didn't understand the reasons for the violence in Europe. He realized probably no one in the Party did, which meant they didn't understand their enemy. Mark remembered he'd once read in school a book by an ancient Chinese general that said such a circumstance was extremely dangerous.

The clip of Veronica's high heels alerted Mark that was approaching. Veronica shot him a wry grin, "Looks like things will be busy for a while."

Mark nodded. "I was just thinking the same thing myself. I

hope the French have the sense to pull back. They've been stuck trying to push into Brittany as it is. Hopefully, seeing our troops joining the other side will be enough to convince them it's not worth it."

Veronica motioned him to come closer. She leaned in and spoke softly. "I know that's what the Party is hoping, too. But I think the people at the top aren't counting on it. The French are proud, and they see Brittany as part of France. It's the same way with the German Islamic Republic and the East German Republic. War in Europe has been brewing for a while now; the fact that they invaded might mean they intend to see things through whether or not we intervene. After the holiday I want you to make plans for recruiting for a full war. Start thinking about it now so you can hit the ground running when we go back."

"Definitely. I'm sure I'll have some ideas ready." Mark replied. Veronica gave him a nod and patted his shoulder before turning and walking toward a guest Mark didn't recognize. Leslie had pretended to be absorbed by the parade when Veronica approached. She now turned back to him.

She gave him a look, raised her eyebrow, and said, "No pressure or anything." Then she laughed nervously. Mark laughed along with her.

The people at the party tried to get things back to normal. Mark and Leslie split up for a bit to socialize with more people separately. People knew they were here together, but there was no need to broadcast it further by socializing as a couple. The news was the main of conversation. A few, however, seemed uncomfortable and tried to change the topic back to the parade or hopes for the New Year.

One woman who Mark couldn't quite recognize seemed intent on asking everyone what resolutions they had for the New Year. (Mark surreptitiously instructed the C-All to display a summary in small letters. Her name was Margaret and she was a Party member in the downtown headquarters' basement working in package routing.) Mark had heard her talking about it to several other people before she approached him. However, before Mark could answer, she launched into her own plans to work with IT to improve the efficiency of the delivery drones in Milwaukee. Mark suspected she saw this party as a vehicle to help her career. She didn't realize how her aggressive pitch was off-putting and, consequently, hurting her standing.

Finally, the announcement that the ball was about to drop drew the crowd back to the main screen presentation. A countdown began. Mark made sure to be next to Leslie. A kiss at New Year's was traditional and wouldn't be considered unusual. The ball began to drop. The countdown roared louder and louder from everyone's C-Alls. Some people at the party began to join in. When the countdown ended, the ball's fall arrested, and fireworks came shooting out in all directions. The crowd cheered both in New York and at the party. Mark and Leslie kissed.

"Happy New Year," Mark said.

"Happy New Year," Leslie replied.

The next day, Mark woke up in Leslie's apartment to the sound of the slowly rising crescendo of, "Together We Are Better." Affixing his C-All, he saw Leslie was doing the same. One of Leslie's friends from work had messaged her after the party about getting together today. Apparently, the possibility of war could mean significant changes to some ongoing plot lines they were using in their current programs. She was hoping to get a few key writers and producers together to brainstorm outside of work so they could go in better prepared the next day. Leslie felt she could hardly say no.

Mark agreed and commented he could use some time to think about his own approach when going back in. He was also hoping to follow the news a little to see if there were more updates. Golden Republic soldiers would land in Brittany today. It wouldn't be long before they would see if the French Caliphate would back down. Today could easily be the day a major war broke out.

It felt strange. There was a heaviness to the air. The thought that today was likely to be historic hung tangibly. This was a day the world might really *remember*. So many days were forgettable, and you knew when you woke up that you'd probably never remember what had happened that day. It was strange to wake up to a day you might remember the rest of your life. Such were Mark's thoughts as he and Leslie got ready and departed. He didn't bring it up with her. The thoughts were probably harmless enough on the surface as far as the Party was concerned. But he sensed there was probably still good reason not to discuss such things with the C-Alls monitoring.

Mark walked home. As he made his way through the cold, he wondered what Christopher thought everything. He realized it didn't hurt to ask, at least superficially. Obviously, a deeper discussion would have to wait until they were in the VR. The thought that he might really talk to someone about a topic like this was exciting. Sure, someone like Don at work loved to talk about these matters, but you always had to be careful not to

ANNO DOMINI 2064

say anything the Party might not like. Even accidentally, a slip of the tongue or an opinion that might later be seen as critical of Party policy could lead to trouble. As a result, you could mostly speculate on what foreigners would do. Speculation on the Party's policy and what it could or should do was fraught with risk. Mark felt it made for very incomplete conversations.

Mark sent Chris a message. "Quite the news last night! What do you make of it?" He got a couple blocks closer to home before receiving the reply. "I know! The French are in for it if they don't pull back. Maybe we could talk about it during some laser tag. I'm free today."

Mark replied, "Leslie ended up with other plans, so I'm free. I'll be home in a few minutes. I'll message you then." Receiving an acknowledgement, Mark hastened his steps toward home. Once there, he attached a few VR peripherals, and then signaled to Chris he was ready. Chris promptly sent a link. Within seconds, Mark found himself in a strange building.

It was dark, lit only by candles and starlight through a missing roof. The moon added its glow through windows but was hidden behind a stone wall from where Mark was seated. The building appeared to be a ruin. Wind swept through occasionally in gusts and whistled overhead where the roof should be. As he looked around, he could tell the building was mostly stone. He noted also a few old timbers, burned but still in place, hanging from walls or standing beneath the missing roof. The building was rectangular, but near one end contained significant outpouchings to each side. Windows were set along each side but were empty.

The wind was audible and seen in blowing motes of dust and cobwebs, and the flicker of candles, but not felt because of the limits of the VR. Oddly, within the gusts there seemed to be stray sounds of singing. Mark could just barely hear many men singing in a solemn coordinated fashion using a language he could not recognize. It was there only for moments before dis-

121

appearing with the breeze.

Christopher was standing about twenty feet away and approached. "What is this place?" Mark asked.

Christopher gave a sad, wry grin. "It's the world right now. At least most of it."

Mark looked at him quizzically. "Sorry, it's a melancholy place, but there's also beauty here. The same is true in our world right now. I suspect it was more beautiful though when there was less decay and more grandeur."

"I think you've lost me." Mark replied.

Chris nodded. "Not fair of me, I suppose. Still, if we're going to discuss war and violence, I think it doesn't hurt to do so in a place that suffered its fair share of such things."

Mark could see the sense in that he supposed. "So, I know we were talking about other things last time, but now with this likely war coming I thought it might be worth changing the subject for a bit. Obviously, I still want to talk about those other things, but with war possibly coming, I thought it would be nice to talk with someone about it more in depth. You know it's not something we can *really* talk about with the C-All's."

A gentle breeze stirred. Again, the sound of men singing. It sounded somber. When it ended, a profound stillness descended.

Chris paused before answering. He then began in a slightly halting, very thoughtful manner, "People naturally see war as an important topic. War is almost universally seen as something of importance, regardless whether people see it as a positive or negative. Most people see war as negative in the abstract but might see specific wars as necessary or even good, at least in terms of effect. In any case, it's seen as important, yes?"

Mark replied, "Well, yes. War brings death and destruction, but also can bring great change. It makes people afraid but can bring hope too." A raven cawed in the distance. This startled Mark. He hadn't realized the simulation included animals. In the candle-lit ruins, it was a creepy effect.

"So, what you're saying is that war affects people, and that's what makes it important. The implication is that people are important. Even if a person doesn't see others as important, they likely see war as important because it could affect them directly. It's the rare person who doesn't value themselves as somehow important, at least to themselves."

"Well, yeah. That all makes sense," Mark agreed.

"But, have we established yet that people are important? We've been talking about how someone can be happy. However, you probably noticed our conversation quickly got caught up in whether life has any meaning to it. If life has no meaning, it's hard to argue that people are important. If people aren't important, it's hard to argue that war is important either." Mark wanted to argue with this but wasn't sure how. It seemed obvious to him that war was important. But he had to agree that its importance came from its impact on people. He'd never considered his doubts about the value of his life and life in general as somehow pointing to war being unimportant.

Chris continued, "I'm not trying to argue that war isn't significant or important to talk about. I'm just arguing it's important that we define *why* war is so significant. War matters because people are important, but we haven't gotten to why they are important. So, we could talk about the war, but I think without an understanding of that context, there wouldn't be much point to it."

Mark raised an eyebrow. "So what you're really saying is, we should go back to our last conversation." It made sense. Chris was clearly trying to tell him his overarching worldview. Mark supposed that to understand Chris's view on war he'd probably need to know that view in a more general sense before it could be applied more specifically. It was still frustrating, though. Ever since the news report, Mark's thoughts had been alive with speculations, fears, and thoughts of how the world might change. It had been, in truth, a nice distraction from his usual thoughts and concerns.

Chris nodded, "Let's keep that conversation going for now. We can talk more about the war, should it come, later." He gestured around the ruins. "Do you know what this place is?" he asked.

Mark shook his head, "I honestly don't have the slightest idea. It looks old, ancient even, and very much abandoned. I noticed the weird singing in the wind, too."

Chris smiled. "A small effect I added. I like to think of it as a reminder of what used to go on in places like this, before they were destroyed and left to rot." He paused. "Once upon a time people might have called it a 'ghost in the wind,' which brings me back rather nicely to our topic last time."

"Last time you said one idea people came up with was that there are invisible entities that exist. That there are things beyond what we can see and experience in this world. I know many people outside of the Golden Republic still believe that. The Muslims, for instance, believe in some kind of omnipotent being that they worship," Mark replied.

"That's true, though discussing them skips us rather far ahead. The idea of entities existing without a visible presence in the world is ancient beyond reckoning. Ancient far beyond the point where mankind began to record words and thoughts. However, once written records began, we have some idea what people were thinking. There was initially a great deal of variety in what people came up with. In general, people believed there were beings who were powerful and responsible for the existence of the world and the way the world was. The number of beings ranged from one to countless. The characteristics of those beings were variable, though one might remark that often people imagined them to be still something like human beings. The belief in such entities and the systems of belief around them came to be considered 'religion.'"

"Now, people naturally developed an array of beliefs about these beings, and very commonly imagined that such beings might desire something from humans and could be bargained with or appeased so they would make good things happen for the people bargaining with or appeasing them. Myths and legends developed about these beings and their interactions with mankind. It's in fact a shame that a great deal of enjoyable literature is no longer taught within the Golden Republic to help keep people from thinking about such concepts."

"In time, though, a new concept arose: philosophy. People began to believe that through rational thought, they could better understand the world. This concept would interact with the idea of entities existing beyond our senses. Philosophers quickly came to understand that our universe does not make sense existing as it does without something transcendent outside of it causing it to."

"Interestingly, the philosophical approach seemed to point to the existence of a primary force, sometimes called an "unmoved mover" who could cause the universe to exist without needing a cause itself. My group is very fortunate to have saved a book by Dr. Edward Feser that details the main philosophical arguments that came to this conclusion. You'll have a chance to read it. For now, it's enough to note that the concept was created, and this concept would be tied back into what was happening amongst religions."

"Although the philosophers were coming to the idea that there must be an entity that is causing the universe to exist, they could not really do more than speculate on the nature of such an entity and whether it interacted with human beings. However, there was a nation made up of twelve tribes who all claimed that just such an entity, who we will refer to as "God" had spoken to them through the centuries using different leaders, prophets, and other religious figures of theirs. They

JACOB CLEARFIELD

claimed that this God cared about them, had even forged a great covenant with them, and had given them laws to follow so they could know what He asked of them in life."

"They claimed even more: that this God had worked miracles for them; at times miracles so great they were responsible for the freedom and even survival of their people. More than that, they had this idea that God worked through history to at times reward them, but at other times chastise them when they failed to keep God's law. They had a concept of 'sin' regarding disobeying God's law, and a concept that such sin caused negative consequences within our world. A sin sort of marked you, almost like a curse, and they would sacrifice animals and perform acts of apology to atone for it."

"It was a religion seen as strange to most of the world. It existed for a long time without spreading very far from a small corner of the Middle East where the peoples of the twelve tribes lived. In time they recorded that a great number of the tribes began to ignore God's law. The kingdom the tribes had built became divided, with the kingdom in rebellion against God's law soon being destroyed by external enemies. The remaining kingdom was predominantly of a tribe named Judah, named for the patriarch that was said to have founded the tribe in the early days of that people's history. In time, the ancestors of that tribe would become known as the Jews, who you may have heard of."

Mark nodded, "I've known several people who are Jewish, but I never heard about any of this. To be Jewish I thought was just supposed to be belonging to a specific race. I never heard about Jews worshipping some sort of, 'God.' I can't imagine the Golden Republic would allow that, anyway."

"It's true that there are very few Jews who still worship God. To be Jewish now is mainly thought of a racial identifier, and this is something that the Golden Republic enforces. Even before the age of the Golden Republic, most Jews saw themselves as a race descended from that ancient tribe, rather than a religion. The Golden Republic then tried to snuff out the religious beliefs of the few worshipping Jews just as it did all other types of religious belief. However, while the Jews are mostly more a race than a religion now, in the ancient world they were more a religion than a race. Importantly, they did not really try to spread their religion, believing themselves a chosen people set apart from the world."

"One of the more interesting beliefs they held was that the world existed in a fallen state and that God had a plan to redeem it. Many ancient Jews believed a Messiah would come who would somehow put things to right. However, they were rather foggy on just what that might entail. Some thought perhaps the Messiah would conquer the world and then put things to right, with the Jews as the Chosen people who would administer his kingdom and serve as an example for all the rest of the world on how to act."

"None of this would have probably mattered much, except that a little over two thousand years ago a Jewish man began to preach amongst the Jews that he was the Messiah. His teachings were extraordinarily controversial. He spoke about matters of morality with authority, making the bold pronouncement that the law given by the Jewish God was in places incomplete, and, worse for the Jews, that it was given to them incomplete because of the hardness of their hearts and their unwillingness to truly follow their God's law."

"But now he said he was giving the full law to them. He even seemed to hint that he was directly from God, even divine Himself. This was incredibly blasphemous to the Jews. You might ask why anyone would have listened to him, and it would be a fair question. The writings we have, though, say that he performed great miracles in the sight of huge crowds. People therefore felt they couldn't just dismiss him as a mere madman, as anyone who could perform such miracles it seemed had to at least have favor with God."

JACOB CLEARFIELD

"Still, this man named Jesus gave laws that were in many ways harder to keep than the old laws. He also criticized the leaders of the Jews for failing to keep their God's commandments and failing in their leadership of the Jews. This really grated on the Jewish leadership. As he became more and more famous and as word spread of his miracles, they saw him increasingly as a threat."

At this point, Chris paused. He walked over to an alcove in the ruins and pushed aside a loose stone, then reached in and pulled something out. Mark had been listening intently and had been surprised by the sudden stop. It was an interesting story. He wasn't sure how much of it he believed. Having heard this much, he was curious how it ended.

As Chris returned with the item, Mark prompted, "I take it, given the world we live in, that this Jesus did not live to conquer the world."

Chris sat down and smiled. "At least he didn't in the way the Jews were expecting." He opened his right hand in which he'd been holding the object. It was a small item that looked like a man in a loincloth nailed to a pair of crossed beams. Mark looked up quizzically from the object to Chris.

"We call this a crucifix," Chris began. "In the ancient Roman empire, it was a means of execution reserved for rebels, traitors, and the worst sorts of criminals. It was a combination of torture and execution that was meant to send a message very publicly to the enemies of Rome. The Jews at that time lived under the Roman Empire, and the Jewish leadership arranged to have Jesus crucified. They figured that would be the end of the threat he posed, and then things could go back to normal for them."

"Jesus's followers probably were very distraught after the crucifixion. It was reasonable for the Jewish leadership to think such a public and humiliating execution would prove to people that this Jesus had merely been a fraud. A few of his followers might have thought about the times Jesus had showed he would have to suffer and die. This was something they had even objected to him about when he'd said this."

"They might have also remembered the time John the Baptist, another famous preacher amongst the Jews, had pointed to Jesus and called him 'The Lamb of God who takes away the sins of the world.' For the Jews, a lamb was a potent offering that was sacrificed to atone for sin, so perhaps this striking statement by John the Baptist would have been haunting them now."

"It might have further struck them that Jesus had been killed just before the great Jewish feast of Passover, which included the ritual sacrifice of a lamb. Even with these warnings of Jesus's death, his followers likely had very little idea what to do or why, if Jesus was the Messiah, he would die like that."

Chris set the crucifix down beside him. A distant look came over him and he paused. "It's all too easy, in these dark days, to imagine what it must have been like for his followers. They'd lost someone they'd loved and believed in. They were probably fearful the authorities might come for them too. They were likely in hiding, huddled together, each fearful they would be the next to die...."

Mark could tell that just thinking about the story somehow struck a deep chord for Chris. If this was something Chris believed in, Mark knew it meant he'd likely already spent much of his life hiding it in fear of being found out. Who knew what experiences he might have had that he could be thinking about now?

"Thankfully, and it's so important to remember this in our own time, the story did not end there," Chris said. "Three days after the authorities had killed him, Jesus came back to life."

"Wait, what?" Mark replied. This was ridiculous. It was hard enough for him to take in the talk of things existing that you couldn't see, a God that gave laws and did miracles, and then a man somehow connected to this God doing miracles. But then he's killed and can just come back to life?

Chris nodded. "It sounds crazy, I know, which is why his followers were shocked and overjoyed. He appeared to them many times. At first not all of them were together when he appeared. At least one of them who was not initially present forcibly doubted. Until, Jesus appeared while he was there and had him touch the places in his hands where the nails had been placed, and the place in his side where during his crucifixion he'd been stabbed with a spear. He even ate with them to further prove he wasn't merely a spirit or ghost. He gave them further instruction and teaching, told them he would now ascend to be with his Father, that he would send the Holy Spirit to give them strength, and that they were to carry his message to the entire world."

"Remarkably, the small band of followers who after Jesus's death had been in hiding, were before long publicly preaching that Jesus had been resurrected, and that his death and resurrection had been the divine sacrifice that had redeemed mankind. They taught that this Jesus had conquered both sin and death, and through following his teachings one could now live on spiritually after death in paradise. They also claimed in time at the end of the world that all people would be resurrected bodily as Christ had. To the Jewish leadership, it must have been bewildering. Worse for them, people began to report that Jesus' followers were also working miracles. Thousands were believing them. Attempts were made to suppress this new religion, but ultimately nothing worked."

"Of special note, Jesus' followers taught that God had chosen the Jews to lead up to the coming of Jesus, but that the salvation he'd brought was not just for the Jews but for all the world. So, unlike the Jews, His followers began to spread their religion across the world. What then followed were two millennia of tremendous ups and downs for this religion historically.

ANNO DOMINI 2064

For a time, it seemed nearly triumphant spreading across the world with billions of followers. However, things changed, and we find ourselves in these dark times now. In this country and in most of the world, His followers are mostly in hiding, and those left now all but hope for the world's ending, if only to put an end to the terrible state mankind now finds itself in."

"The story of how we got from there to here would be longer than the one I just told you. While important, it's nowhere near as important as the one I just told you. So, I think all of that is more than enough for today. We can talk later about how all of this will tie back to our original question regarding happiness. But I think you've got enough to contemplate now."

Mark was too staggered to reply. His first instinct was to dismiss all of it. However, it was too much new information to discard without thinking about. Obviously, this religion existed, as clearly Chris believed in it. A God, miracles, this Jesus, and coming back from the dead. It was just too much to take in.

"Well, thank you for telling me that," Mark managed. He suddenly felt somewhat awkward. What was expected here? Did Chris expect him to just believe all of that right now?

Chris laughed. "You should see the look on your face. I don't expect you to believe all of this all at once. My just saying so is hardly enough for you to go off. I had to give you a basic outline though. After today, I will send you a link to what we call 'the library.' You'll find a set of books I recommend. You'd be very hard pressed to find these books in the physical world, but we managed to save them in a virtual form. Take your time, read, and give what you read some thought. There are a lot of other books there too, you can read, but I recommend starting with the set I'll have ready for you. If you read them first, the rest will make more sense."

"I guess I might as well," Mark answered. "Honestly, I don't know what I think at this point. I will say that that is an incredible story. If it is true, then I guess it really changes everything. I was miserable before. While I'm not thrilled to now have to hide something that could get me killed, I guess I have little to lose either if I investigate this more now."

"I know I've put you in danger. I wish it weren't the case, but I only took the risk because I believe it will be worth it for you. Thank you for listening today. When I log out, you'll get a permanent channel invite. Wait until you have some time, and then access it when you are ready to try out the library. Oh, and happy New Year's." With that, Chris gave him a last smile and logged out.

With Chris gone, the desolate nature of the ruins suddenly felt much lonelier. Mark quickly decided to log out. As he reached for the log out button, a last gust of wind struck. He thought he heard words, but he didn't recognize their meaning. "Agnus Dei…" The log out started, and the ruins melted back into his apartment.

10.

The next few days took on a surreal quality. At work, Mark found himself busy as never before. Events overseas began to happen so quickly that the news felt more like some fantastic movie plot rather than real life. The French Caliphate refused to fall back in the face of the Golden Republic's forces. Instead, they opened fire as GR forces approached. Suddenly the Golden Republic was officially at war. The German Islamic Republic declared itself in alliance with France, and Eastern Germany together with Russia and the Eastern League all declared war on the GIR and French Caliphate. All of this had been somewhat expected if the French fought. What was surprising was that the Spanish Islamic Republic and the Southern Italian Islamic Emirates had joined for France as well. Turkey meanwhile stayed out of the fighting in Europe, but suddenly invaded both Syria and Iraq, moving specifically to capture oil fields while knocking out military installations and besieging major population centers without entering them.

The UK, although basing GR troops, declared itself neutral. This was tested when terrorist attacks from unidentified sources struck the airport and seaports of Gibraltar, and Spanish troops moved in to "restore order." The Spanish had stealthily moved missiles into Southern Spain, and suddenly the straits were heavily defended against both air and naval attacks.

The Golden Republic responded by blockading the Persian Gulf to prevent any oil tankers from moving through the Suez Canal. Some limited oil could make its way by land to the Mediterranean and up from there through the southern coasts of Italy, France, and Spain to the heart of the French Caliphate and GIR. But with Russian oil and gas being cut off, it was clear the forces of Western Europe would only have a short amount of time before they depleted their oil reserves and would have to settle for peace.

A wave of terror attacks on Russian and Eastern European oil fields and pipelines followed, meant to at least hamper the supply of oil to the Eastern League. Meanwhile, hordes of small infantry units began launching raids into Eastern Germany and the Eastern League nations, coordinating with larger and better organized formal military divisions of the French and Germans in numbers not seen since the last World War. The Golden Republic troops found themselves vastly outnumbered in Brittany and barely holding on by using air and naval support. In Eastern Europe, vast and bloody battles began to be waged between formal armies, while local militias tangled with invading guerrillas up and down the border regions of the Eastern Front.

The Golden Republic acted quickly to reinforce its troops in Brittany. However, it was clear they would need a larger force to push into France and help the Eastern states. The French appeared to have nearly a million troops on the Western Front alone, with nearly half already involved in the fighting in Brittany. Meanwhile, the Golden Republic had barely gotten 50,000 troops stationed, with another 100,000 being actively mobilized to the front.

Suddenly the draft was being activated. Instead of recruitment efforts, Mark's office now oversaw local war propaganda. His office was coordinating more than ever before with Leslie's department so they could turn the media programming over to wartime propaganda needs. At the same time, the Party still needed propaganda praising the Party's ideals to inspire unity at home.

The recruiting stations had to be converted almost overnight into large scale rally points for the draftees who had to

ANNO DOMINI 2064

be organized and processed before joining their training units. Doctors were drafted and trained to provide military specific fitness exams for the new draftees at each station. Even the logistics of acquiring the transportation for each recruiting center to send men along *en masse* to the training camps needed organizing.

Mark didn't envy the job of the military quartermasters who were suddenly responsible for the rapid equipping and organizing of all the troops his office was sending their way. During the first week, Mark's department oversaw the drafting and initial processing of a thousand men. In the second week, they processed three thousand. Their goal was to draft twenty thousand men by the end of the month.

The pace was frenetic during practically every minute of work. Despite this pace, Mark also worked longer and longer hours. Ten-hour days had become standard, and occasionally twelve and even fourteen-hour days were necessary. Party communications began to make it increasingly clear that a long war might be possible. European investments in nuclear and alternative energy sources together with their rationing of oil and enough shipping getting through the Mediterranean from Turkey, meant that cutting off oil from the Persian Gulf and Russia would not be enough to dry out the Western European armies. Efforts to dismantle communications amongst the enemy states had also proven harder than expected, despite the destruction of enemy satellites and communication towers via the GR's superior airpower. Meanwhile, it was taking time for the Russians and the Eastern League to fully mobilize, though their support had at least kept Eastern Germany from being overrun. However, if GR forces were overrun in Brittany, and the French could then sufficiently reinforce the Germans in the East, Eastern Germany and even Poland could come under mortal danger.

Amidst all this, it was easy to forget about the conversations with Christopher. Mark could lose himself in his work

135

for practically days at a time. However, occasionally, exhausted after a day at work yet not ready to sleep, Mark would find himself in his apartment alone with his thoughts. He still had the link to the library that Christopher had given him, but never felt he had the time or energy to really check it out. Instead, he mulled over what they had discussed so far.

He couldn't really believe all the stuff Christopher had told him at the last visit. However, it was such an incredible story he felt a curiosity toward it. There was obviously more to it than the short summation Chris had given him. Chris made it sound like the story was a major part of world history and knowing more about that would be interesting. That the Party had purposefully suppressed the knowledge made it that much more tantalizing. At this point he'd already broken the rules; why not learn more about what the Party was hiding from everyone?

The idea of there being something more than this world was also attractive. He knew he'd been struggling with the concept of death and the possibility that life held no meaning. If there was something out there beyond this world, there was the possibility there was some greater meaning to life. Even if he would not accept Chris's beliefs about what was out there, it interested him to learn more about what ideas people had about existence beyond this world. Maybe if he could learn more, he could discover some sort of truth for himself.

With these thoughts in mind, he considered opening the library link several times. It wasn't until a full three weeks had gone by and Mark could finally take a day off on a Saturday that he had enough time he felt like it would be worth accessing it. Leslie had taken a day off several days earlier which meant she would be busy today. Most of Mark's other friends were likewise occupied. Everyone was so busy that no one was trying to plan social events outside of work. Mark found himself with a day alone and nothing scheduled.

ANNO DOMINI 2064

Once, he might have gone to a club to meet women if he had no woman in the Party he was attached to at the time. Or, he might have spent the day playing VR games. He might have even watched VR porn. He realized none of that really appealed to him at this point. He'd done it so many times, and none of it had really satisfied in the end. It filled the time perhaps, but he had nothing to show for it. The stories Christopher had told him had seemed ridiculous. But at this point he supposed it wouldn't hurt to read more about them. At least Mark told himself, there was a novelty to it, which was more than he could say for his old pastimes.

He pulled up the link Chris had left him. The surrounding room faded briefly to black, and then loaded into the image of a quiet room with stone walls, timber floors and ceiling, and rows of books on rough wooden bookcases. Opened glass pane windows looked out over a rural countryside brightly lit by a noonday sun. Out of curiosity Mark went to the window and was surprised to see the room was set several stories up within a castle on a hill. He wondered whether this was a place in real life, or from someone's imagination. In the middle of the room was a stack of books on a desk with a letter sitting next to them.

Mark went to examine the letter. Someone had designed it to look like old-fashioned parchment. On it was lettering that appeared handwritten:

Dear Mark,

I recommend the books on this table as a beginning. However, all the books in this library are yours to read. The link to this library is a copy made only for you. You need not worry about encountering anyone else here. I hope you find it to be a place of comfort and learning. Your friend,

-Chris

He saw at the top of the pile the book Chris had mentioned earlier "Five Proofs of the Existence of God" by Edward Feser. Beneath it was a book titled "The Gospel of Luke." Next was a book titled "The Acts of the Apostles." Then there was a book titled, "Walking with God, A Journey Through the Bible" by Tim Gray and Jeff Cavins. Finally, below it was a much larger book than the others titled "The Holy Bible."

It was a formidable amount of homework Chris had left him; Mark mused. Still, he might as well read some of it. He picked up the first on the pile, "Five Proofs of the Existence of God" and sat himself down to read. Skimming the book cover he saw that the author was a philosopher. Obviously, he was from the pre-Golden Republic period as it used his last name, a custom which had been eliminated early in the Republic. He worried that the book would be too technical a place to start. He had hardly bothered with philosophy beyond the required intro classes. However, as he read the introduction, he learned the book had been designed with non-philosophers in mind and would start each proof with a more casual argument meant to be easy to grasp, before moving to summarize each of the five arguments as a formal philosophical proof.

He started in on the first, which the author called "The Aristotelian Proof." He vaguely remembered something from school about Aristotle being a famous ancient philosopher, but one who had been discredited by later philosophers. His class had therefore not studied Aristotle's writings. He thought it was perhaps a poor sign if the book started with a proof by a philosopher who was so ancient and discredited. Surely any thoughts from such a philosopher would have to be obsolete.

However, as he read, he could quickly see that the ideas discussed didn't seem obsolete at all. The chapter discussed thinking of the world in terms of actuals that can change into something that had before been merely potential. To change to become something that was before a potential, an actual always needed an actualizer to do so. As he thought about it, this made sense. It was a little harder to grasp that everything had the potential to exist or not exist, and that something must actualize existence, but ultimately, this also made sense.

What struck Mark then was the argument that for anything to exist would require something that was purely an actualizer that did not need to be actualized. If something like this did not exist, you relied on an infinite regress of actualizers to explain existence. He admitted this didn't make sense. It would be like having infinite train cars with no engine to push them. There would never be any movement no matter how many cars were added. The more he read, the more Mark had to take his time and think, but he could see the logic behind the arguments being made.

As Mark continued to read, he found himself continually agreeing with the logic. When he got to the part of the chapter giving answers to historical objections to the first proof, he could often see the flaws in the objections before even reading the answers Dr. Feser gave. He hadn't expected to be agreeing so readily with the author. After all, the implications of the argument were astonishing.

Mark found himself increasingly engrossed in what he was reading. He'd never read anything like this before. He devoured the chapters as if famished. He realized that the world he'd been living in was a lie. Why that lie had been told he didn't yet know. But that it was a lie was becoming increasingly clear. The arguments he was reading had been hidden away and dismissed as mere superstition and idiocy. However, when read, it was obvious that the people who had thought about these things were far from stupid or superstitious. There was depth and intellectual rigor here. Hours passed, and Mark had nearly finished the book before realizing he was both ravenously hungry and exceedingly in need of a toilet.

JACOB CLEARFIELD

He somewhat regretfully logged out from the library. He had Sarah prepare him a meal while making a trip to the bathroom. After washing up a bit, he sat down to the swiftly prepared meal Sarah had microwaved for him.

As he ate, he pondered what he'd read. After going through the proofs, it seemed almost impossible to deny that there was a transcendent being making existence possible. However, he couldn't really know the nature of such a being from the proofs, and the author said as much in the introduction. Logic alone wouldn't tell you much about such a being other than the most fundamental characteristics such a being would have to possess for existence to exist. He supposed the nature of that being was what the other books Chris had left for him would be about. After all, Chris had already given him a quick version of events supposedly about this being called, "God."

What really made him wonder though, was why was this idea so suppressed in the Golden Republic? What was it about the idea of this God that the Golden Republic was so determined to eliminate it from the mind of humanity? He'd been struggling now for years with a feeling of emptiness thinking about the lack of meaning in his life. Surely other people struggled with this, too. Wouldn't it be good to know there was something more out there? Why would so many people be against this idea that a whole country like the Golden Republic could oppose it? Mark felt like there was too much he just didn't know yet.

Finishing his meal, he could tell he'd strained his eyes a bit with all the reading. He felt his body could use some stretching and a walk. Further reading could wait, and really, he'd read enough to think over as it was. He had a few more hours to himself to relax before bed, and then his nose would be back to the grindstone the next day. Mark put aside the library for the rest of the day.

ANNO DOMINI 2064

The next few days proved even more trying than the previous three weeks. The war remained at a stalemate in Brittany. In some areas, the GR forces had even had to retreat to take up more defensible positions. While they had delivered reinforcements, the military was now fully engaged with its regular forces. It would still be some time before the drafted troops were ready to see action. Meanwhile, the casualty count was climbing. As it looked like the war might become prolonged, the recruitment staff began to deal with a new problem: draft dodging.

Mark would never have thought draft dodging would be a problem given the amount of surveillance employed by the Golden Republic. In the first few weeks as the draft caught people by surprise, draft dodging was not seen at all. But as time went by, people began to find ways to escape the system. Non-party members did not wear C-All's, and so it was only non-party members who could escape the draft. Most Party members had vital positions that exempted them from the draft anyway.

Mark would have thought the facial recognition systems used by the general surveillance cameras and party member C-All's would have caught people right away, since the system had all drafted persons targeted for ID'ing immediately if they did not arrive for muster at their appointed time and place. However, people were using facial prosthetics, changes in facial hair, tattoos, and sometimes even simple make-up to fool the facial recognition software.

Mark's office was often still able to find draft dodgers by searching out friends and relatives. Simple interviews and a few choice threats usually gave the draft dodgers away. But sometimes family and friends did not know where the draft dodgers had gone. There were rumors of enterprising civilians who were charging significant sums to house draft dodgers who were complete strangers and thus not easily traced to them. As a result, even with investigation there were an ever-increasing number of unresolved cases building up for Mark's office.

All of these tasks were taking up time and resources from an already overburdened staff. Mark tried to involve more traditional law enforcement agencies. But they were little interested in devoting their own staff to something they saw as being outside their own duties. This was particularly frustrating, as what he needed were detectives. His staff were mostly former recruiting agents with little to no experience in such areas. He was sure as a result there were a lot of mistakes being made, but there wasn't even enough time to figure out what the mistakes were.

Still, massive numbers of new draftees continued to arrive as scheduled and needed to be processed. He'd been able to requisition a few more staff for this, and they were managing so far to meet their processing goals. He didn't have much time to socialize at work anymore. He grabbed food at irregular hours when time allowed. He rarely saw Leslie, and he saw Chris even less.

As much as he had to think about the problems he was working on now for the war, he increasingly thought about Chris and the library. He would hear a news report discussing casualties and wonder, "What happens to all those young men when they die?" The idea that existence rested on a purely causal being was a very abstract thought. Even though it made perfect sense, he realized he needed to know more. If there was a being like that who could explain existence, how did that being then relate to the world Mark himself knew? Was such a being just undergirding existence but not playing a role in it? Dr. Feser had argued against this notion in his book, and it seemed strange. At the same time, if such a being existed and had complete power to change things however so desired, why was there suffering and death in the world?

To Mark, those questions seemed more pressing each day as he saw images of bloodied soldiers, bombed out towns and villages, and increasing stories of raids and terrorist attacks against civilians across both Northwestern France and all along the borders of Eastern and Central Europe. He wondered, too, when he visited the old recruiting, now "processing" centers, as he looked at the faces of the scared men being put into service. Almost to a man their faces showed signs of fear and entrapment. A lifetime of propaganda about the greatness of the Golden Republic had done little to make them desire to go die for its interests.

He could hardly blame them either. He'd be feeling just as scared and as trapped were he in their shoes. Why should they want to die for the Golden Republic? The Golden Republic was built on providing safety and comfort for everyone. But what good was that to you if you were stuck in a war zone, or worse, dead in one? As far as any of them knew, they would now go spend a miserable and undetermined amount of time in a foreign country where would be shot at and might die. The best they could hope for was to come back someday. If they died, then their existence was over with and they'd have likely died in miserable conditions. They only went because the alternative was facing the justice of the Golden Republic.

That justice proved harsh remarkably quickly. Within the first week of the war, the Republic declared deserters and draft dodgers to be traitors, "as deadly to the Republic as those proponents of the Old Order who first resisted the Republic's birth." After a meeting discussing searching for draft dodgers, Veronica confided in Mark that when the declaration was made declaring draft dodgers to be traitors, the main debate amongst the Inner Party was whether draft dodgers and deserters should be executed immediately or worked to death in camps to help further the war effort.

Initially, many Inner Party members had favored work camps, hoping they could still put the traitors to work for the war effort. However, a committee was formed to review the question with a week to research past efforts. Apparently, the work camps of the Soviet Union in the 20th century were examined especially closely. It was determined that even in an era before robots where there was plentiful manual labor to be done, the expense of guarding and providing for prisoners largely outweighed the fruits of their labor. Now, with robots easily out competing humans for most manual tasks, work camps would be a clear drain on the State's resources. As such, immediate execution was voted for overwhelmingly.

Faced with execution, most soldiers took their chances on the front line, where at least they would have a chance of returning home someday. It was a grim calculus that motivated the Golden Republic's soldiers into battle. Mark did not at all enjoy being part of the system forcing the soldiers into it. But he faced the same choice, really. If he suddenly stopped, he'd be forced into the Army. If he tried to sabotage the State's draft efforts, he would be caught eventually and then face execution.

So, the grim work continued. The war stretched on into the spring. Increasingly, though he sacrificed sleep to do so, Mark would take an hour out of his day to spend time in the library. Though often exhausted, he found the fatigue was not his greatest problem. He felt sick at heart. He now sensed there had been a sickness within him for a long time. Now serving a system that sent men to the front lines possibly to die, while also telling them their lives held no meaning, had exacerbated that sickness beyond what he could bear. With his time in the library, he felt like he was uncovering a mystery that held the remedy for him. With each visit, he found a small measure of comfort that somehow was helping him get through his days.

Chris had outlined some of the most basic elements of the Christian story. Having now read the philosophical argument for God summarized by Dr. Feser, he approached the stories in the Gospel of Luke and in Acts with a greater openness. He found this radically changed his perception of them. It did not always make it easy to read them. He could see that if he wanted to live in a way that conformed to the messages therein, he would need

ANNO DOMINI 2064

to fundamentally change his life in ways that would not be easy.

As time went on, he increasingly felt a keen sense of loss that he'd grown up in a world where none of this information had been presented to him before. He'd been living his life in such a way that he now had many habits he'd need to break with great difficulty. If he'd known all of this before, perhaps he would have never begun those habits in the first place.

In particular; while he'd noticed a lack of satisfaction or real happiness from the pornography on offer from the Party, he'd still taken his sexual gratification as a need that had to be fulfilled just like eating or sleeping. This was what the Party had taught what him from an early age, and self-gratification had been encouraged starting in middle school.

As he read about Christian morality from the Gospel and Acts, he asked Chris about it and was amazed to learn the Christian teachings on the matter. The idea that, far from a need that had to be fulfilled, lust was a temptation that needed to be kept in check, astonished him. That doing so made one a stronger person, more in command of one's body and one's life, was an even greater surprise to him.

Chris explained that a disordered sexuality was one of the most common ways a person could be enslaved to sin. Mark tried going without and was shocked at the way his body responded. He realized the Party had made him a sort of addict. Struggling through the additional stress of his body's demand for gratification only made pushing through work more difficult. At times he slipped, but his will was determined to be as little controlled by the Party as possible.

His new course of action led to an encounter he didn't expect. For a moment, he almost thought the Party had caught him in his secret treason against the state. In early March, he received a summons to see his primary care doctor. This seemed strange, as he was up to date on all his vaccinations. Though he was stressed at work, he had not been ill. However, there was nothing for it but to keep his appointment.

There were physician offices on the 4th floor of the Downtown Party headquarters. He was summoned to a 1 PM appointment. After lunch, he took the elevator down. It opened to a plain hallway with a sign posted on the wall with an arrow to the right marking "primary care" and an arrow to the left marking "occupational medicine." The medical floor here was primarily for simple office visits. Anything more complicated would require going to one of the local medical office complexes or hospital campuses in the city.

Mark was to see a Dr. Leandra in primary care, and so he took a right. Halfway down the hall he came to an open door with Dr. Leandra's name on it and beyond saw a reception desk with a small waiting area in front of it. The room appeared deserted. He stepped to the desk and saw a touchscreen displaying a "press here to check in" button. He pressed and a residual fingerprint scan showed on the screen. It flashed then to an image of his employee ID and a question came up asking "is this you?" with yes and no buttons beside it. He pressed yes, and a message came up letting him know he'd be roomed in approximately five minutes.

Mark took a seat in the waiting room. He felt vaguely nervous given he didn't know what he was here for. To avoid fidgeting, he checked the news while he waited and flashed through the most recent headlines on his C-All. Apparently, a significant aerial battle had taken place on the eastern front in which the Russians were claiming a victory. The analysts declared that with the additional air cover this would provide Russian and Eastern League forces; they expected a general offensive to begin into Germany as the winter now thawed into spring.

"Mark?" came a young woman's voice. A medical assistant stood waiting at the door beside the reception desk. Mark stood up and followed the woman into a nondescript examining room. She checked his blood pressure, pulse, and temperature, and then told him that Dr. Leandra would be in shortly.

Mark waited in a small white plastic chair with a metal frame. The exam table was to his right and a small desk with a monitor and keyboard were to the left. His chair did not include armrests. He caught himself drumming his fingers on his thigh. He was sure he looked nervous, but then, that was only natural. Who wouldn't be nervous being called in to see a doctor without an explanation? He considered the possibility that his C-All had detected some sign of poor health. While he hadn't been feeling sick of late, he'd been very stressed and extraordinarily busy at work. Perhaps some of the fatigue he'd been feeling was due to some underlying malady instead?

Mark continued to wait nervously for another minute before a knock came at the door. "Yes?" Mark responded, then realizing why the knock had come said, "uh, I mean, I'm ready." The door opened. A short woman in a white lab coat entered. She wore thin rounded glasses and had tightly bound her hair at the back. Mark noticed she wore little make-up. Her appearance did not fit with the current style trends of the Inner Party. She nodded and gave him a small smile. She was thin and reasonably attractive with a friendly face but held herself awkwardly and appeared slightly nervous.

"Hello, I'm Dr. Leandra." She washed her hands using a cleansing chemical dispenser and then shook his hand. "Thank you for coming in today." She sat at the computer and pressed her fingertip to the monitor. A screen opened, and he could see his name at the top. She turned back to him.

Mark felt he should say something. "Well, I'm not sure why I'm here, but I received the notification that I was supposed to come. I figured it must be important if the Party was willing to take me away from my duties to see you."

Dr. Leandra nodded. "Yes, I'm aware you're doing important work. I think that's why they had you see me. We wouldn't want someone like you to run into trouble. It's always best to head things off before there are any problems."

Mark was unsure what to make of this, although it was relieving to hear that whatever the problem was it sounded like it must be early and treatable. "Is there some health problem developing that I need to know about?" he asked.

Dr. Leandra hesitated for a moment and then began, "Not physically, but the Party understands its members are being put under extra stress now as we deal with the added duties that come with the war. We monitor for signs of adaptation to that stress and look for indications of poor adaptation. Your C-All noted an anomaly that might be a cause for concern, although it's unusual enough that I'm uncertain what it means. That's why you are here for this interview."

Mark wasn't sure how to respond, but his puzzled look must have been answer enough. Dr. Leandra seemed to hesitate before beginning, "Your C-All has noted a significant decrease in your frequency of ejaculations. Specifically, you had a pattern of daily to semi-daily masturbation combined with intermittent intercourse with female partners, most recently on a semi-regular basis with Leslie in the media division here for over a year now."

Mark now felt intensely awkward. Even though masturbation was taught as something normal during school, it wasn't something people discussed in polite company. To have a stranger recount his previous habits to him was an experience he'd not been expecting at all. He felt a strong sense of something being wrong about this. But he had a hard time fully understanding the emotion in the moment.

Dr. Leandra sensed his discomfort. "Please, I know most patients don't enjoy this topic being brought up. But the Party recognizes healthy sexuality as being important to long term mental health. So, it's important that we talk about these things." She spoke automatically, as though she'd been trained to use this phrasing and she was falling back upon the training

ANNO DOMINI 2064

now to help her continue. Her voice kept a similarly rehearsed pattern as she said, "Studies show that during periods of stress individuals engage in increased rates of sexual activity, which is thought to be for the purpose of stress relief. This is a general trend, and there is a broad range of behaviors with it. It is rare, however, to see such a large drop in activity as was logged by your C-All. There is the concern in your case that this may indicate an underlying pathology."

"I see," Mark managed. His thoughts raced. He could hardly tell her the real reason for the sudden change. He had no idea whether the Party suspected him. Probably not, given that they'd sent him to the doctor and tipped their hand about the concern. However, it would be like them to also use something like this as a chance to see whether he'd slip and say something he shouldn't that would give him away. It seemed less likely, but still a possibility.

Dr. Leandra interrupted his thoughts. "If there has been some kind of.... organic change, you should let me know, as such things are usually treatable." Her statement presented Mark with a new problem. Should he lie and say things weren't functioning right? He rejected the thought almost immediately. It would be too easy for them to test. He inwardly shuddered at the thought of the testing the Party would likely then force on him.

"No, no," he began. "Things are still working fine, in that regard anyway." If he wasn't going to go the organic route, he'd need to lean into the psychiatric side, but he'd have to do it in a way that didn't lead to some serious diagnosis being placed on him.

"Are you sure? We could test today to find out. The equipment for the testing is portable and it would only take a few minutes. It's not painful, quite the opposite actually." Dr. Leandra was trying her best to sound friendly and supportive, even trying to joke with him. He smiled in response, even as the

149

suggestion left him cold. He had, however, decided how to approach the situation.

"No, it's nothing like that. I'm sure the equipment is still functioning, if you will." He let out a slightly dramatic sigh. "The truth is, it's definitely been a struggle lately. Obviously, I'm not seeing Leslie as often because of how busy we both are right now, which is part of the equation. But as far as the, uh, 'individual' side of the equation goes, I just haven't found it to be as satisfying of late."

Dr. Leandra looked a little confused. "What do you mean by not satisfying? If things are working as you say, I assume you're able to achieve an ejaculation, yes?" Mark almost laughed at her confusion. He realized he'd changed a lot in the last few weeks. But even before then he'd been moving away from the paradigm of thinking this doctor lived in.

"This isn't something that just started since the war, to be honest. I think the war just pushed it along a lot faster. I'm sure if you check my C-All files, you'll notice I was already using the pornography programs much less often. Over the last few years, you'll likely notice a trend. I'd been feeling, I guess, a malaise towards sex. I just wasn't finding it to be all that gratifying anymore."

Dr. Leandra seemed to perk up. "Interesting, that would explain the findings from your C-All. I think I know what's going on." A palpable relief seemed to show across her face, together with a clear satisfaction of solving a difficult puzzle. Mark couldn't help but be interested in what she had surmised, relieved that whatever it was it would provide a cover to the real reason he was no longer masturbating.

"What you are describing sounds like the symptoms of 'sexual anhedonia.' It's a condition where a patient no longer experiences pleasure from orgasms. It frequently goes together with a loss of interest in sex. It is often experienced together with a more general loss of pleasure in life in the setting of depression. But it can be experienced separately as well. The main question then is whether this is something on its own or is this part of a larger problem like depression?" Dr. Leandra took a breath. "Have you had trouble with feelings of sadness or depressed mood?" Mark shook his head no.

Dr. Leandra continued, "Have you had decreased interest in your normal activities?" Mark replied that no, in fact he was spending as much time playing laser tag and other VR sports as he could now to relax after work. He felt rather clever about the added level of cover he was giving himself here.

Dr. Leandra pressed forward with questions, "Have you had trouble with feeling increased guilt or unworthiness? Trouble with energy level? Decreased concentration at work or at home? Decreased appetite? Increased irritability or agitation? Trouble sleeping?" Mark answered that he'd been more fatigued of late, but he attributed that to the intensity and hours of work he was now putting in. He denied the rest.

Mark could tell that the visit was ending. He could see the doctor relaxing as he answered. She made a few more notes and then turned back to him. "I think overall that this is likely a case of isolated sexual anhedonia. This isn't serious unless it causes psychological distress to the person experiencing it. It seems like in your case it is not. Sometimes the condition can spontaneously resolve. In other cases, it can be a lifelong diagnosis. If you find it beginning to affect your life in a negative way, I'd be happy to make a referral to a sex therapist who could explore treatment options with you."

Mark assured her he didn't think this would be necessary. She created a summary and transferred it to his C-All for reviewing whenever he'd wish. It included contact links if he decided to seek treatment. Then, with a few pleasantries exchanged, the visit was over. Mark found himself making his way back to his office to resume work. He felt a palpable sense of relief flow over him as he exited the doctor's office. He decided later that night he'd try contacting Chris. He wondered if there were other pit-falls he would need to avoid.

11.

Thankfully, the rest of the day after the exam went normally. Around 8 PM, he was able to head home. After a quick meal and a shower (a necessity after work lately given how grubby he felt by the time he got home), he sent Chris a message, "Had a weird day, feel like kicking back with some laser tag to forget it. Free?"

A message soon came back that Chris would be free in about 20 minutes. Mark decided it might look suspicious if he didn't also contact Leslie. He shot her a message, "Hey, going to play some laser tag with Chris in 20 or so, but realized we haven't touched base lately. Want to chat for a bit?"

A few seconds later a call came in through the C-All from Leslie. Mark answered. "Hi Mark." Leslie's face came in through a video feed. A pang shot through Mark at the sight of her face; it was a feeling of both love and loneliness at the same time. "Hi Leslie, did I catch you at a good time?"

Leslie nodded. "You did. I just finished eating after getting home. I'm tired, but I was going to just read a bit or something before going to bed. I could talk instead, though. I feel kind of bad that I didn't think to message you. I know I've been bad about staying in touch lately."

She sighed. "Honestly, I've been pretty bad about that with just about everyone really. But it sucks I'm even being bad about it with you." Mark could see lines of exhaustion around her eyes. He thought she looked a little thinner than usual, which given she was thin to begin with, gave her a slightly unhealthy appearance. Mark had noticed he'd been going in the opposite direction. He'd been exercising less and eating more.

153

While he was hardly fat, he had gained about five pounds and his body was taking on a less defined physique.

"I know how you feel." Mark replied. "I think everyone is being less social right now. It'll get better when the war is over."

Leslie nodded. "I just hope it's soon. I still don't understand why the Europeans are acting this way. For the sake of some little peninsula they lit the whole continent on fire!"

Mark agreed. He thought he had a little better understanding now from his time in the library. At intervals he'd left the initial suggested books to look up other topics of interest. He'd been reading a little about Islam and its history. He could now better see why the Muslims were so committed to wiping out the last remnants of Christianity in France. Of course, the Party didn't want to explain that. More and more, he also suspected that the Inner Party members were so ignorant of religion and religious history that they didn't understand it themselves. They saw this war as being about maintaining a balance of power in Europe. They probably primarily hoped that after the war the Golden Republic could have a toehold on the continent to further maintain order. They never suspected the French would see their actions as a Western defense of Christianity in Europe (even if the reality couldn't be further from the truth.)

In his office, they'd been sent some examples of the propaganda being used by the French for recruiting. Golden Republic spies had photographed and sent it. His coworkers had been mystified to see so many pamphlets referring to GR troops as "les croisés" which translated as "crusaders." Mark had had to hide a laugh at the irony. The description was apt for the Eastern League, especially many of the Polish soldiers, but was completely false for the GR troops.

"I don't think we really understand the people over there," Mark opined. "It's honestly what worries me the most about this war. There haven't been any nukes used yet, but who

ANNO DOMINI 2064

knows how far things could go now? The war has become much larger than anyone expected already."

Leslie's eyes widened. "Do you really think they might use nuclear weapons? That would be suicide! I heard from a friend in the air force they think they have barely a dozen hidden away, while we have hundreds we could use. We don't have as many as in the pre-Golden Republic era, thank goodness. But we still have enough to wipe them out if it came to it."

"I guess my concern is, we didn't think they'd make a fight out of Brittany remaining independent. Now there are literally hundreds of thousands, if not millions of men fighting across Europe. So how can we be sure they wouldn't go to the next step as well? Granted, we'd probably intercept a few. At most, they'd probably wipe out a few major cities on the Eastern Seaboard. But that would be enough to kill tens of millions of people. Maybe they'd think that would be enough to make us back down. Maybe they'd think it was worth dying in the retaliation strikes if it meant they could kill a few million infidels. Who knows?" Mark realized as soon as he'd finished speaking that he probably shouldn't have aired these fears. Leslie looked visibly shaken.

"I really hadn't thought about it like that. I guess we just have to hope it never happens." A long pause came over the next minute. Mark wasn't sure what to say. He thought about apologizing but knew Leslie would dismiss it. It wasn't like the risk of what he'd said wasn't there.

Leslie broke the silence. "Mark, I'm sorry I haven't made more time with you lately. This has all just been really tough. But it's made tougher by being apart from people rather than being with them. I'm glad I have you in my life. I don't know what will happen in the future, but right now, I'm just glad I have you."

In that moment, for a brief second, Mark thought about bringing Leslie into the library. The temptation passed as

155

quickly as it came. With its absence, he felt more keenly the separation now between them.

"I'm glad too, Leslie. You're right, we need to get through these things together instead of apart." Maybe, just maybe he could change Leslie's mind about going off service together. Maybe they could live as man and wife, and in time he could share his new secret with her. It would take time, but, it felt like something worth hoping for.

"You know," he continued, "I've been thinking. All this craziness, being so busy with the war on, it makes me wonder; is this really what I want long term? I know in the past we never really thought going off rotation would be something we'd want, but now I'm wondering..."

Leslie looked at him measuringly for a moment. "Mark, you're one of the brightest stars in Milwaukee right now. I know some of the work you're doing probably feels thankless, but believe me, you're doing well. The war won't last forever. If you keep it up, you're almost certain to enter the Inner Party. Would you really want to give that up?"

Mark looked away for a second and gathered his thoughts. He really didn't want that anymore. The more time he'd spent in the library, the more he had seen what it meant to live a good life. He knew that joining the Inner Party would mean walking into a lion's den of temptations and worldly distractions. None of it would make him happy, quite the opposite in fact, and he was glad to know this at last. He almost shuddered thinking of the person he might have become if he'd given himself over to that ambition. Of course, he'd have to do something. He'd given that some thought, though he wasn't sure what Leslie would think of it.

"I don't think I'd be happy in the Inner Party, Leslie. I think I want to do something a little simpler. I want to help people more directly. What Christopher does in IT is like that, he uses a talent in a way that directly helps people. I want that kind of job. I've always been kind of handy with tools; maybe I could go back and train to be a technician for robots. We all rely on robots; the Golden Republic basically runs on them. Maybe I could just live right here in Milwaukee and fix robots."

Leslie looked stunned. "That's crazy. You'd give up being in the Inner Party to be a robot technician? You're not thinking straight. You need more sleep. I think I'll get going."

Mark answered, "Leslie, I love you. We can't be together if we stay on rotation. If we stayed in Milwaukee, took simpler jobs, we could be together. I think that would be more than worth it. Please, just think about it at least."

Leslie's eyes began to tear up. "This," she paused. "This is just too much right now. I'm exhausted too. I, I love you too." She paused again, longer this time. "But I love the Party and I'm not sure going off rotation would be the right way to serve it. I'm not sure being a robot technician is the best way you could serve the Party either. You have so many more skills as an administrator and a leader. If you really don't think you could do it though, maybe you're right for yourself. But I don't know if the same would be true for me." She took a deep breath, then dabbed her eyes with a tissue she grabbed. "I'll think about it. That's all I can say for now."

They said good-bye, and the call ended. Mark stood and stretched. He realized that had been a far more emotional call than he'd expected. He debated whether he should call off meeting Christopher. He felt a need to process some of his emotions. He decided, though, that he'd already committed himself. Also, he had too much he needed to talk about with Christopher to put off any longer. This would have been true even if he hadn't had the experience at the doctor.

He checked the time. Twenty minutes had nearly passed. He sat down again and logged into his library. Once the library had loaded into view, he looked over at his recent reading, considering starting something briefly until Chris could join him. Once he'd finished the book "Walking with God, A Journey Through the Bible" he'd opened the Bible and found a note. It had encouraged him to spend a little time each day reading from the Bible, and to start exploring the various other works in the library as well. He'd most recently started reading the "Dialogue of St. Catherine of Sienna." It was an incredible text, but he found he needed to take his time and think when he read it to absorb what was being said. He probably didn't have time now with Chris coming soon.

Almost as if reading his thoughts, a message came in from Chris. Mark invited him to the library, and in a moment, he had loaded in. Chris looked about a bit to get his bearings, and then nodded to Mark as he spotted him sitting in his favorite reading chair by the window.

Chris positioned himself, so he could sit in a chair across from Mark. "So, what's going on?" he asked. His face bore traces of fear and concern.

"Nothing terrible, or least I'm pretty sure not. But I thought I'd better talk to you about it," Mark answered. He could tell his answer wasn't comforting to Chris. Realizing there wasn't much point in trying to couch his story any further before presenting it, Mark told Chris about his summons to the doctor and the encounter that followed. He'd been a little worried about being embarrassed by it. But as he told Chris, he felt more embarrassed about the fact that he had previously been masturbating and viewing pornography than anything else. The part about having stopped and this being noticed by the Party was probably the only part that wasn't uncomfortable to relate.

Chris was very understanding throughout. He listened intently, only occasionally interrupting to question a detail here and there. When Mark had finished, he looked at Chris somewhat intently, waiting to hear what he thought of the story.

Chris took a moment to respond. "I think I should start by apologizing. Usually when someone is reading from the library,

I try to meet with them more regularly to discuss what they've read and how it affects their lives. I can see you've gained some profound insights in the last few months, on top of ones I believe you were making on your own beforehand. You've started to change your life to match. I'm sorry I wasn't there to offer guidance on how this might affect things."

"So, you've helped people with this before then?" Mark asked. He'd figured as much, but Chris hadn't given him much insight into his past. Mark was happy to grab at the opportunity to learn more.

Chris nodded. "By this point, you've read a bit about the structure of the Church. I'm what's called a 'deacon.' I try to minister to the faithful as best I can wherever I happen to be assigned." He paused for a moment. "I've only helped initiate people into the Church a few times, though. Several of them were married couples. A few others were single women. I had one other single man. The Party didn't seem to notice anything when the single women joined. They hadn't been sexually active outside of a few relationships that they'd already exited.

The other man though, something similar happened, he was still struggling with chastity, so the Party merely noticed a dip and some periods of chastity and then periods where he again struggled more. He was able to give an excuse at first, much as you did today. Then thankfully I found a good woman interested in marrying a faithful man, and he went off rotation. The Party thought he'd fallen in love. While many of his co-workers and previous friends were condescending to him, he escaped with little trouble last I heard."

Mark answered, "Escape seems a good word for it. I've been thinking I'd like to escape as well. I think this war and how busy I've been will make a good excuse. I can claim to be burned out and looking for a change. This 'anhedonia' thing the doctor came up with could play into that. Maybe I can go off cycle and stay here in Milwaukee. Maybe Leslie would even join me, and eventually I could share with her what I know..."

"Be careful," Chris cautioned him. "Your desire to live as man and wife with Leslie is natural, and your desire to share what you've learned is entirely good and reasonable. You must be careful, though. Many people are not open to the good news. If you try to share it with them, they are all too likely to turn you in to the Party. Talking with Leslie, I've sensed she is nowhere close to being ready at this point. God alone can say if she ever will be. If you lived with her, you'd have a hard time hiding all this from her. I truly fear it would not go well in the end."

Mark hadn't really thought about that. He considered what they were doing right now. It would be impossible with Leslie around. Even spending time in the library would appear suspicious. There'd been several times in the last few months he'd worried whether things could work out with Leslie. Now once again he began to feel like ending their relationship would prove inevitable. His chest ached at the thought of it.

"I'm sorry, Mark. I know it's difficult to think about." A long pause ensued. Mark appreciated the time as he processed this. He thought about what would happen now if he tried to go back to his old life. Inevitably, he'd still lose Leslie as the Party moved them to new rotations in a couple of years. Meanwhile, the same emptiness he'd felt in his life would be there. In fact, it would be worse now. Having read what he'd read and felt the truth in it, going back to that life, willfully choosing it, would be to enter a foretaste of hell knowing that the true suffering waited just beyond his last breath.

Mark knew what his decision was. He'd been thinking about it more and more, and he felt at this point truly committed. "Christopher, I want to be Baptized."

Chris smiled. "I'm glad to hear it. I suspected as much when you told me why the doctor summoned you. People don't make that kind of change in their lives without the Holy Spirit being at work in them. I can tell you've been hearing God's call, and I'm glad you wish to answer it."

Chris thought for a moment. "Easter is about a month away. Before the Church had to go underground in this country, the Church baptized catechumenates like you during the midnight Mass that led into Easter. It would be nice to keep with that tradition. But times being what they are, there are other considerations. Every day there is the danger of being caught and arrested. Granted, if you were caught and died a martyr, you'd be baptized by the blood of your martyrdom, and in that way saved. However, should it come to it, I think it would be best to face martyrdom already possessing the Grace that comes with the Sacraments. If you are ready, I would propose we arrange your Baptism as soon as possible."

"I have a day off next Saturday. I could make sure there was a time set aside if you can be free," Mark offered.

"That should work." Chris replied. "I'm scheduled to work that morning but will be free in the afternoon."

"Where should we meet for it?" Mark asked.

Chris seemed to have already thought this through. He seemed rather animated as he replied, "We need to make things seem as natural as possible, so the C-All doesn't flag anything. We should use the pretext of getting together socially at your apartment. We could have a meal and talk about things like work, innocuous topics that the C-All won't notice. Then we decide we will play some laser tag together. I'll send you a link. Once we are safe in the program, we can then perform the sacrament."

Mark could tell Chris had been through this a few times. It made sense and seemed simple enough, though he realized it would require a bit of acting on both their parts. Still, it was straightforward enough that it should work.

"There is more," Chris continued. "Once we baptize you, I'll send you a link you can use to update your library. We have priests scattered about the country who offer Mass. Usually we can offer at least one daily you can join if you are free when it is being said. Your library will show when the next one is likely to be offered. When it goes live, you'll be able to connect to it from your library. We try to have a few offerings on Saturdays and Sundays and to give some lead time on when those will be, so that people can try to find a time they can join to honor the Sabbath. Obviously, it's not the same as being there, and you can't receive Eucharist this way. But most of the time, it's the best we can do."

"In order to still follow the Ten Commandments..." It impressed Mark this could still be done. It would take a little planning and might not always be possible. But Mark figured it likely he could make a time work at least once each weekend. He said as much to Chris.

"Finally," Chris continued, "when you are baptized, it cleanses you of your past sins. Unfortunately, it's all too human to fall back into sin. You've read about the Sacrament of Reconciliation. We do what we can to have priests offer it. Your library will show if a confessor is available, and if not, when one will probably next be available."

Mark still had one question. "So, I've read again and again about the importance of the Eucharist. Is there any chance of attaining it here?" Chris had already said he was a Deacon and not a priest which had lowered Chris's hopes. He'd been secretly hoping Chris would be a priest, as that would make receiving Eucharist much more likely.

"You're right to ask. The Eucharist is the greatest of the sacraments, and the nearest we come to God while in this life. Unfortunately, in these times, it is profoundly difficult in this nation to receive it. It's not impossible, deo gratias. The faithful Japanese once went hundreds of years without the Eucharist after their government drove all the priests from those islands. But sometimes in this age it can be a long time before an oppor-

ANNO DOMINI 2064

tunity presents itself. Priests are few. By necessity, only a few people at most can be present physically at any given Mass.

We have too often been reduced to the ignominy of relying on 'dead drops' to pass Sacred Hosts from priests who offered the sacrifice of the Mass to deacons and even some lay extraordinary ministers so that communion services can be offered later with the faithful who are being persecuted. I can tell you; I've spoken to priests who have lamented that there is no more terrible duty then to have to leave Christ hidden and alone, and then to walk away fearful that the Sacred Host might be found and desecrated. Yet, we know our Lord desires to be with his people. Terrible as it is, to do nothing would be worse."

This practice seemed extremely dangerous to Mark. "How do you keep the C-All's and security cameras from noticing people leaving and then picking up something like that?" Mark asked.

"There's a reason we can't do it often. Too frequently and people would more likely be caught. Most of the priests are outside the party and at least don't have to wear C-Alls. Still, they are forced to leave the Blessed Hosts in nondescript items. Often the priest must pretend to lose the item chosen or misplace it so that if a security camera is present, it is less likely to take notice. The receiver meanwhile must be equally careful to be nondescript in 'finding' the items we place the Blessed Hosts in. Again, most of the deacons aren't party members like I am, so it's a little easier for them. But even then, they have to be very careful."

Chris paused, seeing the troubled look on Mark's face. "All of that said, I do still manage to hold a communion service a few times a year with a few of the faithful at a time. We try to make sure everyone has a chance to receive the Eucharist at least once a year. Being newly baptized, you would be first on the list to attend a communion service when I can next minister one. If we're lucky, I might even be able to arrange it so you can attend

163

a Mass in person."

Mark thanked him. He didn't really know what such an experience would be like. Given the effort involved and the risks people were taking, he felt grateful even for the offer. They discussed the details a little more for Saturday afternoon and then bid each other farewell.

The C-All program ended, and the screen dissolved back into a transparent lens. Mark expected to feel the weight of the decision he had made tonight. Instead, he felt a strange lightness. The decision was made. He now just had to carry through with it. His life would change forever. Despite the danger involved, he felt a tremendous relief wash through him. If a year ago someone had told him he would give up his career and risk his life to join a forbidden religion he'd never heard of before, he'd have said the person was crazy. Yet, here he was. The more he thought about it the better he felt. An almost giddy feeling of joy began to well up within him. He wanted to shout, to sing, and to dance, though he was aware enough of how that would look to the C-All to hold back.

Though he couldn't sing, he remembered that the library had a book about songs for worship. He'd only opened it briefly and had been surprised to see it broke the medieval motif of the library by including playable links of the songs it talked about. He resolved that the next opportunity he had time to spend there he would look up songs of joy and listen to them. With that happy thought, he turned in for the night.

12.

During the days leading up to Saturday, Mark had a hard time concentrating on his work. He had little motivation to make the recruiting centers process draftees faster, nor did he want to optimize the investigations to hunt draft dodgers. To a large extent, he'd previously done what could he could do in these areas, anyway. As the war continued, what had started out as a hurried effort to slap together a working system had now taken on the contours of a functioning program with increasingly normalized operations. Some of the urgency within the department was declining, and he noted he could more consistently give employees time off. He almost wondered whether, if the war went on long enough, the Party might continue pressing warfare simply to prolong the new normal that had developed.

Thankfully, as the workings of day-to-day recruit processing became normalized, besides having days off, both he and his employees began to work more regular hours. The increased time at home allowed him to spend more time in the library. He was spending less time directly studying Instead, he had listened to some of the sacred music that had been preserved. He found it moved him in ways he'd never felt his whole life. There were mighty hymns of inspiration, gorgeous songs of hope and longing, and perhaps his favorite, beautiful chants filled with serenity and deep reverence.

He had also started to pray. It felt awkward at first, but as he continued, he found it more and more natural to talk to God. He started with a few of the formal prayers he found in the library and then also began to pray more informally. He even sometimes said mental prayers outside of the library, though he

JACOB CLEARFIELD

was careful not to give any sign in his face or body language that he was praying so that the C-All could not notice.

The night before his Baptism, he experimented with one of the longer forms of prayer he had read about: the Rosary. He'd finished work around 6 PM that day, and after arriving home to his apartment and eating supper, he composed himself and entered the library. The library mirrored the time in the real world, and so outside the windows was a dark but star filled night. The moon was a thin crescent that shone down on snow-covered fields abutting pine forests. Mark reflected on how well the simulation captured the look of snow caught within pine tree branches. Turning back to the library itself, he also admired the peaceful glow created by the candlelight illuminating the stone walls and bookshelves. He turned on some Gregorian chant. As the deep harmonies began, he felt almost like he really was in a monastery library listening to monks at chapel.

He'd read about the Rosary several times now, and he'd come across multiple sources that recommended praying it daily. Given the importance many of the saints seemed to put on the rosary, he'd learned more about it, and ultimately thought it would be worth trying to pray himself. He had found a guide in the library, and now, with the guide in front of him and making do with a virtual rosary, he started.

At first, he felt a little awkward. He had to rely heavily on the guide for the Apostles Creed, and even the "Our Father", "Hail Mary", and "Glory Be" he didn't have completely memorized yet. When he came to the first mystery though, he appreciated how the guide took him through the Gospel passage related to the mystery. In this case, he was praying the Glorious Mysteries and started with the Resurrection of Jesus. As he continued and repeated the prayers, he became more comfortable with them and could think more about the mysteries from the Gospels as he prayed.

As he reached the mystery of the descent of the Holy

ANNO DOMINI 2064

Spirit at Pentecost, he was struck by the fact that tomorrow, God willing, would be his own Baptism. He wondered what it would mean for him, what it might feel like or how it might change him. He wasn't sure on this point. Most of what he'd read on the subject had talked about the cleansing of sin and opening of the way to Heaven. But he'd also read of how it could provide a person with graces to better resist sin and be a better person. He wondered how much he might tell that it changed him.

He also wondered if this would be what would finally lead him to happiness. Christopher had talked with him more on their original topic of happiness. Now exploring the concepts of Christianity, Mark had asked Christopher if following Jesus would really make him happy. Christopher had explained to him that beyond the levels of happiness they'd discussed before, those of immediate gratification and of prestige, there was a third level encompassing the happiness that came from helping other people. Even this was not an end though, as it relied on fallible and mortal people for one's happiness.

However, because God is both perfect and eternal, the happiness that comes from serving Him provides a happiness that lasts and that can truly fulfill a person. In life, both the third level of happiness from serving others and the fourth level of serving God could blend, as serving others is a way to serve God. However, because God is eternal, the good that comes from serving others lasts beyond their death. It also lasts beyond the death of the individual and contributes towards happiness into eternity. Christopher had explained that, for this reason, serving God could give Mark the meaning he needed to find true happiness both in this life and the next.

Returning his thoughts to the rosary, he thought about the men who had been gathered when the Spirit came upon them. Most of those men had later gone out to preach the Gospel and had later suffered martyrdom. They must have known that would be a possibility. They had already witnessed the crucifixion. Something about receiving the Spirit had made them willing to risk, and even accept, violent deaths. Again, he wondered what kind of change Baptism might bring for him.

He continued through to the end of the five mysteries and the "Hail Holy Queen." He had imagined praying so many prayers would take a long time, but upon checking he was surprised to see only twenty minutes had elapsed. He continued to sit and closed his eyes, listening to the sound of the harmonies reverberating across the stone from the Gregorian Chant. In all his adult years, even in those times after his greatest achievements for the Party, he realized he had never felt so at peace as in this moment.

This thought alone was enough to tell Mark there was Truth in what he'd found here. But there was more than that. He was keenly aware of the idea that he at this moment was still outside, standing in the gloomy cold and looking through a doorway into a brightly lit-up house where a joyous feast was being celebrated. Tomorrow he was to cross the threshold and enter the feast. The idea was nothing less than thrilling to contemplate. Just looking in made him feel better than he ever had in his life. What would it be to enter through the door?

With that happy thought, Mark called it a night. He exited out from the library. Still thinking about the events of the next day, he took his time and got ready for bed. Finally, once fully ready and laying in bed, he removed his C-All. As he heard the click from the microphones, the noise did not irritate him as it so often had. Sleep quickly found him.

The next day, he tried to do things as normally as possible. He slept in until 9 AM. He was sure to get ready and dress the same as any other day. He spent some time reading the news. It seemed there had been no major changes in the war the last few days. A few Party leaders were working on a peace proposal they hoped the French might accept, though thus far the French continued to demand all of Brittany for there to be peace. The Eastern League and Russian forces were slowly pushing westward, and with the heavy fortifications now guarding the border of Brittany having largely curtailed raids and terror attacks, the Golden Republic was increasingly sending supplies to the Russians and Poles while further building up forces on the Continent as a threat to Paris. It was hoped that through increased pressure on the Eastern Front and the threat of a direct Golden Republic invasion of France, the Islamic powers of Europe would soon be brought to the negotiating table.

Christopher would come over for lunch around noon. At 11 Mark decided to go for a walk. The weather was slowly beginning to improve. Today had proven unusually warm, such that there was the rejuvenating feeling of Spring in the air. He made his way east to the lake. It was a little colder, as a brisk wind carried the lower temperatures of the water up onto the beaches and the easternmost blocks of the city. It had been a cold winter, and Mark could still see blocks of ice on the lake, though they were now broken and floated atop the waves. Winter had filled the beaches with bits of ice that had washed up onto shore and now were melting and returning in rivulets to the lake.

As it always did, the lake struck him with its beauty. Season by season, and even day by day and hour by hour, the lake was constantly changing its appearance. Sometimes it would appear calm and majestic. At other times, it became fierce and terrible. Sometimes it would be lit with incredible oranges and pinks from the rising or setting sun, and at other times it would be dark and mysterious, lit only by the reflection of the moon and stars. Always though, he found a sense of wonder present in it. A connection to things much larger than himself.

He thought how fitting it was then, that today they would mark him using water. Christopher had told him they used to use water that had been blessed ahead of time, but this was now too risky. Instead, a prayer of blessing would be said over the water to be used, and this would then suffice for the Baptism. Christopher realized that, this being the case, the water would come from his own tap, and so would in fact be coming from the very lake in front of him now. Again, it felt fitting.

He stayed until he knew he would have to start back to be home ahead of Christopher. As he walked he received a message from Leslie. She had gone into work that morning, but things had gone well, and she would have the rest of the day off. She was wondering if he wanted to get together that night.

Mark was careful to suggest meeting to go out to eat that night. Leslie happily agreed, but Mark worried she would expect to spend the night afterwards. They hadn't slept with each other now in several months. In that time, the war and their resultant work hours had provided a convenient excuse to avoid this. However, both of their hours were improving, and Leslie had even been dropping hints lately when they'd talk or message each other that she was feeling restless. Mark knew a reckoning was coming. He wasn't going to be baptized just to fall into fornication again immediately. Given Leslie wasn't likely to have decided to marry him and wasn't likely to accept a life of chastity outside of marriage either, there did not seem to be much hope for their relationship.

It would be a day of big life changes, Mark reflected. Some would be more pleasant than others, but they would all be for the best, Mark decided. He reached his apartment building and was relieved to see Christopher was not waiting for him. He had timed it well though, as no sooner did he get up to his apartment than Christopher was ringing from the entrance. Mark buzzed him in.

"Good to see you, Mark!" Chris greeted as Mark let him in. As Chris entered, he appeared slightly weather-beaten, with the brown skin of his cheeks slightly reddened from the wind. He began to remove his gloves and coat.

"Good to see you too! Things go okay at work this morning?" Mark asked.

"Oh ya, things went fine, just little fires here and there to put out." Chris answered.

Mark took Chris's garments and hung them up in the small closet near the entrance. Mark then gestured to the dining table where he'd had "Sarah" put out some snacks before returning to the kitchen to prepare their lunch.

"I was working over in the media division. They were having some trouble with the rendering software for one of the children's shows. I ran into Leslie while I was there, and she said hello." Chris smiled. "She also said I was taking up so much of your time with playing laser tag, she hardly ever saw you anymore. Apparently, if I don't make sure you call her a little more often, I may have to watch my back."

Mark laughed, trying to hide his real emotions. Chris no doubt sensed it and tried to shift the conversation. "So, obviously I didn't tell her what we were planning on doing this afternoon. Her complaints aside, I feel like your aim has been getting sloppy lately, so I don't think you've been spending nearly as much time practicing as she makes out. You keep missing those shots when people move out of cover, we'll have to put you onto our second-string roster..."

Mark took up the cue, though it had in fact been weeks since they'd really played any actual laser tag together. As far as the C-All knew though, they played laser tag together regularly and Mark was practicing daily. "Please, I miss one good shot, and suddenly my aim is sloppy. You go through the actual shot accuracy data, most days I'm the best on the team."

Chris shook his head. "That statistic is meaningless. It can't account for covering fire. Most of the time, the people with the highest accuracy ratings are some of the worst players, because they don't know how to use covering fire to support teammates." Mark shot him a look. They hadn't played laser tag together in a while, but even so. This was sounding a little too real.

"Are you implying I'm a bad teammate? I wasn't expect-

171

JACOB CLEARFIELD

ing to have you over just to get grilled here, man," Mark replied.

Chris put out his hands in a calming gesture. "Whoa, whoa. I wasn't trying to accuse you. I'm just saying there are plenty of players who are very good shots who don't end up with high accuracy ratings because they shoot a lot for covering fire. Not trying to say you don't, just saying you can't use the accuracy rating to say whether you're a better shot than other people."

Mark nodded. "Okay, that's fair. I'm still a better shot than you give me credit for, though." He grinned, refusing to concede entirely.

The robotic sounds of Sarah bringing lunch interrupted the conversation. Once she had placed their plates and drinks, Mark instructed her to return to her charging station. Over lunch Mark and Chris decided they would settle the accuracy matter this afternoon with some time on a virtual shooting range, though Mark couldn't tell whether this was something they would really have to do later or was just for show. He supposed the fact that he couldn't tell would at least mean the C-All wouldn't be able to tell either.

Finally, with lunch finished, they could pretend to enter a laser tag match and start what they had really planned for today. They positioned themselves in Mark's living room. Chris first grabbed a bottle of water, "in case he got thirsty during play." Bottle in hand, Chris looked toward Mark and said, "I'll go in first, and then send you the link." Mark nodded and waited. Chris's glasses darkened as the program began. A moment later, a link came up on Mark's C-All, which he accepted.

The interior of a soaring Cathedral replaced his living room. A brilliant sun shone through tremendous stained-glass windows, displaying images of Gospel stories and holy Saints in vivid color. It surprised Mark to find he and Chris were not alone. A small crowd had gathered, and they stood at the entrance of the cathedral in front of a fount of water. Mark recog-

ANNO DOMINI 2064

nized most of the faces from the times Chris had invited him to play VR games with some of his friends. A few others though he did not recognize, and they wore strange clothes. Four were men and two were women.

Chris also wore strange clothing, though Mark recognized the garments from his reading about the ceremonial vestments worn by clergy for Mass and the Sacraments. Chris wore a white garment with full length sleeves and a tunic that stretched to his feet without leggings. Over this he wore a sash over one shoulder. Two of the men he didn't recognize wore similar garments, while the other two wore the white garment but wore sashes that wrapped around the back of their neck and hung down over both shoulders. The women meanwhile wore black veils over their heads, with a white headdress underneath and around their necks. They wore garments similar to the ones the men wore covering their arms and bodies, but in black.

Christopher introduced the men as Fathers Thomas and Sebastian together with deacons Paul and Timothy and the women as sisters Mari and Ruth. They all greeted him as did the young men Mark recognized from games with Chris in the past.

Fr. Thomas appeared to be leading the group. He looked to be a little past middle age, though still healthy in appearance. His blond hair was graying, and he kept a clean-shaven face. Mark noted the deep, almost piercing blue of his eyes. He exuded a calm reverence, but as he greeted Mark, he gave a smile that hinted at an almost childlike joy. After the introductions, Fr. Thomas told Mark that he would lead the opening prayer and ceremonies. Then Deacon Christopher would perform the essential rites of the Baptism itself as he was physically present with Mark.

"I understand... Thank you for being here." Mark replied.

Fr. Thomas gave him a friendly smile in response, and then addressed the group. "Let us begin in the name of the Father, the Son, and the Holy Spirit." Mark joined the group as

JACOB CLEARFIELD

they made the sign of the cross over themselves with this invocation.

Fr. Thomas then began, "We gather today to welcome a soul into the One, Holy, Catholic, and Apostolic Church. In doing so, we are reminded of our own Baptismal vows, and in our charge to bring the healing light of the Gospel to all people." He turned to Mark. "What is your name?"

Mark was a little surprised, but after a second's hesitation he replied, "Mark."

Fr. Thomas nodded. "And what do you seek here today?"

Catching on that this was a part of the ritual, Mark replied, "Baptism."

"Our brother Mark seeks Baptism from the Church. Let us hear the words of our Lord and let their wisdom guide us this day." Fr. Thomas nodded toward Deacon Paul, who produced a book and read.

"A reading from the holy Gospel according to John

Jesus came to a town of Samaria called Sychar,

near the plot of land that Jacob had given to his son Joseph.

Jacob's well was there.

Jesus, tired from his journey, sat down there at the well.

It was about noon.

A woman of Samaria came to draw water.

Jesus said to her,

'Give me a drink.'

His disciples had gone into the town to buy food.

The Samaritan woman said to him,

ANNO DOMINI 2064

'How can you, a Jew, ask me, a Samaritan woman, for a drink?'

—For Jews use nothing in common with Samaritans.—

Jesus answered and said to her,

'If you knew the gift of God

and who is saying to you, "Give me a drink,"

you would have asked him

and he would have given you living water.'

The woman said to him,

'Sir, you do not even have a bucket and the cistern is deep;

where then can you get this living water?

Are you greater than our father Jacob,

who gave us this cistern and drank from it himself

with his children and his flocks?'

Jesus answered and said to her,

'Everyone who drinks this water will be thirsty again;

but whoever drinks the water I shall give will never thirst;

the water I shall give will become in him

a spring of water welling up to eternal life.'

The Gospel of the Lord."

The other participants responded, "Praise be to our Lord, Jesus Christ."

After this, Fr. Thomas turned again to Mark and stretched out his hands. Chris also approached and placed his hands over

JACOB CLEARFIELD

Mark's shoulders. Fr. Thomas then began to pray, "Almighty and ever-living God, you sent your only Son into the world to cast out the power of Satan, spirit of evil, to rescue man from the kingdom of darkness, and bring him into the splendor of your kingdom of light. We pray for Mark. Set him free from original sin, make him a temple of your glory, and send your Holy Spirit to dwell within him. We ask this through Christ our Lord. Amen."

Christopher then brought out the bottle of water, which he held before Fr. Thomas. Again, extending out his hands, Fr. Thomas began, "Let us pray. Holy Lord, almighty Father, ever-lasting God, we earnestly entreat you, the sanctifier of supernatural water, to look with favor on our lowly ministry, and to send your Holy Messenger down on this water, which we are making ready to cleanse and purify the human race. Holy Father, through Your Son may the power of the Holy Spirit be sent upon this water, so that those who will be baptized may be born of water and the Spirit, and once they have been cleansed of the sins of their former life, freed of their guilt, and given a new birth, may they remain a clean dwelling for your Holy Spirit; through Christ our Lord." The group then responded, "Amen."

Turning again to Mark, Fr. Thomas asked, "Mark, do you reject Satan?" Mark was a little taken aback by the bluntness of the question, but replied, "I do." Fr. Thomas proceeded, "And all his works?" Again, Mark said, "I do." The questions continued "and all his empty promises?", again Mark affirmed.

A slight pause and then, "Do you believe in God, the Father Almighty, Creator of heaven and earth?" Mark was ready now. "I do." Feeling more confident in his part of the ritual, Mark could focus a little more on the questions, each time answering, "I do."

"Do you believe in Jesus Christ, his only Son, our Lord, who was born of the Virgin Mary, was crucified, died, and was buried, rose from the dead, and is now seated at the right hand of the Father? Do you believe in the Holy Spirit, the Holy Catholic Church, the communion of saints, the forgiveness of sins, the resurrection of the body, and life everlasting?" After Mark had answered the last question with "I do", Father Thomas ended saying, "God, the all-powerful Father of our Lord Jesus Christ has given us a new birth by water and the Holy Spirit and forgiven all our sins. May he also keep us faithful to our Lord Jesus Christ for ever and ever." Mark and the assembled responded, "Amen."

Fr. Thomas then nodded to Christopher who came forward. He laid his left hand on Mark's shoulder, which Mark suspected was as much to make sure they were matched up in the real world as closely as they appeared in this virtual setting. Christopher then began, "Mark, I baptize you in the name of the Father." At this he allowed some water to drip from the bottle onto Mark's head. He then tipped the bottle back up, "and of the Son" again water was poured briefly, "and of the Holy Spirit." Water was then poured a final time.

Christopher then seemed to reach down into his pocket. He came back up with his thumb, and Mark could smell a faint sweet odor. "Mark, with this sacred chrism I anoint you that you may be marked forever as a member of God's people and of Christ who is Prophet, Priest, and King."

They then brought a white garment forward. Chris explained that while they could not give him a white garment physically, he could wear this here as a symbol that he had put on Christ and was to be clothed in his love. "May you keep this garment unstained with sin." Chris intoned.

The group then processed up to the altar. Mark hadn't really been prepared for how the ritual would go. He realized that with the blessing of the water, he was now baptized. It fit that now he'd be welcome to come forward with the group toward the altar. The group paused before the altar and bowed. Mark was sure to do likewise. Fr. Thomas then took a small candle and went up to a large candle that was burning beside the altar. He lit the candle, came back down, and gave it to Mark. "This candle represents the light of Christ that you have received. Let it also be a reminder to all of us that as Christians we are ever called to be a light to the world." Everyone responded, "Amen." Mark was a little belated but managed to keep up.

The group bowed again before the altar and returned to the back of the church. This time, they did not stop at the fountain but continued processing all the way out into a courtyard beyond the church's doors. Once out, everyone seemed to take on a more informal air. Person after person came up to Mark to wish him congratulations. He thanked them in turn, trying to remember names or learn them as much as possible as they came up to him. A couple of the men noted they lived in Milwaukee and offered to try to get together socially at some point, using VR gaming as an excuse for how they would know each other. One also mentioned that now that he was officially baptized, he could join a VR board game group he managed that met every Sunday after Mass.

The offers were friendly, but it was a little jarring for Mark to go so quickly from the serious and reverent ritual they'd been part of to such light, social conversation. When Christopher came up, Mark quietly mentioned the feeling.

Chris smiled. "Wherever the Catholic sun doth shine, there you will find music and laughter and good red wine." Mark looked at him quizzically. Chris laughed. "It's generally our way. We are serious and reverent before God within the church. But we know God calls us to be lights to the world and that includes joy and merrymaking as well. So outside of the church, it's good to be friendly and convivial whenever possible. Especially in this day and age, where so much of the time we must keep our joy hidden just to stay alive."

For the next half an hour, the group continued to talk. One by one, people had to go due to their own schedules. Finally, when only about half the original group was remaining,

ANNO DOMINI 2064

it was decided they should call it a day. Fr. Thomas approached Mark before leaving.

"Mark, in better times when an adult was baptized into the Church, they would receive the Eucharist and Confirmation on the same day. I'm sorry we could not arrange that for you today. I will work with Chris to arrange it as soon as possible. The bishop prefers to do confirmations himself, but because of the difficulty in arranging it safely, it can take a while to do. Eucharist is easier to arrange, though still dangerous. We will probably be able to have that for you sooner. In the meantime, you can still commune spiritually with our Lord at Mass. I'll expect to see you there tomorrow, in fact." At this he smiled.

"Yes, of course." Mark replied.

Fr. Thomas grinned. "Good man. I'll see you tomorrow then." At this, he logged off.

The rest of the group also gave their farewells, and everyone logged out. Mark and Christopher were back in Mark's apartment.

Mark wasn't sure what to say. He was still taking in everything that had happened. Chris, however, quickly spoke up after the log off completed. "Well, that was quite the victory!" he said.

Mark's first thought was Chris meant the Baptism and worried he'd somehow slipped having exited the VR simulation. His second thought was, of course Chris meant the baptism. But the C-All had no way to know that and would assume he was referring to a VR game they'd played. Mark grinned in relief and joined the deception. "Still worried whether I can hit the mark?"

This seemed to sober Chris for a moment, and in a very serious voice he replied, "We should always be worried about that. Today we had a victory, and it was a great one, but there's always another fight ahead. It will not be easy; our opponents are very good at what they do. Stay sharp."

Christopher caught Mark off guard for a moment. There was a double meaning to what Chris was saying, though the words would still fool the C-All. He'd have to think about it more later. Meanwhile, Chris began to excuse himself as he had some further plans that day. Mark wondered whether he'd be seeing other Christians who needed him. The two exchanged farewells and Chris left.

Mark spent the rest of the afternoon careful to do things he would normally do on a day off. He watched some Party programs on his C-All, exercised for half an hour, and read a little more of the news. When the time came to leave for dinner, the summoned car was on time. After Mark got himself seated and belted and the car pulled into traffic, he began to sense butterflies in his stomach. It had been a whirlwind of a day. He still felt an incredible sense of cleansing and relief. He knew though, that what lay ahead would be a first test following his baptism.

He thought about the temptations he would face. The simplest temptation, or at least the most obvious, was that Leslie was a very attractive woman who likely would push him to have sex with her tonight. While he had been doing well in the last few months avoiding pornography and masturbation, and avoiding sex with Leslie as well, she also hadn't been pushing for it. He realized now this would put an extra level of temptation on him tonight.

Beyond that, Mark loved Leslie and didn't want to lose her. He didn't see a way to deny continuing to have sex with her without also losing the relationship. He would be lonelier without her. Even as he hoped to find new relationships now within the Church, he still knew there would be a real loneliness to come from a break-up. Also, she would feel hurt by what would seem to be a rejection to her. The thought of hurting her was in some ways the hardest thing to bear about the whole situation.

The buildings of the Third Ward continued to flit by as

Mark sat in silence and reflected. He could turn on some music but felt a need for silence. Suddenly, he realized he didn't need to be alone in this anymore. He offered a short mental prayer. "God, give me the strength to get through this. Fill me with your Grace so I can do your will. Help me find the words to hurt Leslie as little as I can while still avoiding sin."

He felt a little better. The thought came to him that, so long as he was doing what was right, he could feel good about himself in the end. He considered what would happen if he gave in to the temptations he was facing. He would feel dirty and weak. He knew he could still find forgiveness. But having fallen to the temptation once, it would be that much harder the next time he faced the same temptation. He needed to face and conquer the temptation now. He knew he would not be perfect now just because he'd been baptized, but he felt with a sense of tremendous certainty that if he failed now, when he was so strengthened coming right off his baptism, he would probably lose his soul for good.

The thought galvanized him. He even thought for a moment it wouldn't be that hard to do the right thing. The car pulled up to the restaurant precisely on time at 6:30 PM. As he stepped out onto the sidewalk in front of the restaurant, he saw Leslie in the next car pulling up to the curb.

As she stepped out, he almost lost his breath. They had chosen an upscale restaurant on the northeast side of the city. Mark had dressed well for the occasion. It was the kind of fine dining establishment almost exclusively frequented by Party members, and generally the more well-to-do ones at that. However, Leslie had clearly taken the outing as an excuse to dress to the nines. Her hair was perfectly coiffed in the sharp, modern style she preferred. Mark suspected she'd found time to go to her hairdresser today. Meanwhile, her make-up brought out the already fine feminine features of her face and added a vibrancy that absolutely radiated sex appeal.

On top of the stunning beauty of her face, she wore a tasteful but still slightly risqué evening gown with one leg cut just above the knee and a neckline just low enough to show a hint of cleavage. The hint was all it took to remind Mark of those temptations he'd indulged in in the past that now enticed him from just behind the fabric. As Leslie walked toward him, the dress held tightly to her frame, covering everything vital but doing nothing to hide her overall firm and trim figure.

Mark's reaction must have shown on his face because Leslie hit him with a knowing smile. She was gorgeous, and she knew it. Clearly, she was expecting a romantic evening and was enjoying herself. A small voice in Mark seemed to say, "You're giving THIS up? A few philosophical words, some books, and a sprinkling of water, and now you're ready to throw THIS away?" There seemed to be something very immediate about her proximity. As she came up, she extended her arms for a hug. The warmth and press from her body were almost intoxicating. A part of him asked whether anything of the spirit could really compete.

Thankfully, just thinking of the spiritual brought him back to that feeling of peace and cleansing he'd felt with his baptism. The answer was yes; an emphatic yes, that the spiritual could offer far more than the physical ever could. This thought grounded him. As they released each other from the hug, Mark had found his balance again. He smiled back at her.

"I love you, Leslie. I love you so much it hurts." It took Leslie a little off guard, but after a moment's thought she replied with an amused tone, "Save it for later tonight, honey. If you think you're hurting now, wait until tomorrow morning to see how sore you are." Mark almost laughed. He would be feeling some pain the next day, but not for the reason she thought. He motioned towards the restaurant and they went in together.

13.

Halfway through the meal, Mark felt utterly adrift. Leslie was vivacious and full of energy. Mark was grateful she was carrying the conversation, but he had a sense that the night was heading out of control in the wrong direction. Leslie talked excitedly about how things were finally under better control at work and everyone had more time again. People were in a good mood at work because it seemed like the borders in Europe were solidifying and maybe peace talks could begin soon. Her office's entire media plan had initially been spun out of control by the need for programs for the war. Now they had caught up. When peace arrived, some of their previous programming could be used as well. This would mean they would be ahead of schedule for a while. Her boss had hinted if peace arrived, in celebration the Party would give her entire department extra days off.

The idea of extra time off had given her the idea of a real vacation. She imagined time in Hawaii or the Bahamas. Several times now she had given vague hints about how romantic such places would be and how much "fun" they might have there. The hints had made Mark feel uneasy, especially as Leslie had been looking at him with hungry, eager eyes throughout the dinner.

Once, such looks and such energy from Leslie would have had Mark practically counting the seconds until he could call for the check and lead Leslie back to his place. Now though, it made him feel vaguely queasy. Leslie wanted to have him and his body, but with no commitment attached. Mark felt like she was seeing him as a cheap and disposable object. It occurred to him that though he'd barely spoken the entire night, and in fact his discomfort throughout the meal was probably not all that well hidden, this hadn't slowed Leslie down at all.

The realization annoyed Mark, and it gave him the desire to begin what he'd set out to do tonight. There really was no sense letting Leslie go on like this anyway given what he knew was coming. Mark waited for a pause in Leslie's speech and then began, "You know, I like the idea of a vacation, but I don't think I'll have time to go. I think once the war ends, I will enroll in robotics repair classes."

Leslie's face immediately fell. "You can't still be serious about that." She shook her head with a rueful grin, as if hearing someone tell a bad joke. "Why would you want to just spend all day fixing up a bunch of broken machines? You have real talent, Mark. Everyone sees it. You know how to organize and lead people. That's not something just anyone can do. It would be a shame to throw it away." Her words carried genuine admiration, and Mark could tell she thought she was trying to help him.

Mark collected his thoughts for a moment before replying. "I hear what you are saying, and I don't disagree. It seems like a shame to stop doing something you happen to be good at. The question I've been struggling with lately, though, has been, even if I'm good at something, is that enough to mean it's what I *should* do?"

Leslie looked at him with quizzical eyes. She bent forward and looked like she would argue the point. Before she could object, Mark hastened to go on. "It's not just purely about the work itself. It's a question of what I want to do with my life. I've been thinking about that a lot lately, and I've realized that I want a family. Obviously, that's not something I can really have with this career."

Mark paused and watched Leslie react. A silence descended on the table even as the normal buzz of conversation and light classical music continued to surround them in the restaurant. Leslie held still for a moment, then with a small, "Oh,"

ANNO DOMINI 2064

she shifted back into her chair.

After a long pause, Leslie began, "Mark, you still have your parents. You grew up with them. I'm sure that must have been nice. Maybe that's why this is something you want. Understand though, that's not where I'm coming from at all."

Mark nodded. "I really can't imagine what it was like losing your parents growing up. I can see why that would make it hard to really know what it might be like to have a family."

Leslie shook her head. "You really do not understand." She lowered her voice. "My parents were traitors! My family has been nothing but a cloud of shame over my head since I was a little girl. How could I want to start a family of my own after that?" She paused and took a sip of water. "Beyond that, I enjoy being a Party member. The Party forgave me and gave me a chance, even after what my parents did. I owe them. Working for them is the least I can do. In return, they continue to treat me well. I mean, look around you. Good food, nice clothes, a steady job with good pay after getting an excellent education. You expect me to walk away?"

Shaking his head sadly, Mark smiled. "Not really, no. It would be great to start a family with you, but I didn't really think it was something you'd want. I felt I owed it to you, though, to try."

At this, Leslie's face hardened. "So what, you came here figuring we'd break up? You let me talk on and on about taking vacations together and the whole time, you were planning to break up with me?" She pushed her chair back. "Honestly, and to think I was planning to have sex with you tonight. I guess I should be glad you weren't enough of a pig to screw me and then break up with me."

Mark tried to remain calm and bear her anger. "I would never do that to you. I really do care about you. We just want different things."

185

JACOB CLEARFIELD

"Ugh, it would probably be better if you had just screwed me one more time and then broke up to go off with another woman. At least that I'd understand. It wouldn't be the first time. I could just call you a pig and forget about you." Leslie sat back down. Suddenly, she broke into sobs.

"Leslie, I'm sorry. I didn't want to hurt you tonight. It's just that I've realized this is what I want, and if I stay with you when we won't be making a future together, then I'd just be using you." He reached out a hand to put on her shoulder.

Leslie batted the hand away. "Damn it, don't you realize how much worse you're making it? You're not leaving me because you're a pig. You're leaving me because you want a future with me, and because I don't want to go along with it, now you have to break up with me. So here I am getting dumped, and it gets to be MY fault, because I didn't want a future with you. Oh, and if you stay with me, then you're just using me, so your hands are tied. Isn't that convenient for you!"

Mark wasn't sure if he had ever seen Leslie this angry or this sad. He realized people around the restaurant were casting glances toward their table, then quickly looking away. More than a few held a smirk or a grin. One man even seemed to shoot him a wink, though Mark couldn't be sure if he imagined it.

Leslie took a deep breath. "Fine. Fine. You don't want to use me. Well, guess what? That's all this ever was to me. I was using you and you were using me. You know why? Because that's how life works. You think people just do things for each other to be nice? Hell no. Life is a series of transactions. If you make good transactions, you come out ahead. You, sir are making a terrible transaction right now. You are throwing away your career, throwing away your hot girlfriend, and throwing away any chance at getting further ahead in life. What are you getting in return for it? Some stupid dream of fixing robots and finding a girl to settle down with and plop out babies for you? Great, go do that for five years. Then when you are bored with your ugly

186

wife and your ugly kids and your worthless little job, remember tonight and everything you threw away." Leslie stood up.

Mark could tell Leslie was finished. She'd hit on her exit speech and intended to leave having delivered it. There was no sense in chasing her. As she turned and began to leave, Mark felt the need to at least say goodbye. He felt sorry for Leslie. She was lost in such a sad world. "Goodbye, Leslie. I hope you find happiness," he said.

Leslie turned, her face a mask of fury. Lost for words, she let out a cry of frustration and then turned again and marched away. Once she'd left, the waiter courteously asked if he'd like the check. Mark nodded and then waited quietly at the table. He breathed a sigh of relief. It was done.

The rest of the night passed by in blissful quiet. As he rode home, it began to rain. Mark appreciated the gentle sound of the rain pattering against the windshield. There was an option to use wipers to better see out the windows, but Mark was happy to focus on the drops as they collected, appreciating the beauty in the little dots as they formed up, connected, and then eventually began to run in rivulets as the car pressed forward toward his apartment.

The next day he put in his request for transfer into robotics repair training pending the end of the war. He knew Leslie would talk about their breakup, and she would have no reason to hide the reasons he'd given her. It surprised Veronica. Much like Leslie, she tried to talk him out of it. Ultimately, when she could see he'd made his mind up about it, she consented to the idea. She noted she would expect him to continue to work his hardest in his current position until the war ended. Mark assured her that this was his intention.

In the weeks that followed, thankfully the war continued to go well. The Golden Republic adopted a new strategy in France. While there was no desire to take and hold territory outside of the Breton region, the army began to aggressively strike at any forces that attempted to gather near the border of Breton. Once they had dispersed the French Caliphate forces, they followed this by launching raids deeper into French territory. This forced the French to pull forces back from the Eastern front to face the GR forces. More than that, the GR forces were successful in inflicting heavy casualties on the French.

At the same time as pressing the attack on the Western front, the GR had increased its material support for the Eastern League and Russia. Eastern theatre victories multiplied. The final blow came at sea, with a huge GR victory off the coast of Gibraltar that gave the GR the ability to attack at will up and down the coasts of the Mediterranean.

By June, a ceasefire was announced, and a general peace conference was being planned. Mark was ecstatic. He was scheduled to train at the Milwaukee School of Engineering in July. Meanwhile, his new life in the Church had been flourishing. Every day he found time to pray and study in the library. Sometimes he could attend Masses during the work week, and weekly he had always found a time for Mass on either Saturday or Sunday. He continued to see Christopher and had also been able to spend more time in VR with new people he had met after Mass or through Chris.

Once, he'd even received communion. Chris had, through tremendous effort, set up a physical safe zone that would fool local C-All's. Mark and several other area Catholics were able to meet and celebrate Mass with a priest physically present. They had to use the basement of an old warehouse, and the only light was from candles they had brought with them, but it was still one of the most beautiful experiences of Mark's life.

One of the other lay Catholics that had been there was a young woman named Rosa who Mark had seen a few times after virtual Masses. Chris introduced them, and they had found an excuse for a way he could "meet" her in the world of the Golden Republic. She worked at a small grocery that sold artisanal cheese. Mark "developed" an intense interest in cheeses, and so just happened to meet her at her work and got into a conversation with her about local cheese blends. He'd been back a few more times. Once he was out of his position at the Party headquarters and downgraded from a full Party member, they planned to court.

The last day of June, Mark was to have his last day at work. A small party was planned. While some of his coworkers had been stand-offish when they learned what Mark planned, a surprising number had been understanding. More than a few had expressed to him in some form or another how they could sympathize with the desire for something simpler. Many people felt burned out. A few had even mentioned they were also thinking of finding something new. Leslie, meanwhile, had studiously avoided him since the break-up.

As he got into the auto-car to take him to work, he wondered if Leslie would come to the party. It would be awkward, but he hoped they could leave things on a better note than when she'd stormed out of the restaurant. He could still see her face, beautiful and furious, as she turned and stormed out. At first when he'd thought of her he had felt a sense of loss. Increasingly since then, he simply felt pity. Her last words to him, about seeing life as transactional, had stuck with him. He realized he'd used to think about life the same way.

He was so grateful he'd escaped that world. In finding Christianity, he'd found a world of incredible joy. Christians loved each other and even loved the non-Christians who persecuted them. Also, they loved as much as they could because they were trying to follow the example of Christ, who had loved mankind so much that he became man and died for the sins of humanity. As a result, life wasn't transactional at all. Life was a gift from a God who loved creation into being and then sacrificed Himself for his beloved creations. In turn, they were called to love each other. The gift of that love gave further joy to life.

He would soon have to give up his comfortable apartment. He wouldn't be able to have a "Sarah" personal assistant robot, so he'd have to cook his own meals and attend to things like cleaning and laundry. Overall, his physical comfort was likely to go down and his chances for personal advancement and wealth had been all but eliminated. He already knew it was worth it.

He wondered, sometimes, if there had been anything he could have said to Leslie that might have led her to seeing things this way. He felt bad for her, trapped in the dark world he'd once been locked into. He supposed though that there was nothing he could have done. He'd thought about it several times since they'd broken up. Nothing he could think of seemed likely to have made a difference.

Looking out the window, Mark realized the auto-car was taking a different route than usual. Sometimes the auto-cars changed routes if there was heavy traffic or construction taking place. In rare instances accidents between auto-cars occurred which could lead to traffic re-routes. Still, it was a little strange.

Mark began to watch more carefully. His alarm spiked when he saw the car not turning at Wells Street but continuing north. This meant the car was now actively taking him further from the City Hall, which would be very unusual. "Auto-car, why are we taking this route?" Mark asked.

The slightly mechanical female voice of the car replied, "An error has occurred. This car is being re-routed. Please stand-by." Mark began to feel his heart race. "Auto-car, please pull over and stop. I will walk the rest of the way." The car continued driving. The mechanical female voice replied, "This car is being re-routed. Please remain seated."

Mark tried the doors, thinking the car was going slow enough he could still make a jump for it. He was not surprised, though, to find the doors were locked. The windows, too, would not go down. He was trapped. Oddly, one of the first thoughts to go through his mind was "what would the people at work think when he missed his party?" There was also a small part of him that felt annoyed people would initially think he was late for work when it was not his fault at all that he couldn't be there.

He almost tried to hold on to these thoughts as the auto-car turned onto State street and continued toward the target he suspected: the Milwaukee County jail. The Golden Republic had renovated and expanded the original building. The facade was now an imposing mix of concrete and steel. The Party had detailed it with soaring bronze and gold leaf friezes, statues, and imagery glorifying the Golden Republic and its founders.

The auto-car turned off into a descending driveway that led into a basement garage. As the garage door opened, Mark could see only a dark void. Mark reflected on how this design feature so easily inspired terror and hopelessness. There was something primordially terrifying about descending into a dark place. While he was sure the designers didn't think of it, there seemed an obvious connection with a descent into hell.

The auto-car did not need to see to drive, and so it descended swiftly into the abyss. As it entered, the garage door closed behind them. At first, it appeared to Mark as if he were in total darkness. As the car continued, however, Mark noticed occasional faint lights. As his eyes adjusted, he could see these were small square windows placed in heavy steel doors from which light on the other side came through. They were entrances to the garage. As the car wound its way through, there were only a few of them and so the car went from pitch black to dim light, to pitch black again as it continued to wind deeper down.

At last the car came to a stop in front of one of these doors. As it stopped, the door opened, and two large men came out. One held a gun at the ready. The other was brandishing a set of handcuffs. The auto-car door swung open. "Come out with your hands up," the man with the gun ordered.

Mark complied, and the other man swiftly came forward and pulled his hands down behind him, smoothly putting the handcuffs into place. They roughly led him through the steel door into a featureless antechamber. The door closed behind him and he heard the auto-car speed off. The guards then led Mark into another room where a third guard awaited with gloved hands. Mark's clothing and C-All was removed, and they thoroughly searched him. He was given a plane orange jumper. As he dressed, Mark noted somewhat absently that there were no pockets. He thought to himself how pockets are only useful if you own something to put in them. Mark wondered whether he'd ever own anything again.

Once dressed, the guards led Mark down a hallway that abutted the body searching room. This hallway was as featureless as the other rooms he'd seen so far. Deep underground, the only light came from plain white LED bulbs behind steel cages spaced along the ceiling of the hall. They turned a corner, and here Mark began to see adjacent hallways on either side. As they walked past the first set, Mark could see these were very short, maybe ten feet, and ended with a featureless door. The hallway intersections were spaced maybe five feet apart and there appeared to be at least five sets before the hall appeared to again turn to the right up ahead. At the third intersection, the guards halted. They turned left and pushed Mark in front. They then directed him to the door at the end of the small hall. Here one guard activated something on his C-All, and the door opened.

Mark could see a small room only about eight feet deep and three feet wide. At the far end of it was a toilet. The walls and toilet appeared to be coated in rubber. Curved plastic bowls in each upper corner, strategically place up out of reach of even the tallest man, assuredly protected security cameras behind them.

Mark's handcuffs were released, and they pushed him into the room. The door closed behind him. Immediately, the room went dark. The only illumination of the space had come from the hallway, and with the door closed no light came through. Mark felt his way along the wall until he came to the toilet at the other end. It was the only piece of furniture in the room, and so Mark sat down on it.

He took a moment to gather his thoughts. He was imprisoned, locked in a lightless cell somewhere several levels underground and with hardly any room. He could only guess that somehow, they'd found out about his conversion to Christianity. He could only hope he was the only one who had been caught. Christopher would be in great danger. Hopefully, they had not found him out yet. Mark's own disappearance at work would serve as a warning to him. Mark could only hope.

There was little Mark could do besides pray, and so he resolved to do just that. He noted his prison suit had a small elastic cord at the waste for fitting. The cord was thin and pliable, Mark was sure no one could ever hang himself with it (not that he wanted to, but from the rubber padding in the cell he'd guessed this was a concern of his captors). He could use the cord to tie small knots. In this way, he could easily use his fingers to keep track to ten while using knots to track the decades. Using this method, Mark began to pray a rosary.

As he prayed, Mark struggled to focus on the prayers and not think of what was likely ahead for him. He couldn't help but wonder whether he was to be left in this cell to die of hunger or thirst. It was possible, he supposed, though it seemed needlessly cruel even for the Golden Republic. A single bullet would suffice if they wanted him dead and would obviate the need for such little cells. Having said the first few prayers and entering the first decade, Mark decided the sorrowful mysteries would be most appropriate.

Thinking of Jesus in the garden of Gethsemane, Mark reflected on Christ's total willingness to sacrifice Himself when faced with His impending death. He thought about how Jesus had had the option to escape, or even more, to use His power directly to humble those who planned to kill Him. Mark thought of how tempting it would be, if he had such power, to simply blow the door of the cell off its hinges and walk out, subduing any guard who tried to stop him. He wondered, if he knew God were asking him to be here but he had the power like that to escape, if he could really stand to simply sit and wait for the end.

He continued to pray and meditate on the sorrowful mysteries. Thinking of Christ's sacrifice helped calm him. When he finished the rosary, he continued to think about his situation. It was likely the Party still wanted something from him, or they'd have killed him immediately. Whether they had some use for his life still, or intended to put him through a trial to satisfy their own consciences was hard to guess.

It appeared obvious to Mark that they had arrested him for his Christianity. Aside from this, he had done nothing illegal or betrayed the Party in any way that he could think of. Trying to take a demotion and give up his career he was sure had looked suspicious and may even have led to him being caught. But there was nothing about it specifically that would warrant arrest. Then again, maybe it was? The fact that they'd taken him on the last day of his work was certain to have a chilling effect on any of his coworkers who had also been thinking of changing careers.

However, this scenario seemed less likely to Mark. If the Party had been so opposed to him leaving his position, he'd have received more resistance when he'd first requested the transfer into robotics. Besides, there were always plenty of people looking to climb the ranks of the Party; one Party member bowing out would hardly make a difference.

Mark continued to wait. The time stretched. To fill it, he alternated between prayer and simple meditation. With no light, it was all but impossible to keep track of time. He had relieved himself twice and guessed by this that perhaps four or five hours had passed. He had been thankful to find that at least the toilet worked. He began to grow thirsty. He worried that perhaps the guards intended the toilet water to serve for his drink. He would wait as long as he could before so debasing himself. He had heard you could only live two days without water. Perhaps if he pushed himself then, he could go a day before he would get very sick from not drinking. He realized, though, that eventually he would have little choice. To purposefully refuse to drink would be a sort of suicide, and he could not countenance that. If Christ had humbled Himself to die on a cross, then Mark realized he could at least humble himself to drink from a toilet.

As he continued to wait, his many discomforts struggled with each other to take up most of his attention. With the walls side to side barely being wide enough to turn around in, and the length of the room barely long enough to lie down without hitting the toilet or the door, finding a comfortable position became more and more difficult. The floor was tiled with hard rubber, just like the walls. It felt cold and was unyielding enough that staying in one position for too long soon became painful or caused his limbs to go numb. He eventually found the most comfortable position was simply laying flat on his back.

Meanwhile, his mouth became drier and his lips parched. He was becoming hungry. Each of these discomforts clawed at his attention. Worse however, was the thought he wasn't sure what would be worse: if they left him in here to die of thirst or hunger, or if they provided food and water but otherwise just left him here. He tried to imagine what it would mean to live out his life in this lightless room, all alone. He'd heard men could go mad by being left alone for too long. He could see why. All alone with his thoughts and left blind by the dark, he could see where the sense of powerlessness and loneliness could overwhelm a person.

He took comfort from the knowledge that he was neither truly alone nor truly powerless. He decided that if his captors kept him alive here, then there was no other worthwhile option than to give his life over to one of prayer. He'd read about monks who took a vow of silence and spent their entire life in prayer. Apparently, many of them had seemed to exude peace and contentment. Mark hoped he could find that here.

He spent the next few hours focusing on meditative prayer. As he prayed, he found his anxiety abated, and even his thirst did not bother him as much. He was feeling tired and felt himself drifting towards sleep. He considered whether he should at this point drink from the toilet before sleeping. He felt a little faint besides being tired and suspected it was from dehydration. It had been quite a while since that second time in the cell he'd urinated, and he had felt no further urge from his bladder since.

Mark started to pull himself up from the floor. He found it much more difficult than he'd expected, and as he stood, he immediately felt dizzy. He bent back down onto his knees and slowly crawled to the toilet. He reached his cupped hands in, and as he felt the cold liquid within touch his hands, an abrupt metallic sliding sound from the door could be heard as it unlocked. Mark was glad he was facing the toilet, as the sudden glare of light entering as the door cracked open was almost blinding, and when fully opened, Mark had to shut his eyes tightly even facing away from the light.

"Well, well, thirsty, eh?" A man stepped into the cell. "Why didn't you say something? It's an odd guest that drinks from the toilet rather than asking the host for water." Mark carefully opened an eye, though he still found himself blinking and squinting even to get a glimpse of the man. He did not appear to be a guard. He was dressed in a suit that appeared tailored exactly to his frame and was in the most modern style. He wore an angular and thinly cut beard together with slick jet-black hair that seemed to form multiple points all angling forward toward a single point above his forehead.

ANNO DOMINI 2064

"Really now, it's hardly becoming of a Party member to be drinking from a toilet. Here, take my hand. If you want some water, just say so." He extended his hand outwards. Mark was caught off guard by the odd friendliness the man seemed to treat him with. He was sure it wasn't genuine, and he was sure the man knew he wouldn't see it to be, so Mark couldn't tell what the point of it was. Just to further disorient him?

Not seeing any better option, Mark took the man's hand. The man helped him up and then steadied him. He began to lead Mark out of the cell. "Very good, now, tell me if you are thirsty," the man said.

Not seeing any reason not to go along with the little routine, Mark answered, "Yes, I'm thirsty."

The man nodded in agreement. "After 21 hours, I should think so. You'll have to forgive us for the rather poor accommodations here. We don't get such distinguished guests as yourself very often. We mostly deal with thieves, rapists, and murderers. Until recently, we had a good many draft dodgers as well. Indeed, quite a few were sent here by you. Your name has come across my desk many times. Imagine my surprise when your name came up and it was as a prisoner!"

The man took Mark around a corner and into a small office. He motioned Mark to a chair in front of a desk and then took the larger chair on the other side. On the desk was a glass filled with water. Mark's eyes immediately went to it, and the man nodded in response. Mark took the water. For a split second, he wondered if it might be drugged or poisoned. He then realized if they wished to do either of these things to him there was really nothing he could do about it anyway. He drank the cup greedily. The water was cold and tasted pure. He doubted he'd ever tasted anything so good before in his life.

The man motioned again to the chair and so Mark sat. The man peered at him intensely for a few seconds, as if trying to get a better read on Mark. Finally, he looked down to the side next

197

to his chair and pulled open a drawer from the desk. He pulled out a piece of paper and a pen and laid them out in front of Mark.

"Well, I've been instructed to inform you that due to your years of faithful service to the Party, the justice administration has decided to be lenient. Write out on this paper your confession, including all persons you encountered who likewise committed treason, and the Party will release you under 10 years of close probation. You will be allowed to learn robotics repair as you desired and then will work in this field. You will be sent to the Rockford Institute of Robotics in Illinois and once finished with your training, you will then be reassigned as needed for your expertise. Congratulations. Considering the charges, this is quite generous." The man again looked at him appraisingly.

Mark stared at the piece of paper. The tactics now made sense. They had given him a little taste of what they could do to him and now offered freedom from it in return for names. He almost wanted to laugh. He supposed he could really, as it would hardly make a difference what he said at this point. Still, he was curious enough he decided he would rather play this drama a little further before finding out what the Party would next have in store for him.

He started to respond, but found his voice still parched. The man pulled out a bottle of water and poured him another glass. Mark again drank the cup and then asked, "What is it I'm supposed to be confessing to?"

The man shook his head. "Now, now. You know what you did. You don't think we don't know?" He leaned in, a diabolical smile across his face, "Do you really think once you started acting strangely with your idea of starting a new career that we wouldn't double check what might be happening? We double bugged your house and set live watchers to examine you while you were at home. It was obvious right away when you were supposedly playing 'laser tag' but not moving to match it."

He shook his head ruefully, "It took a while for our IT

ANNO DOMINI 2064

people to find the little software modification in your C-All. Whoever put it in there was slick. It kept changing itself and hiding again and again. If we didn't know to look for it, we'd have never found it. Even once we found it, we still had a devil of a time containing it long enough to erase it." He shook his head. "Whoever your friends are, if they have that kind of technical skill with our software, they are too dangerous to be allowed to remain free."

Mark grinned. "I was told people in the Inner Party use such software all the time. I was just being given access to it a little early." For a moment, Mark wondered whether he might throw the Party off the trail a bit. Perhaps he could even get the party to investigate Inner Party members.

"That may be. Maybe your friends just stole the software. Maybe your friends have friends of their own in the Inner Party making this stuff. Or maybe you're just full of crap or the people who gave you the software were. It doesn't really matter. Once we were watching you live, we spotted some funny movements you made. We had to bring in one of our dissident experts to figure out what you were doing. It quite surprised her when she saw the footage. She said you were 'crossing' yourself. Apparently, she hadn't seen it in years. She'd never seen it from a Party member. You're quite the novelty, I guess."

Mark nodded. "So, I'm being tried for possessing illegal software?"

The man snorted. He could tell Mark was not going along with the confession, and his face began to show his irritation.

"The illegal software would be enough to charge you. But it's what you were doing with that software that is the real treason. The dissident expert said you were, 'praying.' She said it was something like what the Muslims do, but not quite the same. Some old superstition from before the founding of the Republic. It means, though, that you are putting some invisible god above the Party. To give your loyalty to any entity above

199

the Party is treason!" The man said this last line with enthusiasm. He seemed pleased, as if he felt he'd made a point beyond reproach and was proud of his own cleverness in doing so.

Mark thought for a moment and then replied, "If the Party worshipped the God I served, it would help the Party and the Golden Republic. It would be the best thing possible for every member of the Party and every member of the nation. So, in worshipping God, I was in no way a traitor to the Party."

The man's face turned to one of revulsion. "You confess your crimes even as you deny their wrongness? That only makes things worse. The dissident expert said the worship you engaged in was common among the enemies of the Party at the time of the founding. The suppression of your superstition was one of the necessary steps in the Republic's founding."

Mark shook his head. "My God is all loving. He desires the best for all people. There is no crime in worshipping Him. To spurn His love is the worst thing the Party can do for itself. Before I knew Him, my life was miserable and meaningless. I shudder to think how many people in the world are like how I was."

The man pushed the paper toward him. "Write your confession, stop your fruitless 'worship', and name those like you whom you know. Do this, and you go free. Don't, and you will face the full justice of the Party."

Mark sighed. Choosing his words carefully, he answered, "I will happily confess my love for my Lord and Redeemer, His Father, my Creator, and the Holy Spirit, my Sanctifier. Meanwhile, if the Party punishes me for worshipping the ultimate Good, then it calls true Justice down upon itself. If not in this world, then in the next. My duty compels me to offer God what is His just due, for that is true justice. Therefore, I cannot stop worshipping Him. Finally, if it is the Party's intent to punish others for offering God the worship he is due, then I cannot in good conscience reveal them to the Party."

With that he took the pen and wrote his confession of

worshipping God and having become a Christian. He added nothing beyond this and instead signed his name after the confession. The man meanwhile watched him with cold fury in his eyes. Without a word, he took the confession and then stood Mark up and led him back to his cell.

When they reached the cell, a guard was waiting who took hold of Mark roughly and shoved him inward. Before the door closed, the man said, "Tomorrow, the judge will see you. You have until then to change your mind. Knock on the door if you decide to be reasonable."

14.

Bereft of a way to tell time, Mark alternated between prayer and sleep. Mainly, he prayed for the strength to stay true to his faith and not to give in to the temptations laid before him. Hunger gnawed at his stomach, and it was not long before his throat was once more parched. Images of beatings, electrocutions, and many other torments intruded on his prayers. Alone in the darkness, it was easy also to picture being left to starve. He prayed fervently that whatever was to come, his will could endure to the end.

A small part of Mark considered the temptation set before him. He reminded himself fervently though of what it would mean to deny Christ. He would be re-entering his life of emptiness. He would again face the slow monotony of a life without real purpose. Only now it would be worse. Now, he would know the truth but would have denied it out of cowardice. Yes, redemption and forgiveness would be possible, but inevitably, that would lead him back to the fate he faced now. Would he prove any truer the next time then? If he was to face torment and death, what good would it do to space it out with a period of misery in this life?

No, it would be much better to face whatever torment awaited him now, with the hope of salvation in the life to come. He had read of the "glorious martyrs" and how so many of them had considered it an honor to die for Christ. He took some consolation from that. He tried to hold that thought in mind as he attempted to rest.

Then, while he was dozing, the sound of his door unlocking suddenly roused him. This time it was a pair of guards standing outside the door. They stood him up, and immediately he felt lightheaded and his legs began to give out on him. The guards roughly pulled him upward and handcuffed him.

They kept hold of him once they were outside of the cell, and they led him through several hallways until they reached an elevator. One guard underwent an optical scan. After a minute's wait, the elevator arrived. The inside was made of smooth reflective metal throughout with several LED bulbs implanted in the ceiling for light. The multiple mirrors the walls created led to looped reflections in every direction. It was an eerily unsettling space, and Mark thought he noticed a guard grimace as they stepped into the elevator.

A few seconds after they entered, the door closed, and the elevator began to move. Mark had expected some creaks and groans as the elevator started up, but it was utterly quiet and smooth. Neither of the guards spoke. Mark likewise kept quiet. Even had his parched throat not been too sore for speech, he would have had nothing to say in that moment. There were no buttons on the walls of the elevator, and so Mark surmised that it was controlled by C-All, or the routes for each guard were pre-programmed ahead of time.

After another minute, the elevator reached its destination. The doors opened onto a small lobby with a bank of elevators. The walls here were richly decorated, and symbols of the Golden Republic and the Party abounded. Signs indicated the directions to various courtrooms. It was clear the area had been designed for the comfort of the Party members who worked here. After his time in the cell and the featureless walls of the hallways that surrounded it, this felt like a different world.

Ever since the auto-car had taken him into the blackness of the garage below the prison, Mark had felt like he had been in a world apart. Just seeing signs of art and comfort felt like a momentary reprieve. They led him to a small waiting area outside of a courtroom. One guard produced a bottle of water and pressed it to his lips. He began to drink it almost before he realized what was happening. He drained the full bottle. Next, the guard produced a packet of shake that could be sucked from a straw. Mark likewise drank from this. It was foul tasting, but contained a heavy mix of proteins and fat mixed with salt. Not knowing when he'd next have nutrition, and half-starved, Mark gulped it down. It left him feeling a little thirsty again by the time he finished, and he rasped, "May I have a little more water?"

The two guards look at each other for a moment. Then, one guard nodded and took the water bottle over to a nearby water fountain and filled it about a third of the way. Coming back, he offered Mark the bottle. Mark drained it and then nodded at the guard in appreciation. The three then sat and waited, Mark flanked by a guard on each side. They waited on a long bench sat against a wall. Mark guessed they wouldn't have brought him until the judge was nearly ready for him, and this proved true. After only two minutes, the guards seemed to receive a message in their C-Alls. They both looked up suddenly. They then stood up and hauled Mark upward, leading him into the court.

The courtroom was austere. Rows of wooden benches were arranged along a central aisle. Mark was led down the aisle to a seat placed in front of and below the judge. The guards placed Mark in the seat. Above him sat the judge, a woman likely in her late fifties with dyed black hair that did not quite hide her gray roots. Her face was smooth, but in a slightly unnatural way that betrayed the use of botulinum toxin to smooth her wrinkles.

An officer presented her with a data tablet. She took it and began to read, "Citizen P-927-19-4781, otherwise known as 'Mark.' You have been charged by the state with treason. I have reviewed the evidence of the state provided against you together with your written confession. Do you have any words in your defense?"

ANNO DOMINI 2064

Mark cleared his throat, "Only that, as I explained to the man who took my confession, I at no time acted against the interests of the Golden Republic, believe in fact my actions to have been for its good, and therefore do not consider myself to be a traitor."

The judge snorted. "Your personal sentiments notwithstanding, I hereby find you guilty of treason." Mark had expected it, but still felt something like a stone drop in the pit of his stomach at her words.

The judge continued, "Because of your lack of repentance and cooperation, your punishment will be not less than 10 years of imprisonment, but with further lack of cooperation may range up to the penalty of death. You will be given two weeks during which you will undergo interrogation. If you do not comply with your interrogators, then you will face the death penalty. Compliance may lead to lesser penalties, though because of your obstinance so far you will face not less than 10 years imprisonment. You are to be brought before this court in two weeks' time to assess final penalty." She banged the gavel.

The guards came forward and picked Mark back up by the arms. He was led from the courtroom. They took him through a separate exit that led to another elevator. This elevator appeared to be more of a service elevator, and there was no waiting area or lobby around it. It opened almost immediately. The rest of the return trip to his cell passed in what seemed an instant. Suddenly he was back in the pitch black of his cell.

The days that followed became a blur to Mark. Most of the time he was in his cell. He tried to use the time to sleep and to pray. Occasionally, small amounts of food and water were given to him. However, whenever the door opened, he never knew if it was for sustenance or to bring him to the interrogator.

His first encounter with the interrogator was brutal. It appeared the Party hoped that raw pain would be enough to break him. Guards had led him to a featureless room of rubber tiled flooring and walls. Handcuffed and shackled, they threw him in the middle of the floor. The interrogator then dismissed the guards.

The interrogator did not even bother to ask a question, but started immediately beating him using a rubber truncheon. Blow after blow landed striking his limbs, chest, and back. The interrogator was careful to avoid areas that might cause serious internal injuries or muddle his awareness.

The pain was shocking. Sometimes the rubber truncheon smashed just over top of a nerve and fire would zing down an arm or a leg. Other times it was the shock of an already bruised section being struck again that would come to dominate his pain.

Mark felt a part of him weakening. It would be so easy to give a name or a place. Something to make the beating end. However, more than the pain, it was giving in that scared Mark. The thought he might cause other innocents to suffer the same fate was terrifying. A line from the "Pater Noster," the Latin version of the "Our Father," he'd been studying, sprang to mind. He began to recite it to himself again and again. "Libera nos a malo." Sometimes he interchanged it with the English "Deliver us from evil." It became a refrain in his head. With each blow, with each spike of pain atop the dull bruising that now seemed to encompass his whole body, he prayed silently "Libera nos a malo."

Suddenly the beating stopped. The interrogator was sweating and breathing hard. Mark was left handcuffed laying on a cold tile floor. The interrogator turned and exited. Mark lay there, feeling like every inch of his body was bruised. He was grateful of the reprieve, but fearful of what further torments might be coming. Only minutes later the interrogator returned. He looked at Mark with hate in his eyes. "You think you're a tough little bastard, don't you? Unfortunately for you, we've barely started."

The interrogator began to use electric currents instead of

the truncheon. He seemed to vary the amperage and the location of the shocks, careful not to let Mark lose consciousness or endanger his cardiac rhythm. Where before when a nerve was struck he would feel a sense of fire running through a limb, now it would feel like his entire body was alight. Mark lost all sense of time. Oddly though, he felt less and less compulsion to give in to the torture. He continued, when he could pull his thoughts away from the pain enough, to pray. The thought came to him that likely, no matter what he said, they would continue this to him anyway. There was likely no amount of information that would stop them from torturing him for more.

As the waves of pain claimed his body, he progressively felt a sense of disconnection. He almost felt like an outside observer witnessing some poor soul being tortured and feeling the utmost pity for him. Oddly, he also felt like he was not the only one observing and that the other observers shared his pity. He felt a sense of warmth emanating from them, though he saw no one.

The interrogator began to lose his patience. Where before he had tortured him in silence, now he began shouting and swearing at Mark. He began to demand Mark tell him who had given him the C-All program. When Mark didn't answer, the interrogator suddenly turned the dial on the amperage up precipitously. The world seemed to explode, and spots formed before Mark's eyes as his body went taut with muscle contractions.

"Not so pleasant, eh? That's not even the maximum on this thing. Now tell me, who are the other traitors? Give me names!" the man demanded.

Mark struggled to find his voice and gasped, "I... am... not a traitor!" At this the interrogator literally growled in frustration and Mark saw him adjust the amperage still higher. He applied it to Mark's chest and Mark briefly felt his whole body convulse before his vision went black.

Mark woke on the interrogation chamber's floor. His hands and feet were still bound. His eyes were closed, and he could hear the interrogator arguing with a woman he had not heard before.

"You idiot!" she was saying. "You seized his heart for a moment. You're lucky he went back into sinus rhythm, or you might have killed him! The Inner Party wants to make an example of him, and meanwhile you haven't even gotten any information from him!" Her voice was high-pitched but held the tone of practiced authority and biting condescension.

The interrogator's voice was petulant and wheedling, "I've never had someone like this before! I've just been dealing with draft dodgers and petty crooks. We don't normally get political traitors like this. I do not understand what makes this guy tick. Whatever it is, pain isn't making him talk."

There was a brief pause, then the woman sighed and replied, "Fine, take him back to his cell. Maybe his will can be weakened with further dehydration and starvation. Meanwhile, we can try other things to break him." Mark heard an electric door unlock and open and the click of a woman's heels exiting the room. After this, what sounded like two sets of guard boots approached, and Mark felt himself being lifted by the shoulders and dragged from the room.

He must have passed out again, as the next thing he knew he was waking up in his cell. The restraints on his wrists and legs were gone, and he was once more in complete darkness laying on rubber tiles. A wave of nausea took hold, and he struggled feebly to the toilet feeling about to vomit. Dry heaves wracked him, but nothing came up. Exhausted, he slunk back onto the floor and fell asleep.

Time continued to pass. He tried his best when waking to at least stand and stretch. His body was so stiff and bruised that the pain of standing was almost enough to cause him to pass out. It didn't help that he was profoundly thirsty and lightheaded. Small amounts of water and nutrition continued to be given to him at intervals, but Mark could tell it was a starvation ration and barely enough water to keep him alive and conscious.

In his prayers, he thanked God for giving him the strength not to give in so far and begged for continued strength to hold until the end. In mentioning the possibility of a death sentence, the judge had done him an unexpected service. Now, Mark could concentrate on simply holding out a little longer. There was an end in sight.

He suspected the judge thought he would fear death, and that this fear would motivate him to give up his fellow Christians to the interrogators. He reflected that he feared the pain being inflicted on him, but death no longer seemed dreadful. He felt a deep assurance that on the other side of death was a God waiting for him with love and patience. A God who had loved humanity so much that He had become a man so He could suffer and die so that men could be saved. Most of all, a God who, as a man, rose from the dead so that those who died in Him could also be resurrected.

There was still that little voice seeming to whisper in his ear asking, "What if none of it is true? What if you're just being a fool and suffering for nothing?" The voice seemed much weaker than it once had. The idea seemed less fearsome and instead, almost ludicrous now. For all that, a ready answer came to his mind. His life without God had felt empty and meaningless. Such a life was hardly worth living anyway, so what was he losing by dying? Much more importantly, he knew what he was gaining, and deep to his core he felt it was worth his present pain.

Finally, after what must have been days, his cell door opened, and guards once more retrieved him. He lacked the strength to walk, and so he was again lifted by his shoulders and dragged to a set of elevators. This time they brought him to a

JACOB CLEARFIELD

floor he didn't recognize and went past several normal looking offices before they deposited Mark in what seemed to be just a regular conference room. He was cuffed to one of the office chairs, and the guards departed.

A moment later, a stern-faced woman entered the room. She wore a high-end, fashionable C-All and a professional suit that was tailored to hug her figure. Her dark red hair was tied tightly into a bob in the back. Far from a guard, she reminded Mark of many of the hierarchy-climbing Party women he'd met during his life. She turned on a screen placed in the middle of the wall across from him. The woman then turned and left. Mark noted the click of her heels and wondered if she was the same woman from the interrogation chamber. In front of him, two containers with straws were placed. He tried one and found it had water. Almost draining it, he tried the other and found it contained a protein shake.

As he drank the shake greedily, the screen switched into a video presentation. A narrator came on. "Welcome to the Golden Republic!" a proud voice boomed. "Congratulations on being accepted to the immigration candidacy program. With hard work and loyalty, in time, you too may one day become a citizen of the greatest nation on Earth!" The film cut to a scene of the Capital, then scenes of city after city from the Golden Republic were shown as the narrator continued, "The Golden Republic is the wealthiest and most advanced civilization in human history. Our cities are clean, organized, and safe. Through the efforts of our administrators and the Party, together with our advanced technology, everyone's material needs are met. Food is plentiful." Scenes of bountiful farms were shown, followed by fully stocked grocery stores and then citizens enjoying meals in their homes and at restaurants. "Clothing, housing, transportation, are all provided by the state." The screen showed citizens walking in fine clothing, resting in homes and apartments, and entering auto-cars that came and went. "Medical care is state-of-the art and easily accessible." A

ANNO DOMINI 2064

brief image of a doctor in a white coat counselling a patient. "What about entertainment? You'll find no finer entertainment in the world than that produced here and made abundantly available to the citizenry." Now images of big budget movies, virtual reality games, theater productions, and symphony concerts were shown in rapid succession.

The screen cut away to an image of the globe. "While much of the world remains in chaos, here in the Golden Republic the faulty superstitions and selfish politics of the past have been jettisoned, and a society of order and plenty has been achieved." Mark couldn't help but smirk. The Golden Republic had order all right, order through constant surveillance and fear. It had plenty, but mostly plenty for the Party and Inner Party members. Sure, everyone else was given enough to get by, but he'd seen the housing and food most people were being given and knew it was hardly as rosy as the film made it sound. He wondered how many "immigration candidates" had watched this movie only to soon live in a dilapidated little ranch built a hundred years before the founding of the Golden Republic?

The screen now cut to an image of the Golden Republic flag waving proudly in a breeze. "Serve this great country well, and you and all your descendants can come to know what it is to live in a place of true security and prosperity: The Golden Republic!" The video ended with the fanfare of "Together We Are Better" playing in the background as the Golden Republic flag continued to wave. Mark reflected that the one blessing of his cell was that he could now wake up without that irritating melody playing in his ears.

The film having ended, the woman returned to the room. She turned off the screen and then sat down across from him. Mark watched her with mild curiosity. She levelled a condescending gaze at him. "So, Mark, what do you have to say to that?"

Mark laughed. He realized he'd probably pay for it, but he

couldn't help himself. Seeing the irritated look on the woman's face, he replied, "I'm sorry, it's just a very odd form of torture is all." He smiled at her, wondering how she'd respond to the joke.

She was not amused. "This is hardly a joke. The Golden Republic is the greatest civilization mankind has ever produced, and you think it's a good thing to betray it!"

Mark shook his head. "As I told the judge and the interrogator, I'm no traitor. The Golden Republic does a good job of providing bread and circuses..."

The woman interrupted, "We provide a fair bit more than that!" She was indignant to have the efforts of the Republic so brusquely summarized.

"But man cannot live on bread alone," Mark finished. Again, the woman did not seem to take Mark's meaning. She shook her head.

"What a dumb response. You know full well we provide a balanced diet to our citizens. No one in the Golden Republic is suffering from malnourishment, much less starvation!"

Mark nodded. "I was a Party member. I know very well what the Golden Republic does and doesn't do. It's true that everyone has their basic needs met. Obviously, a lot more creature comforts go to the Party members and Inner Party members, but every society in history has done something similar so I can hardly fault the Republic for that. That's not the point, though. You've given people everything they need to live but denied them anything to live *for*."

The woman scrunched her face in confusion. "Well, of course we have! They can live for the Party, for the Republic! This is a great nation. Why shouldn't they live for it?"

Mark replied, "Because all the Party and the Republic stand for is keeping people alive and comfortable. But no one stays alive forever, and comfort becomes boring and empty. People need something more to make life worth living, and the

Party not only does not provide it, you outlaw and prevent it. I said I'm no traitor, and I meant it. If the Golden Republic is to survive, it needs to learn what I've learned and change in response. Otherwise, eventually it is doomed, and its life will be hardly 'life' at all meanwhile."

At this the woman stood up. "I can see we're not getting anywhere. I'm beginning to think you are too far gone to see reason. I'm glad this country is nearly rid of your type." With this, she began to walk out.

"May you find God's peace," Mark replied. She paused for a moment, seeming to consider responding, then continued away with her back to him and left the room. The guards who brought him returned to the room and took him back to his cell.

More time passed. Mark could only wonder how close he was to the end of the two weeks. Given what the woman had said, he hoped vaguely that the Party would give up on getting information from him, and allow him to wait in the cell until they were ready to pass their final sentence on him. As it happened, though, it felt like much less time passed before the door to his cell opened again. Mark reckoned it could not have been more than a day at most.

This time they brought him to a small room with a square table only a couple feet on each side. On either end was a chair, and they again left Mark in a chair handcuffed and shackled. He wondered what new tactic the interrogators might try.

It surprised him when rather than an interrogator, the door to the room opened and Leslie stepped in. She looked nervous and a little disheveled. A guard followed her. It relieved Mark to see that she wore normal civilian clothes and was not cuffed or bound. The guard indicated to her he would be right outside of the room and they would monitor everything. If there was any threat to her safety, they would intervene right away. Mark had to stifle an eye roll at the idea, as though he were some dangerous criminal who might attack her. It saddened

JACOB CLEARFIELD

him to see Leslie nod fearfully to the guard, though, as if she truly thought it was a possibility.

Leslie sat somewhat stiffly and looked down at the desk. The guard turned and left. An awkward silence ensued. Mark caught Leslie sneak a glance at him and then struggle to cover her emotions in response. He could only guess at his appearance. His body was bruised and yellowed almost everywhere, and he'd lost considerable weight. They had not allowed him to shower or shave, and he was fairly sure his breath must smell like death. Still, as repugnant as he must have appeared, he was somewhat gratified to see it looked more like pity that Leslie was trying to hide than disgust. Mark felt sorry for her. He could not help thinking of how she could not let herself show pity with the Party watching. He suspected what tactic she would have to use to avoid this, and so was not surprised when the contours of her face changed, and she finally said something.

"Look at you, as stubborn as ever. It looks like even the Party can't knock any sense into you. Honestly Mark, what have you been thinking?" She couldn't hide the exasperation in her last sentence overtaking her attempt at anger.

Mark thought about his reply for a moment before answering. "I'm pretty sure if I tried to tell you, they would quickly put a stop to it. All I can say is that I found meaning and purpose in life, and I hope someday you find it, too."

"You find being in prison meaningful? You think getting beaten and handcuffed and half-starved is meaningful? You're being ridiculous Mark!" Leslie replied.

"I find what they are beating me, imprisoning me, shackling me, and starving me for to be meaningful. I would not choose for them to do these things for me, but because I suffer them for the sake of Him Who suffered before me, I do find meaning in these things." Mark looked at her intently, "Truly, don't worry for me. They can destroy my body, but they can't destroy my soul. I'm far more worried for you than you should

ANNO DOMINI 2064

be worried for me."

At this the door opened and the guard came in. Mark expected the session to end, but the guard simply struck him across the face. Leslie gasped. The guard nodded to her and then left. Mark grinned. "I guess I'm not supposed to talk about that."

Leslie shook her head. "Honestly, you've made things difficult enough for me. If you're going to destroy yourself, please don't ruin me any further in the process." She looked at him now with greater anger. "Not that you probably care, but do you realize what you've done to me? It's bad enough my parents were traitors. At least I was a child and couldn't do anything about it. But now, now I'm the woman that *dated* a traitor. No one will talk to me at work unless they have to. You ruined my career. Every night I wonder if they will arrest me just on the general suspicion that I knew something and never reported it. I'm tarnished, radioactive, a danger just to be around!"

Mark hadn't accounted for that. "I'm sorry about that. I really am. It's not right that they are doing any of this, and you shouldn't suffer for it either. To be honest though, I'm a little surprised. The Party disappears people all the time, and their friends and family aren't usually stigmatized much for it. Supposedly most of the people who disappear are just sent for re-education and are reassigned. Why would people think differently about me?"

Leslie let out a little rueful laugh. "I suppose they haven't told you. They're using you as an example. You've been in all the latest news reports. 'The Menace from the Past' they're calling it. The Party has been saying you got mixed up in some cult from before the Revolution and got brainwashed. Official advisories are warning everyone to look out for people who might be trying to give 'subversive messages.' It's really got people on edge. Some people are seeing enemies everywhere, and now I'm a prime suspect to anyone who knows me." She nodded sadly. "You should realize that if you don't talk, they will make a spec-

215

tacle out of your execution. The Party will make sure everyone knows not to cross them, and you'll be exhibit one for why."

Mark sat back. This surprised him. He'd assumed he'd be disposed of quietly. He had felt bad for his parents, and especially for the friends he had found in the Faith who he'd thought would likely never know what exactly had happened to him. He'd thought especially of Rosa, and he regretted never getting to find out if things might have worked with her. She had seemed so joyfully full of life whenever they met. It pained him to think of her now seeing him on the news and knowing exactly what would happen to him.

"Thank you for telling me," he managed. His voice was thick with emotion, and as he pictured the shock people like Christopher and Rosa would have felt on seeing such broadcasts, he had to fight back tears coming to his eyes.

Leslie also became tearful. "Just work with them, Mark! You don't have to die. Maybe with good behavior they'd even let you out some day!" Mark realized she must have thought he was tearful thinking of his death. He shook his head.

"I'm not crying for me. I can't do what you're asking. I'm really sorry that this hurts you. I hope you will someday understand."

Leslie pushed back from the table. "I just can't. I can't watch as you destroy yourself. I don't know what madness has taken over you, but obviously I'm not getting through. I'm sorry, I'm just, I'm done." She began to walk toward the door and before she reached it, the door opened, and the guard came in to escort her. A few minutes later, Mark was dragged back to his cell.

15.

The time in the cell dragged on. Mark slept a lot more. When he was awake, he could barely stand, and just dragging himself onto the toilet was a severe challenge. There were no more visits. Mark was grateful for what Leslie had told him. Otherwise, he would have been afraid the Party might still leave him in the cell indefinitely. As it was, he knew there was to be an end soon. Not knowing how much longer he had to wait was frustrating, but he tried to catch himself when frustrated and bring his thoughts back toward prayer. He knew he would die soon. He felt it was really a blessing to know this with such certainty. He was being given a chance to prepare himself for death. He only wished a priest could visit him to receive penance and a last communion as he'd read was done when the Church could be visible.

Still, he was grateful for the blessings he'd had, and prayed only that he could now see things through faithfully to the end. He prayed also for his friends and loved ones. It had sounded like the Party was redoubling its efforts to persecute the Faith. Likely other Christians would be caught. Even more likely, poor souls who knew nothing of Christ would be implicated and would suffer for the sake of a Savior they did not even know. He prayed that somehow through that suffering they too might come to find Christ.

Finally, the door to his cell opened again and guards dragged Mark out. He did his best to walk as the guards held him up. They passed through the featureless corridors of the prison. Mark silently prayed he would never have to see them again. They reached the elevator Mark recognized from the day of his trial. Sure enough, it led back to the same waiting area outside the courtroom. This time there was no waiting to be brought before the judge. Unlike before, however, the courtroom was packed with cameras and reporters. Leslie had been right about the Party wanting to make an example of him.

They deposited him in the chair before the judge's bench. Apparently, the Party was closely coordinating things for the cameras. Only a second after the guards placed him, the door to the judge's chambers opened, and he recognized the judge from his initial trial coming out. This time she appeared to have a new haircut and more elaborate jewelry. Her robe also appeared to be more formal with more Party insignia. She walked carefully and proudly to her seat. As she entered everyone in the courtroom stood, and somewhat reflexively Mark started to try. However, his legs barely obeyed and before he could lift himself a guard placed a hand on his shoulder. Mark allowed himself to collapse back into the chair. He noticed at least one cameraman smirk.

As the judge seated herself, the courtroom likewise was seated. The judge then addressed him. "Citizen P-927-19-4781, we meet today to determine sentencing for the crime of treason. I have been informed that you have failed to cooperate with the State and have refused even to renounce your crimes." She then seemed to allow a slight pause for effect. "Beyond even this, I am told that during your interrogations you expressed the desire that others might yet join you in your superstitious beliefs, thus further compounding your treason in full view of state witnesses."

This seemed to bring about something of a tumult among the gathered reporters. Mark noted several cameras panning quickly from the judge to him as if to look for his response. He doubted he was giving them the hoped-for response. He had come expecting to be given a death sentence and nothing said so far was surprising to him.

ANNO DOMINI 2064

The judge then cleared her throat and proceeded. Mark saw the cameras mostly turning back toward her. A few remained trained on him. No doubt some feeds were showing both him and the judge simultaneously. "Given your lack of remorse, failure to cooperate with state authorities, persistence in your crime, and obvious desire to further persist, I do hereby sentence you to death. As there is no reason to waste further state resources on your bodily maintenance, the sentence is to be carried out immediately." She punctuated this with a bang of her gavel. She then stood, the courtroom standing with her as she exited. As soon as she left, the guards to either side of Mark grabbed him. He felt the guard who had laid his hand on him earlier was considerably gentler than the other.

The guards brusquely hauled Mark from the courtroom, but rather than return to his cell, this time they led him to the parking garage. Waiting was not merely one squad car, but an entire line of cars with officers on motorcycles at the front and rear. Mark chuckled.

If there had been any doubt that his sentence had been planned, this scene dispelled it. They packed him into the back of the car, and the procession started off. The garage was as dark as he remembered it, but after weeks spent in a lightless cell, it did not seem as dark. Also, this time there was an ascent rather than a descent. The moment the car exited the garage into the light of a noonday sun, Mark felt a small thrill of exhilaration. From the squad car windows, he squinted through the light. The brightness hurt his eyes, but he dared not close them all the way. Instead he fought against the pain to look once more upon the beauty of a blue sky dotted with a few cumulus clouds.

He saw that the motorcade was heading southeast toward the lake. As they got closer, he began to see crowds formed. People jeered and booed as his car passed. The motorcade was approaching the lakeshore festival grounds. The grounds were massive, used for huge festivals dating back over a hundred years. He was surprised to see such crowds gathered. It ap-

219

peared many of them held signs to voice support for the Party, or the Golden Republic, or else announcing "death to traitors." He noted some stages had speakers lecturing to audiences, and others held bands playing patriotic music. Apparently, his execution had given the Party reason to stage some elaborate festival of patriotism. He suspected he was now to play as the main event.

Where there had been some jeers and yells on the way through the city, now the citizens crowded the motorcade. Cries of hate from the crowd were loud even through the glass of the squad car. Mark could only imagine how deafening the noise must be in the crowd itself. He wondered how many of the persons shouting truly hated him, and how many shouted only so they could be seen shouting?

Unfortunately, by the look of it, most of the crowd were passionately enraged. The faces of the people seemed to turn monstrous with hate. Eyes bulged as men and women turned red with shouting. A dark energy seemed to propel the crowd into a frenzy. It was all the motorcade could do to keep them back and press on toward their destination. Looking on the crowd, a sense of cold and heaviness seemed to press on Mark. A primal fear stabbed at his heart, and for a moment Mark questioned his resolve before again steeling himself.

Finally, the motorcade proceeded over a bridge to a small island just east of the main festival grounds. It appeared the bridge was being used to keep the main crowds at bay. Mark could see a stand had been erected at the center of the island. The motorcade pulled to a halt.

He was pulled from the car and again half carried by two guards. His legs were almost on the verge of giving out, but he tried his best to keep pace with the guards so they would not have to drag him. A swarm of media followed his every movement. The stage they led him to had three steps up. Mark nearly tripped as the guards rearranged themselves with one taking

ANNO DOMINI 2064

the lead above to pull him and one stepping behind to push him. Thankfully, the guard behind him, the one who had seemed gentler before, caught him before he fell fully. He then managed to gain the stairs.

Waiting for him at the top was some sort of master of ceremonies. Beyond him were ten men armed with rifles. Beyond the stage lay only the backdrop of the lake and the open sky. "Deo gratias," Mark whispered, thankful God had allowed him to see the lake one more time before he'd die. As the guards led him forward, they came near the men with the rifles. Mark felt a pang of sadness for them at what they were being asked to do. He cleared his throat as best he could, and with a rasp that was quieter than he'd hoped he turned his head and addressed them, "God forgive you for what you must now do, as I now forgive you." He noticed the eyes of the nearest executioner widen in response. The guards then pulled him forward a little more forcefully toward the far end of the stage.

Mark noted a small "X" taped on the ground and was not surprised when he was placed to stand over it. However, whoever had planned this had not accounted for Mark's inability to still stand on his own. Thinking quickly, the MC motioned to one of the media cameramen. Mark watched curiously as they discussed something. Then a couple more men came up to the stage with what appeared to be a large camera tripod. As the guards stood with him, men brought the tripod up and placed it behind him. Then the back of his shirt was used together with a belt they procured and placed around his waist to prop him into a standing position.

This done, the guards relinquished him. The MC then stood next to the squad of soldiers assigned to the execution and read a pronouncement. "In accordance with the verdict passed today on citizen P-927-19-4781, known by the name of 'Mark' we are charged here today to carry out the sentence of death. Due to the severe nature of the charge, it has been decided that the execution is to be carried out by means of firing squad.

221

Soldiers! Take! Aim!" At this, the line of soldiers snapped their rifles to position at their shoulders.

From only about 20 feet away, Mark could see the hollow of the barrels as they pointed at him. The death he had been so long expecting now stared directly at him. Despite himself, his heart began to quaver. The darkness of the barrels seemed to stretch outward and across his sight. A wind picked up from the lake, and a chill ran through him.

The MC paused and turned from addressing the audience of cameras to address Mark directly. "Mark, as the Party is just, so it is also merciful. Even at this late hour, despite all your crimes, you are to be offered one last chance. I have been instructed to tell you that if you will now denounce your false beliefs and swear loyalty to the party, your sentence will be commuted to life imprisonment."

The barrels of the rifles continued to point at him. Mark felt his heart racing in fear. For all his faith, he did not want to die. Not now, not yet. He felt like the darkness of those barrels might consume him as he felt keenly his own weakness. He was exhausted, thirsty, and weak to the point of collapse. Surely God would not fault him for giving in?

A few seconds passed. The MC addressed him again, "Denounce your beliefs and swear loyalty to the Golden Republic. Or, if you wish to die, you need only raise an arm and the soldiers will fire." Mark looked out past the soldiers to the sea of cameras watching him. He thought about the likely millions of people who would see this. He wanted to be brave, especially for his fellow Christians, but fear clawed at him. The icy heaviness he'd felt earlier now seemed to return and press in from all directions. Mark's head swam and he felt like his vision was going dark. "Lord, send me aid. I do not think I can do this alone," he quietly prayed in his mind.

Something caught his eye among the cameras. A flash of light drew his eyes to a woman who was watching him. She held no camera, and tears ran from her eyes. Such tears could be seen as treasonous, but no one around her seemed to notice. More striking than her tears was her beauty. She was easily the most beautiful woman Mark had ever seen. Her gaze radiated love, and she almost seemed to glow in the noonday sun. Below her tears, she gave him a gentle smile. At the sight of it, the darkness and fear that had been weighing on him suddenly vanished.

Mark felt a profound peace settle on him. His limbs seemed to take on new strength. He stood himself straighter. His voice was suddenly clear. A phrase came to mind, and he smiled at the thought of it. He looked out toward the crowd. The woman was gone, but the strength remained. Taking a deep breath, Mark cried out "Vivat Christus Rex!" and raised both arms as if to embrace the world. The rifles roared back a furious world's reply.

ABOUT THE AUTHOR

Jacob Clearfield

A rehab physician (physiatrist) located in Wisconsin, Jacob lives within sight of Lake Michigan. In a crisis he figures that at least his family will always have access to fresh water. (He also admires the view.)

Fiction has been a passion of his since discovering his school library at age 7. While he enjoys history, philosophy, theology, and biographies, he always comes back to fiction when wanting to read for enjoyment. As a kid, when not reading he was usually creating elaborate stories in his mind that would play out as a continuing saga day after day.

It is his great pleasure now as an adult be able to revive that childhood creativity. Aiming to combine it with the discipline and knowledge learned over many years of education and career, he hopes to create stories that will prove both meaningful and entertaining.

Made in the USA
Coppell, TX
24 November 2020